SPIT RO

SPIT ROAST

JASON LEE

ROMAN *Books*
www.roman-books.co.uk

ISBN 978-93-83868-09-4

Typeset in Adobe Garamond Pro

First published in 2015

1 3 5 7 9 8 6 4 2

British Library Cataloguing in Publication Data.
A catalogue record for this book is available from the British Library.

Publisher: Suman Chakraborty

ROMAN Books
26 York Street, London W1U 6PZ, United Kingdom
Unit 49, Park Plaza, South Block, Ground Floor, 71 Park Street, Kolkata 700016, WB, India
2nd Floor, 38/3 Andul Road, Howrah 711109, WB, India
www.roman-books.co.uk | www.romanbooks.co.in

Printed and bound in India by
Repro India Ltd

SPIT ROAST

PREFACE

Spit Roast is a myriad of a mirror concerning the life of footballer John Tao, an everyman, where the inner world and outer world fuse. Augustine Illumines is the ghost in the text, a footballer who committed suicide, the uncanny shadow. We follow Tao's life, from the peak of his success, when every paper and journalist wants a piece of him, to his semi-retirement via Zelig-like incarnations. This is in the same satirical mode of Lee's novels *Dr Cipriano Cell* and *Unholy Days*.

What do you get when William Burroughs, B.S. Johnson and Julio Cortázar do a cut up of James Joyce and *The Sunday Sport*? Granny videos and close-ups of banned old men, brutal with blood. You can do better than that. Get away from identity, from the past, the present and the future. Get, *Spit Roast*. We come to a book, not on a book, hoping it will surprise, not solely in its subject matter, but in form. This can only happen if it breaks a few rules.

Moving on from Bataille, I cannot concur that by breaking the rules you only re-confirm them. That assumes the lachrymose Lacanian Law is always there, crying black tears down my hideously white face, as I watch the native boys splashing in my water. At least fiction, unlike psycho-analysis, admits to being 'made-up', in a lovely Liverpudlian accent, with the birds on the Liver Building still standing, hovering over the horizon, ready to head out west, to defecate on the Antony Gormley bastards below.

If I had the wings of a sparrow, if I had the wings of a dove. . . . Some literature asks you to concentrate, calling you to lose yourself, to be highly conscious, to become more conscious, if such a thing is possible. As your unconscious is always one step ahead of your conscious mind, it needs to stem from this.

Despite living within spitting distance of White Hart Lane, banned chants of 'Yid Army' echoing in my FA cup ears, I've not had a passion for football. You don't need one, to appreciate corruption, lust and greed, and don't feel obliged to get a tattoo of a cock on you hand. Nor have I been spit-roasted (as far as I know). Saves money, and time for everyone; I'm still waiting for the one man who can do this–simultaneously. Even the two hundred million euro player couldn't do this with a banana shot.

Fifty-two cards in the pack, weeks, and chapters in this novel, taking you one step ahead of the conscious, via football, tran-sexuality and the mediated world. This gets under the foreskin, to that grain of sand, that pearl. By doing so it brings on consciousness, but if we don't want to see this then it appears as fate. Treat it like therapy, but without the power relationship, the bullshit.

Places have a character: *Spit Roast* traverses London, Salford, Italy, Tenerife, and Essex. There are traces of David Mitchell, e. e. cummings, Chuck Palahnuik, Jack Kerouac, James Joyce, William S. Burroughs, descending from Virginia Woolf as much as Jake Arnott and Will Self. But the tone, voice and weirdness are unique. Nothing can be taught us of which we didn't have the idea anyway. Treat this as your own. Despite the title, there is nothing that explicit, no need to salivate. Judgements are deceptive, but it is up to you to judge morally and aesthetically. Hopefully you don't really want to do that. Let me judge you. As I say–you can do better than that.

Jackie Reuben, Editorial board, *Transgressive Culture*

> *Oh shit*
> *There goes the charabang*
> *Looks like I'm gonna be stuck here the whole summer*
> *Well what a bummer*
> *I can think of a lot worse places to be*
> *Like down in the streets*
> *Or down in the sewer*
> *Or even on the end of a skewer*
> -The Stranglers, 'Peaches'

> *'Was your first sexual partner a boy or a girl?'*
> *'I was too polite to ask.'*
> -Gore Vidal

Prologue
The 3 Booksellers

'Do you mind removing your hat,' said the shopkeeper.

I found it quite remarkable that I had to remove my headgear in a shop but, being a typical English man, I did what I was told. My grandmother had just passed on, and after spending the last three months assisting her to do so, I was now free to follow my own pursuits. Manoeuvring around the works of fiction which, to be honest, I always found to be rather trashy, once I had circumnavigated these literary obstacles, I made my way hastily towards the famous poetry section. Famous in poetry circles, I mean, which were not enormous, I admit. I was what you might call a 'minor poet'. Small magazines have heard of me, to be sure, probably from my persistence if anything but, apart from a very small pamphlet, I had yet to bring out my first collection. I loved the peace and the smell of bookstores and it was wonderful to be inside, away from the inclement weather and the traffic hurtling into the metropolis. This second-hand bookstore opposite Highgate Woods was the place where I was searching for a book of poetry that had haunted me for years. I had heard Sumner perform on three occasions and, despite meeting the man, I had not been able to purchase a copy of his second major collection, *Looking for Nobody*.

It began with a quotation from Matthew's Gospel that I knew from heart: 'But I say unto you, that whosoever looketh on a woman to lust after her hath committed adultery with her already in his heart.' This King James Version I had always found a bit extreme, akin to the Muslim view about never looking left or right.

'Hello, excuse me, do you mind removing your jacket,' came the storekeeper once more.

There was a way that she said this that took me off guard. Between the first request and the second she had been on the telephone, a black

9

retro number, to what I believed to be another bookstore in New York. There seemed to be a problem with a supply of the latest poetry by another well-known poet that nobody had ever heard of.

She had asked me to do two things, or ordered if you will, but as yet I had failed to ask her the one question that had been preoccupying me. Where was the book by Sumner? Of course, it was easy for me to go to the poetry section to search alphabetically, but it would've been easier still if I asked the bookstore attendant.

Not wanting to get her back up, I removed my jacket, which I must admit did actually make me feel more comfortable. A mouldy smell penetrated me, and, despite my love of old books and bookshops, there was something slightly nauseous about the small space. It felt that, imperceptibly, the walls were closing in. Clearly, this place needed a good clean out, which nobody was prepared to do.

'I've been looking for the collection by Sumner for about two years now, his second full collection, do you think you could help me, or even order it?'

I had been composing this line on the bus, but the look on her face right now meant that any approach seemed futile. She sat back down now on the faded leather chair at the old desk, glaring at the powerful phone, flicking between the 'telling bone' and the ancient computer. The Aztec God of a machine looking like the only thing you could do on it was play tennis, with a vertical line as a player, or count up to nine, at a push.

Stumbling over boxes, filled with still photographs from 1960s films usually starring Peter Sellers, I managed to reach the poetry section, which I was sure was normally quite interesting. But on this occasion there was only one book on the shelf, and 300 copies of it.

Picking this book up and browsing the contents, I read segments of a narrative poem of 92 pages that seems to me to be a story about a secret island that only appeared on certain occasions, when the moon was in a certain position, in alignment with the other elements.

The narrator finds herself on the island listening to the echoes of her dreams. She seems to believe that dreams are the only thing we are not responsible for. I found this difficult, seeing as I realised that we become ourselves when we become our dream. People appear on ships, and she is unsure of her existence, and theirs.

'Hello, excuse me, do you mind watching the spine on that book!

You're bending it back a bit too far. Also, as you've taken your hat and jacket off, I think you should remove your trousers, pronto, A-SAP.'

When you are asked something as absurd as this, you tend to ignore it, mishear it, or deny anything was spoken at all. It wasn't that I was particularly embarrassed. The girl had greasy brown hair, half way down her back, with penetrating bookworm-eyes, and an oval Tudor face. I would not dream of finding her attractive. Indeed, she was the stuff of nightmares. But to suggest I should remove my trousers in front of her was obviously taking it too far.

Was she going to ask me to remove all my clothes, take a photograph and then put it on Facebook?

'I'm not on social media,' she murmured, with a wry smile, as if reading my mind.

At least she hadn't asked me to remove my glasses. There was an old episode of *The Twilight Zone* I remembered, which was set in a post-apocalyptic age, after some kind of nuclear war. One man is happy because the world is destroyed and he is stuck in a huge public library. He now has all the time in the world to read everything. Bending over to pick up a book, there is a smash; his glasses have fallen off, and the lenses have cracked to smithereens. Game over.

I had been in the shop now for about 15 minutes, and nobody else had entered, or even browsed through the window, which was a bit weird really. But the place was not exactly user friendly.

'It's to do with the temperature of the books, you see,' she explained, playing provocatively with a cheap pen.

'The particles from your clothing interfere with the particles that interface, if you like such a techno-phrase, with the books. You may think we're just about selling books, but we are also about preserving them. I like to think this is a library, museum and archive, as well as a bookstore. Anyway, you look like you're searching for something?'

'Isn't everyone?' I replied, cautiously.

At first I surmised her switch to amicability was a trick, a ploy to catch me off guard, so I would really remove everything. Then she would take my clothing to the charity shop next door, the same place I had purchased them. I would then buy my clothes back at a higher price, come back in here to look at books, be forced to do the same again, she would take them next door, and so on. But I might be a poster boy for the shop.

'Yes, I am. I'm looking for the work of the poet Sumner, his major second collection. Have you heard of him? Is it likely you have a copy in stock, or maybe you can acquire a copy, preferably signed, but any will do, as long as it's in good condition?'

She began to rub the cheap pen under her porcelain chin, the gesture starting to arouse me, despite my earlier judgement. At last I could tell she was intelligent and was taking my question very seriously.

'You know, I do know exactly who you mean. I once saw him give a reading at the Jackson Lane Centre. It was slightly embarrassing really, as there were only about six of us there, and one gentleman kept on making a ridiculous noise.'

I was about to confess that man must have been me, when a tall gentleman entered the shop. Despite my attempt to hide myself, adjusting my trousers behind a bookshelf, he caught me with my pants, or should I say undergarments, half-down.

'Don't worry, I've seen it all before fellow, and I know what Clarissa gets up to, setting people up like this. At least it makes her job more interesting. It must get a bit lonely in here.'

But I still couldn't understand what real benefit this gave. Was it just fun at someone else's humiliation? I had my undergarments up now and my trousers on.

'At least you haven't removed or hidden them,' I mumbled.

The face of the new customer seemed vaguely recognisable, although it had withered and changed from my memory.

'So good to see you again, Sumner!' shouted Clarissa, and I stumbled back into shelf.

I couldn't believe it. Could it really be him, the elusive Sumner? I thought he had become a Russian Orthodox priest, and was building a monastery on the Isle of Mull with like-minded people. At least, that's what a friend of a friend had told me.

'Clarissa, you really shouldn't humiliate your customers like this, no wonder there's nobody ever in here. How do you expect to sell any books, my books for example?'

'I offered him the opportunity of gaining your book through removing his clothing. Do you really think it's fair to make people pay for your poetry?'

'That's a cheap dig, Clarissa, something your mother would never even think of!' Sumner chuckled, reaching his big paw out to me.

'Damn good to meet you, young man, I'm Sumner.'

'I know, sir, it really is an honour to meet you, Sumner. I'm Anthony Johnson,' I replied sheepishly, with too much deference, 'I was actually looking for your second collection.'

'Oh that thing, I'd rather forget about that, if you don't mind. It was a bit too close to the bone, if you get my meaning, fuelled by my wife playing away from home, with my best man no-less.'

Clarissa was up now, looking slightly jealous of the intimacy between us.

'I always felt that when you read out your work that you were actually talking about real events, not just putting on a narrative voice. That's why I've been so obsessed with finding your work.'

My enthusiasm was getting the better of me but, for once, I didn't let it lead to an embarrassing silence.

'You mention a teacher in one of your poems who gets a bit too close to a young boy. I love that poem. So delicate and tender, the way the teacher ruffles the boy's hair and the spark it ignites in both of them. Did that happen to you, Sumner?'

Sumner, stepped back, took a big sigh, and shrugged his shoulders.

'Why, did that happen to you as a boy?'

'Happens to all of us, one way or another,' Clarissa laughed, using a phrase my grandmother said constantly, 'one way or another'.

'You poets, you take all this stuff too seriously; stick to prose. You're not reworking the past, and you don't have to cling onto it to redeem it, you just make things up. Forget those idiots who say it's all auto-biography, even fiction.'

'I will tell you the truth, and as we all know the truth sets you free, to set the record straight, and no, it did not happen to me. I was not the young boy in that poem, and I wasn't even the teacher. I just thought it would be a good scenario. I mean the closer you are to a situation, the less you can understand it in many ways.'

I knew what he was talking about. I had studied Buddhism, and once thought seriously about joining a Buddhist community. But at the same time I felt he was talking utter bullshit. Surely, the closer you are to the experience, the deeper you understand it. The subjective and the objective were just as real as each other, depending on which side you looked at it. Any rules set by anybody, one way or another, were just there to reassure them. One way or another again; it was then I remembered it was also the title of a Blondie song. I never knew my grandma had been so with it. 'So you almost did what Clarissa asked you to do, and now I have saved you! What is it you would like me to do for you now?'

'I'd be really grateful if you would sign a copy of your book for me, if you have a spare one. There is none in the shop and Clarissa says she needs to order it from Australia.'

Clarissa went bright red at this. Not stocking Sumner's book was an absolute crime, and she knew it. At least she did not attempt to cover this up with a lie.

'Of course, it depends what you are looking for, whether you just want a rare copy of my book, signed by me, so you can indulge in having the possession, or you're really interested in the content of my work, not just an object.'

I wasn't sure how to answer this one. I was so interested in the content of his work clearly, but I was really interested in possessing an actually copy of the poems. The book itself was important to me.

'I tell you what,' Sumner purred, interrupting my deliberations.

'I will write down a selection of my work for you, new and old, I am sure as a poet you have a notebook on you.'

I could not believe my luck. An original manuscript, by the elusive Sumner was exceedingly valuable. I was not rich, to put it mildly. I stumbled with excitement as I extracted my notebook and laid it in front of him. As soon as I had the manuscript I rushed from the shop and phoned my friend Cedric who worked at the Bodleian.

'I have an original handwritten manuscript from Sumner, I know this sounds unbelievable.'

'Yes, it certainly does, he died last year in a walking accident in East Sussex, I thought you of all people would realise that, what the hell are you talking about, Anthony?'

'Cedric, I just met him, he's aged badly, but it was definitely him, and someone else recognised him as well. I've seen him read. I knew him more than I know myself.'

'That's not saying much. Anyway, perhaps that was someone else who died, or he wanted anonymity, and maybe this was some way of trying to achieve his masterpiece, far away from the maddening crowd.'

The phone box reeked of urine, and without much thought I was hopping on the Northern Line headed south to catch the train to Oxford, diving into the belly of the city.

Cedric wouldn't tell me how much this manuscript was really worth, if anything. I was interested in it academically, of course, but at this stage in life I had to think more practically as well. I didn't have any time to get nostalgic about my old seat of learning, having reached Oxford in no time at all.

'I tell you what Anthony, you leave them all with me, and I'll see what I can do.'

I had no choice. I trusted Cedric. After reading English together at Wadham, we'd stayed close, but at the same time I had a fear of losing all that was now my most treasured possession.

Cedric implored me to leave the manuscripts with him, but knowing him better than he knew himself, I felt it was best to take them with me; just to be on the safe side.

'Come on, my man, let me just show them to my boss. She will be back tomorrow from Michigan, where she's negotiating purchasing the Albert Harvey archive, and she can value them better than I can.'

The train back to London was crowded, and without much choice I loitered near the wider area by the toilet.

'Sorry,' I muttered.

Just before we entered back into dirty old London, a man had banged into me. It was clearly his fault, but typically I had been the one who had apologised. And when I checked my pockets the poems had vanished. My paranoia was now running rampant. Hadn't Cedric told me that today was his day off, that he would be working on his PhD thesis about a poet whose work was about a woman abandoned on an island? And wasn't being mugged on the train just too much of a coincidence, like something out of the novels by Tomás Eloy Martínez, or the short stories of Jorge Luis Borges? Who else, other than Clarissa, Cedric and Sumner himself, knew of my possession of the manuscripts?

That night in my tiny bedsit in Tottenham, images of Clarissa and Sumner were still haunting me, and I tossed and turned.

At first light, I took the bus up to Muswell Hill and waited for Highgate Woods to open so I could march to the other side, to where the shop was situated. Once again, I tried to not gag on the smell of urine in the phone-box on Archway Road, but it was too much. Cedric wasn't answering. It was at times like these that I could see my non-acceptance of modern technology, such as mobile phones, was an impractical insanity.

I went out into the street, preferring the sound of the cars and their smell, to that stench inside the phone-box.

My Timex Expedition shifted to nine AM, and I banged on the door of the quaint shop. A man in his early twenties with a Beatles haircut and a purple broach, glared at me through the front door.

'Keep your hair on, mate, or are you desperate to find a long lost manuscript that you know is kept here, hidden away within the jacket of another book, such as *Cub Scout Annual 1972*?'

'Apologies, but I really need to speak with Clarissa, it's urgent. She was with me and a poet yesterday, right here, when I was looking for his book, and I was mugged on a train back from Oxford. My friend Cedric, we were at Wadham together, he works at the library and . . .'

'OKAY, whatever you say mate, whatever you say, sounds like a right nightmare, but this shop wasn't even open yesterday right, look here.'

Spinning around the open and closed sign, which also showed the times, it was clear the shop was actually shut on Mondays, presumably because it was open on a Sunday.

'But that's absurd. I was here, speaking with both of them. Sumner wrote some poems for me, right here.'

When I considered how to explain the written manuscript, I realised then he would just think I was a mad man. There were plenty of them about, wondering up and down Archway Road, picking up rubbish, as if it was the Crown Jewels.

'Listen, I think you need to get with the programme, mate,' said John, or was it Paul, or maybe even Ringo.

The door automatically shut, the man with the broach pulling the lock back for protection. Not knowing what to do next, I froze, staring in the window at the children's books display.

'Get lost, will you, or I will call the police, and I don't care if you went to Oxford!' shouted the man from behind the door.

If it was true, that the shop had been shut yesterday, then what was the reality? I needed time to think. Luckily, one of my most favourite spots in the world, Highgate Woods, was still directly opposite, at least I was certain about natural geography even if time was playing tricks on me, so I psyched myself up for a good stomp, stopping at the café in the woods for a double espresso.

Going back to the shop, I now came across a closed sign, suggesting the fab one had gone for his luncheon. A small alleyway was situated to the right of the shop, and out front, even though it was shut, cheap books were still displayed in boxes, waiting for their final reader. It dawned on me that there had to be some record in the shop of what went on yesterday. With this in mind, I tiptoed down the alleyway, hoping to find some way into the shop from the back, without anybody noticing.

Getting around the back, I came across what seemed to be a small kitchen, ducking down below the window, voices muttering above me. Even from our brief encounter, I could tell one of them was the young man currently in charge. The other one was a bit was a bit more difficult to make out. Was it Cedric, was it Sumner, or was it even Clarissa, because she did have a rather deep voice, and, if all three of them were involved, then what exactly was going on?

The only thing I could do was conjecture about it, given their conference was going on in the kitchen, and that seemed to be the only way into the shop. I crept back up the alleyway, attempting to plan my next step. I was shocked to find the shop now open, and an elderly woman sitting behind the desk. She seemed to be engrossed in pricing books methodically, and by the look on her face would take umbrage if interrupted.

I stood in the shop waiting for her to acknowledge my presence, feeling like a small boy in front of the headmistress.

'Can I help you?' she asked, without looking up.

'Yes, I was talking to a gentleman just now, a young man who looked like, well it doesn't matter really what he looked like, who tells me you were not open yesterday. I can assure you I was in here and even negotiated the price of some books, and I wondered whether you knew about this.' The old woman looked up, took off her round John Lennon glasses, wrapped them with a loose part of her purple blouse, and then slid the lenses up and down thoughtfully as if summoning a genie.

'David can be very annoying like that, I know. He has some kind of penchant for winding people up, shall we say. Personally, I think it is pretty pathetic. But my daughter Clarissa finds it very amusing. They used to be an item, as they call it, but she is not that stupid any more. What was it again, perhaps I can help you?' Once the woman started talking she was far less ferocious than she looked when silent. Of all the shopkeepers, she seemed the most focused and receptive to me.

'Well, it's about a poet called Sumner, perhaps you've heard of him. I had the fortune to meet him right here, yesterday, but then the misfortune to have been robbed off his poetry manuscripts on a train back from Oxford. I am still willing to purchase one of the books from your associate in Melbourne; your daughter told me there were some copies there. It's his second completed volume of poetry.'

'Let me have a look here, just a moment,' said the kindly old woman, bashing her ringed fingers on the keyboard.

I knew, given the age of the computer, my request would take some time again. As I moved to browse through the collection of still photographs from films, with one face remarkably like hers from a film set on a boat just off an island, she shouted.

'It is better than you thought, young man. One of the copies is signed, in perfect condition. And I have a transcript here of what it says. Would you like to hear it?'

'Yes I would love to, love to.'

'To my best man, Anthony H. Johnson, remember the best poetry is always achieved through nakedness; one way or another.'

I
TRUTH CLOUD

1

KISSING UNDER
THE CAMEL TOE

'John, I'm here, John, waiting for you, John, to unwrap me, kill me.'

Wet white towels (is that allowed?), covering the luxurious cream-pie carpets, rugs more like, cream and cream and cream, black cherry, smooth. Feel the oil on brown skin, hello, reflecting in the champagne cooler. Milky drops of sweat, the City's great cock of a gherkin, but could it be anywhere? Don't say anywhere, but here. Amen.

I'm not talking about orifices. Twelve-inch (give or take), re-enforced steel erection, with a pulsating Piccadilly-line vein, begging to be touched or torched or stopped, gripped or gnashed. Taut steel buns, spidery green and purple symbols, smothering the calfskin canvas that says 'God is love', God knows what? Over six foot three, a boxer's nose, and a full head of oily onyx hair, that with effervescent azul eyes gives an innocent-babies-burnt-in-the-forest look. Forget poetry books and dusty shops.

Take me down, or up the Styx. I was never one for poking the pig's bladder, literally, or metaphorically. A well-kept pitch might be beautiful, granted, to fuck on, that luscious green, one goal to you; the deafening crowd full of passion, two nil; the sublime goal, a hat-trick; plus the nostalgia of being taken, and the yearning for something else over the horizon, or the past, an obsession for league tables and facts, that help you to hold on, to stop exploding see-men everywhere, a means of communication, the ambition and competition, but all an avoidance? A Pink Floyd concert, circa, forgotten now, a giant pig floating above the crowd. Elton John, Rod Stewart, you name it—everyone wants a team, glowing men proving themselves.

'John, please, John!'

I want to tell you a story. Shakesqueer: Merchant of Penis, Two Benders of Verona, As You Like It (Up the Harris), Anus Andronicum, The Queer Temp as Sex Pest, Merry Queers of Windsor, Dicky The Threesome – A History Play in 3 Acts, King Queer, A Midsummer's Night Wet Dream About Elton John with Cliff Richard in the leading role, Total Gay Love's Labour's Lost, CumBeline, Alls Well That Ends Well Into the Rectum, and so on. Let's not try and be so cultured.

Forget the racism and violence, what about those streakers? Why is nude such a ludicrous word, the Dutch or English lass bounding, with their bouncing breasts and their bush or beard the size of a badger, a hedge on legs, eh? No smooth ham here. And in the dustbins, on the way to the ground, aged about ten, I could hear other children having sex inside the bins, I was certain of it. A distant echo, not of far away voices boarding far away trains but of children in cans, next to the dead Indian was buried a baby, one thrown around by Wild Bill at the show.

'Oh John, come on, John, come on, John.'

A dome inside the head, over the city and world and a logo screaming the order, bang-bang-chicken carving the MILF, roasting the GILF, when it comes down to it bad deodorant dominates. But it is always wrong to preach right, to tell it how it is, was, forever shall be, if you don't believe. There is a disclaimer at the start of a book I am reading about unwrapping signs and signifiers that, for a moment, lead us behind the Nandos' Almighty Wrap, like we'd all chomp it down, given half the chance and nobody was looking. Some Nans clearly do. The more you unwrap the less you find; that's what the fear is.

The more you realise what you are seeing is a cover and what you are doing is avoiding every possibility of difference, the more you seek sameness in the crowd. Let me put that more clearly for you if you haven't got it yet carved in your skin, dearly beloved reader. Stories about clones frighten us, because we fear that deep down we are all the same. Worshipping Sartre and Kierkegaard, we develop a false sense of alienation, even from our own family, our clan, our tribe, our football team. In the crowd, I don't see anything, sings Paul Weller.

'Hello, John?'

And we look back in time, over our shoulder, to a period of nostalgia and onto a floating piece of debris because all that remains of our eternity is the past. Proust reading Joyce in the sauna, while a Walter Abish figure creates a new numerical system, the point being: what if every time our side score our family receive goods from the state, the side merely the mirror image of the manager's empire.

'John, oh John, I am here, waiting for you to unwrap me.'

Once upon a cock, as if it was a time and place. Surprisingly, John had not been thinking about his cock, but had been thinking about Raymond Lee, the man in that novel Lisa Fenton had been telling him about. Lee the copper had it all, until one fine day his dirty past caught up with him. Spell dirty for me please.

'DU-R-R-T-E-E-E.'

'Correct.'

John Tao—yes, you—surfacing from a supernatural, or preternatural, run down the left wing, playing for England, about to slot one in past the Brazilian.

'I'm here John, why don't you take me, take me now John, go on, just slip your lovely silky one in my slinky-minky.'

I bet she likes Silk Cut. Feeling down to my cock, I'm pining for my pubes. It's normal for sportsmen to make our bods into freshly felled and de-feathered chicken, OK? I decided to keep my Barnet, a throwback to the days of the Our Lord Keagan.

I'm an ape man, I'm an ape ape man, I'm an ape man.

'The fuckers!'

'John, let's shower together.'

Clutching her muscular, manly, arse, feeling our own way in, in someone else's dream, twenty four to eight, fake chubsterblonde, rubber tits, page three torn out wannabe—the voice spoke, but was it real?

The painting the size of a wall, beasts with human heads, and war melting women; fantasy abandoned by reason produces impossible monsters, united with her, she is the mother of all arts, the origin of their marvels.

Was any of it real? Since signing for Elstree and Borehamwood Football Club, now fifth in the International Bank of China League Division One, you are not so cocksure. Strutting by the crowds into Lately's Nightclub in Hampstead, well West Hampstead, to be sure, Terry, the women just chuck themselves at you, like vomit, or fake sick from a joke set, as if something in them is driving them on and on, beyond themselves.

Some have pale patches under the make-up, they are getting on, and go on, smothered in gold, dripping in it. Show me the money, show me the lizard. The streets outside are layered with cigarette butts, gum, and half-arsed attempts at getting into society.

You sense women don't really know what they're doing. You like to forgive them like that. Darwin only had it half right though, didn't he, John? They're only doing what they've been told, aren't they, John? And, like the men, they're acting with the herd, but they need to get above the herd, don't they, John? There's still that sense of competition. Who can get the best meat, the best pop for their lolly, and while the birds sometimes work together, they know nothing about real team-work, do they?

'John, I am rubbing my clit and am so damn horny!'

When they're working in pairs they want to be the one who really gives all, so they get called back, alone. It's the same with the puckered-up rent boys.

'Make sure you brush your teeth!'

And when I saw that play, a woman being taught by her psychiatrist husband how to work on her throat muscles to perform a blowjob, it was elastically realistic.

'Don't you want to fuck me hard, up the arse, John?' came another finger-pussy cry.

He had to be at the training ground by ten, felt his cock twitch—the radar-divining tool that would find water or a precious mineral that no one knew about yet.

Up the arse, up the Harris—as in Aristotle, Bottle, that is Bottle and Glass—ARSE! What was it again, the age old proverb? Was it you then who gave up on the fanny when it became too saggy? He couldn't see the fascination of the stool tube, as he had once seen it translated in a Korean porn film Andy had on, and on.

'No love. Thanks for the offer, truly I am most grateful, a thousand apologies not enough you might say, but I'm not interested, scouts' honour. I've got to be at work in twenty minutes. Get dressed and get out, will you.'

It's not as if you don't want a fuck, but the offer of the shit hole, even on the hottest chick, is unappealing and, to be honest, you wouldn't have shagged her anyway, but are too polite to say. You hate that word, shag. It has a Fred West ring to it, he who picked up girls and murdered them with his wife. The man who let innumerable old back rams tap his white ewe so he could watch, initiated into sex by his father shagging sheep, trapping their back legs in his Wellington boots out in the fields, who would have been proud. Maybe even prouder when he knew his son had killed his grandchildren, their bones lying under the house, a type of living cemetery, not hung on his walls Rimbaud fashion. Methodical builder, human, all too human, like Dennis Nielsen boiling up his victims, in total more than a football team, then using the same pot to make curry for his work colleagues. Obsessive Compulsive Disorder–OCD; who doesn't have a neighbour who has it?

You've never believed in sleeping around, have you, have you John, never fallen off the wagon that way. Which actually means you once did, doesn't it John Tao, but we won't go into that at the moment, not right at this moment as the sun nudges its way north to another world. Only the Irish repeat things, things, they repeat them, or reverse them, to be sure, or Yoda. The reason being we can never be sure. Some people thought you were right queer. I mean, why just stay with the one woman when you can have a thousand, a million, every man, woman and beast on the planet? Shouldn't that be our goal–our genes declare so, so and so. Why go against what we are born with, the purity. Just to let difference reign? Whoever made difference a good thing? I tried to explain to me mates that it was about love, commitment, about higher values. But they weren't having it. They thought I was a coward, living in fear of an easy screw.

In the notebook he presented lined drawings of his fiancé wearing nothing but a fur coat, although in one she did have a strap-on dildo, so had obviously been fucking him up the arse, at least in his desires. When I told someone this they said I was a prude for even bothering to mention it, or for reading it in his notebook. Perhaps I was wrong, genuinely wrong, to believe another person would be interested in juvenile scribbling.

Cowardice, I'd heard that about smoking once from my English teacher. He offered me a cigarette on my way home. He wasn't looking for any sexual favours or anything, by the way, OK maybe he was, I don't know and don't care, but he was just trying to bring me into his tribe, his secret circle and clan, like a Scottish Laird, and make himself feel larger, I suppose–it doesn't always work that way–the larger the tribe the safer you feel–but you know what I mean.

'Are you leaving, or what?'

Cat's paw padding, camel toe revealed. She's in here with me, right now, on top of me, moaning, writhing like a demented camel. Playing chess with your eyes shut, fucking a whole series of women blindfold, not having a clue who the fuck they are, correct. I was told my friend

25

went to pools where they swam naked; this is when we were kids. His dad had playing cards with people pissing on each other. At least they do that for real, not the symbolic or the imaginary. I mean people all do that in their own way, sometimes from great heights. But getting it out in the open like that. A certain purity, brutal honesty, we never find out, do we, the level of resistance, or how good the cheese on toast was in that early Beckett story, the head in the sand the perfect choice for whoever we need it to be.

Bring me the head, a cigarette who smoked a human, with the silent man with notes posted all over him, telling us who he was an uncle of mine, or something like that; we didn't really bother with accuracies back then. What happened was he died; who doesn't? And then I got a message from his distant relative, five years later, that he was at the airport. This guy didn't talk either. He just had notes sewn into his jacket telling us who he was.

'You mean things like—Sartorial, Pure New Wool?'

'No his name, basic details, but not really why five years later he would show up like this from Ireland, none of it made sense, chaos reigned.'

At least reason did not dictate. England versus Ireland on at Wembley, two days after you were there, and some players need to stay away, as they are fighting for their careers in their national sides. We can all sit out and read, to a degree, and allow ourselves pre-Oedipal fantasies. Hovering over the vagina, seething with divine retribution a lightning rod, the Acts of the Disciples, twelve or so, they actually act, that is the point, unlike a football team. They throw us to the wind, and then watch as our pieces are gathered, inside the vaginain the shape of Jesus on a boat. Nobody can speak about this, or dare scream my name, or allow a branding on their head. The babe slips into the dawn, its skin a manuscript of forgotten alphabets, humbled accessories, taken from the airport, stolen from religions. Not the baby, found in the sewer system in China, flushed down the toilet, still alive. We trace the man who did it back through his mother's womb, her mother's uterus, cry of a Tom cat, a beacon on a hill, bee the size of a zeppelin, diving into your mouth, frog spawn in your ears. The man did nothing wrong, only his lies came true; the police made them come true.

FLASH. FLASH. FLASH.

'Got it, Wendy?'

'So long, mother fucker.'

2

HOW YOU DOING UP THERE

'Murderer!'

'Whore!'

'Spartan dog!'

Every day a woman stands outside on a ladder, hollering over the crowd–'murderer', and 'whore'!

With my brother John Tao a celebrity footballer, raping or being raped, I am not unaware of publicity. I had to wear a bulletproof vest to work. I grew up believing in God, big-time, no questions asked, as it was part of the fabric of everyday life. God was bigger than the Super Bowl, bigger than your Manchester United or your World Cup. God knitted you together in your mother's womb and was the exoskeleton. I went to Africa, saw the devastation of AIDS and then I volunteered in an abortion clinic. This all seemed the right thing to do. I know it was. These women weren't evil, just desperate. One day I went to work and the woman normally up on the ladder hollering wasn't there. I remember thinking, 'I hope she's OK'. In the reception tired eyes looked up at me.

'We all learn from life,' I told her after the operation.

'You know what, doctor, I am not like these other woman, see.'

She and her partner were going through a difficult time, and they didn't have the money for another child.

Next day she was back on her ladder. We're all on our ladders, shouting expletives, pretending we are way better, screaming and yelling, babies, wagging our tails like mad, sperm racing to the finishing line, to get to the ovum God, the goal, the net. Let's penetrate. Sperm can be thick or thin, it depends on what you've been doing. Smoking has really nothing to do with it; it doesn't turn your semen yellow. Seeing it drip from the, you know–cunt is beautiful, a painting about to form that never does form, but it's a waste. Some girls feel guilty about liking it. The anus is more beautiful, like the so definite article, the ineluctable modality of the anus.

The patient spent seven years or so making an architect's model of a building to replace the World Trade Centre. Then she smashed the fucking thing up, like her bitch. She always had these falling dreams, like everyone else. She was a robot, without the intergalactic heart. I could see everything from the high turret, the wind making the trees dance as ghost-ladies, a churning sea full of old iron statues, and Latin American novels, with marble limbs strewn strategically. We were at a distant relative's chateaux on the way back from Holland, azure turrets and a decaying facade, an old European country finally flipping over into oblivion. My parents were amusing themselves and trying to be clever, arguing nonstop like normal, being themselves by not being, acting out what they felt they had to be to assert themselves, so losing themselves to anger.

There was a form of transcendence in this, I could tell even way back then, a meditation, where there's just a blind roar of a mantra repeated infinitely and everyone gets on the same frequency. We are seeking the final frontier while praying it never comes, in a boat travelling towards the horizon that gets further and further away. My grandfather was an ambassador, as well as a thief, my mother felt abandoned. Did she push my father out of the window, or was he drunk, I don't really want to know. Like John, nobody wants to know. I didn't mind being christened John, bound and put in prison for Herodias' sake, Herod's brother Philip's wife. I was christened after a man who had condemned another man for marrying his brother's wife. As a reward for the niece's dancing, my namesake's head was given because, even though he was sorry, he had made his oath, felt he had to carry it out because he was sitting with those at meat.

My four brothers with me, the little toe rags sleeping, us, well supposed to be, three corridors away, in a room stinking of spiders and spilt cognac. But we could still hear them howling and hollering, lost gods in a Greek tragedy. We were tempted to be the chorus, to put on our white sheets, stand on our beds, echo every sound and gesture. The heavens will always mimic the earth, and vice versa, and hell? I didn't want to think about that. I was balling, a big fat Jesse, as if I would never see again as I now

28

was the father and Oedipus had been at me with a flick knife. A fist in the eye, as Nietzsche put it, the German form of like chalk and cheese.

'You just had him to get back at me, didn't you, fucking bitch!'

They were arguing about me. At least I thought they were. Was I adopted? Had my father's career in football ended because of me? Or was it because he was photographed in a hotel room with a transsexual? What else could they be talking about, not the night, where you could see every star ever created, and to be created. My father really hadn't wanted me. It took away his fucking freedom, and his ambition, made him more rooted in the home, the domestic situation as he liked to put it, and that was the very last place he wanted to be.

Even the smell of my mother got to him.

'Can't you ever wash, you slut!'

I was wondering about these words—'bitch' and 'slut'. I knew bitch had something to do with dog. I felt it was unkind of him to call my mother a dog. I mean she wasn't a jackal, like in the story *The Omen*, for if she was, then one of us was the antichrist. Despite how much my brothers annoyed me, it didn't feel right. We had no supernatural powers. I always felt that the obsession with supernatural powers came from a feeling of powerlessness, people praying they could actually influence things through any other means than hard work, seeing things move with their minds, rather than their hands, denying reality.

She was overwhelmingly pretty, a prettiness that can make you sigh and cry simultaneously, make you bite your fists, force you to accept the notion of a divine being. When she entered a room, men stopped what they were doing and found it hard to resume their conversations, or even to know where they were, or who they were; her presence wiped their minds clean, like someone working to remove traces of internet porn from a computer, or a religious exercise that might take decades, and take all your money. Even my usually negative brothers said so. I wasn't sure what 'slut' meant, however. Was it the same as 'whore'? I'd heard the word 'tart' before, which seemed a bit more comic than 'whore'. 'Slut' sounded seedy low-down, encouraging sloppy seconds, but mother never slept around. Looking after us, she never got the chance, even if she'd have wanted to. China probably had the right idea; you should punish people who had more than one child because they clearly weren't grown up enough to look after them if they couldn't be bothered with contraception.

When we got back to England, just before school started for my second year, I was walking with mother through the cemetery next to the stadium, where one day I would beat the living daylights out of the blues, and we viewed three young men doing martial arts, in what seemed a gay way. I was drinking in the dank smell of centuries of corpses that hung around our necks like a noose even in the killing heat of midday. Mother always talked to everyone.

'I need to learn to kill people by doing Pilates,' she barked, laughing, touching her tummy.

She had a flat stomach, not convex or concave, so maybe she could roll on someone and kill them, for it was as tort as the Law. There was always a hidden anger there, which should have been directed at my father, and came out directed at herself, for what she thought was not being good enough. Everyone was looking for love and she did this by conforming to what she believed others wanted. She seemed eternally happy, but underlying was an infinite sadness, or so I wanted to believe. Why would anyone want to believe their mother was unhappy? Because then they could work on saving them from herself and from others. There is very real potency in this, as in praying to Mary to save the world. Mother always said she never was truly a child, and so she was partly a child now, unable to be an adult, to make independent thought-out choices. So this had an impact on us all and on me in particular. In the cemetery we saw many men, just hanging around the gravestones.

'It's a shame the police don't just let them get on with it.'

One had shorts on, all in white, dressed like a tennis player, smiling provocatively and lapping up the sun like a cat on heat. Others were more thoughtful, at ease with the spirit of the place. I couldn't stop thinking about my poster of a tennis player walking towards the net, scratching her bum, and wondering whether it could be a guy. A lost woman, wispy blonde hair, placed flowers on a grave. I wasn't certain if it was appropriate for me to be hanging around, but mother reassured me it was.

'Do you like this plot? Me and your father have it for seventy five years.'

I wanted to answer that I loved it, the fresh deep grass that smelt of paradise, in the view of the stadium, the Almighty Stadium, grander than a church and the coliseum. But I was worried about it. Wouldn't she live at least another thirty years, and then what, would they just dig on top of her, put bodies there, or cement the whole thing over? Where would I go to pay my respects? None of it made any sense.

'You're not going to die, mother, are you?'

'Your father's trying to kill me, but no, I'm not going to die, not ever.'

He made out it was suicide, which isn't death, is it?

Don't say you can't see him turning now, on the spit at the Artichoke pub, with the rest of them, as they dribble. Remember when a virgin policeman is tricked to come to an island, and is sacrificed to enable the crops to grow. The pubs are closing down, all towns are becoming like a ghost town, and the ones that remain all look the same all the people look the same; that is how you remain, all have the same thoughts, do the same jobs, buy the same phones.

'Hello, is there anybody in there?'

3

DEATH OF A HERO

Cum seeping, dribbling, to use the technical term, out of the pussy, certain women you cannot cope with; leather boots, fur coat, the all-match report. Gillingham 1 Carlisle United 0, a great dribbler that player, like eight goals against Sunderland, or three in extra time, in the Liverpool versus QPR game, dribbling around the entire defence in crotch less knickers, with a golden zip. An Egyptian God, regrets, I've had a few, whatever happened to them, you keep moving up and down, broken yellowing Graeme Greene fury teeth, in the Mexican jungle.

Kicking a ball, we watch men fucking women on a pitch, a woman in goal, not gaol, with her legs open, kneeling back to back with a dildo in each others' anus, waiting for the train, a memory of tomorrow, shaven haven, shaven haven, pummelling down the track. What does the Church have to say, what does the fox say? Forget the bee's knees. Men fucking in the showers, we all saw the big dong, king dong, the mong's dong, and the nun's buns. I don't care if people really approve of Bill Burroughs's sciento-logy, but it is a shame that paying hungry Arab boys to have sex is highlighted in the reviews, as if everyone's life is just a Tennessee Williams' play about cannibalism. Remember the fence where they were trapped, and eaten?

John Tao had known Augustine Illumines, who would be in his fifties by now if still alive. As a kid, he looked up to him. Illumines had every-thing then lost it all, a symbol for hubris, an Icarus figure. John's brother, a surgeon, helped him switch off from their parents incessant arguing, engaging him with memorabilia, football scrapbooks and programmes. He went through it all nostalgically tracing a line of heritage, even old tickets. The football stickers and the cuttings appeared to be from another age but made his heart ache.

Augustine Illumines had what we might classify a good childhood, despite being placed with his brother in a foster home with white parents in Norfolk. On an early documentary they both seem very well fed, happy lads, but from today's perspective you always suspect some form of abuse. Who knows, like everyone else they might have been abused, or thought they were. There's the fantasy and the gap, and then the realisation and the lack of anyone to turn to, and the inevitable police cover up. But the issue is the story, and how you tell yourself that story. And Illumines was good at storytelling, porky or pucker pie eyes.

The problem wasn't that he was black, or gay, although for many these were and are insurmountable problems, it was all the money, and he had a big gob. Those at the top with even bigger orifices didn't like one of their minions having a pop. You had to keep it shut. Today you have to wait until you write a warts-and-all autobiography, where you can set the record straight, according to your own accounts, and take all the swipes you want. Isn't that the nature of publishing, the cut and thrust of it all, a game of two halves?

Slave women had their mouths wired up to be starved, or to be force fed, just to keep their traps shut. So-called terrorists were fed up the arse. Food it seemed, as with anorexia, was the only way to take back power. The same can be said of sex. Don't be in denial. Everyone thought it was a bad signing. The press tried to kill him off in their own British vindictive style they reserve for anyone who might have an inkling of star quality, but who is different, and even in the biographies of the manager they are giving Illumines a right good kicking. He was banned from not just sharing showers but from training, as if the team would catch something.

'Where do you go if you want a loaf of bread?'

'A baker's, I suppose.'

'Where do you go if you want a leg of lamb?'

'A butcher's.'

'So why do you keep going to that bloody poof's' club?'

Old Big Head comes across as a paranoid psychotic alcoholic-homophobe of the highest order, so maybe he just fancied him. Repression. John Tao doesn't think so. Raised by a doting mother, with three brothers, an abortionist, an actor, and a computer geek, what does he know? Illumines plays all over the shop after The Wood, in the good old USA and Canada, returning to City, and the rest, and he comes out with an interview in *The Blob*.

It doesn't matter if you have no love of football, or people think about the money. Could you call this exploiting your own sexuality for cash, or coming clean, or even exploiting the sexuality of others? Can you remember any other player doing so since? I can think of one, thinks John, but we are talking about a quarter of a century on. And he went on about his affairs with a married Conservative MP. The Krays did the same, bribing this Lord and that, setting them up with rent boys, the bisexual soap starselling stories to the press. You don't insult a national treasure.

You can fuck the queen backwards, shave her arse and teach her to walk backwards on her hands and knees, queefing the anthem, piss and stamp on her grave, but don't say a bad word about the queen of TV, a bi-sexual blonde bombshell with a beehive, who took over a small pub in the longest running television show, where the stars have been charged with child sexual abuse, then acquitted. Then she went a bit radio rental, to put it mildly, a bit peanut.

Similarly, it became all the more serious when Illumines was accused of sexual assault by some Smiths-loving boy in the USA, all fabricated, perhaps, by some teenager who had heard about him, and just wanted to sell his story.

'I realised that I had already been presumed guilty. I do not want to give any more embarrassment to my friends and family.' This was his suicide note.

At the Artichoke, John Tao reveals the inner secrets of Scientology, the desert island disc favourite scrawled inside the beast. And still the fat of the swine sizzles and spins. You can't help thinking the pig had known it all, swimming with the fishes, the hefty rump spinning, eyes hypnotising.

'Go on, Sanjay, you're into anything, aren't you?'

John Tao is a lizard now, Sandy remains motionless, and the fields sway, the wind brushing by trailing God's ladyfingers a mercurial hyacinth. Over in Greece the foundation of Western democracy 4,000 commit suicide, unable to pay their bills under the austerity regime, and no paper is allowed to write anything that doesn't support the system. Germany lost the war, but millions of Greeks died with the Germans using Greece as their garden to supply food to their troops, starving them to death. Has anything changed?

'Keep him away from the beast, it's still red raw.'

'That's never stopped him before.'

4
TIED UP IN CHANTAL KNOTT

I am the girl everyone remembers from their childhood, the one who always wanted to play strip poker right up until the bitter end always doing the splits as a girl with tight jeans on, people really wanted to carry me in a sedan chair. The camel was revealed getting the boys going, really did. As a journalist this behaviour is still important. Anything a bit extreme gets them going, don't you think? That's why the boys and often the girls fall for the mad ones, the total loony nut-job Prozac-addled fruitcakes, who stand on the roofs of cars and lift their tops up until the police come and bundle them away, better in bed, obviously.

Becoming a journo and getting the snaps of his gherkin was a natural step, bingo. Kids use the word bingo to mean something great as in 'OMG that was so bingo.' I've yet to hear, 'that was sick bingo.' Not that I'm a collector of slang. Once a week when mum went to Bingo, dad fucked me, to put it crudely. I never thought anything of it, honest to John. I just put it out of my mind, as I was more into Ouija boards and tarot cards.

The first time I saw John in Lately's in North London I knew he was a total sucker and he reminded me a bit of that guy who topped himself. All he could do was reminisce about his favourite stars like Augustine Illumines, the one who topped himself. He didn't have the patter and the streetwise nature like the rest of them football folk. We would take the piss, big time—a bloke wakes up with a hard on, a woody as some idiots call it, caused by a full bladder so taking the piss means popping his false pride. Or it might come from when they took piss on the canals around the country. And taking the Mickey? Mickey Bliss, piss. In a bit of a two and eight are we, need to go for a Sherman? We were in this shamanic game of media, where the knob of a knob was worth more than a few bob.

John was just playing the game but the fool wasn't the game. *You had to be the game.* You didn't have to be a great philosopher to know that, it's like with being on the game. Again, you had to be the game. Know that you are sitting on your assets. John really wasn't like other footballer having done a biology degree at Salford playing for his university side, turning professional later than the rest, so on one level he wasn't an idiot. He wasn't one of them gone up through the ranks from a kid knowing fuck all. Some had been sent over from Ireland aged fourteen and had pissed themselves and craved their mommas for a year while the coaches knocked any empathy for their fellow man out of them. Most had dads who'd been in the game at one point of the other. A closed shop, like any other profession: good game, good game. I'm not sure if my mum was on the game. When she went to Bingo she always came back with a lot of cash and an odd scent about her.

He could have gone on and done research, created the perfect team in a test tube, although difference rules regenerating the greatest dead players. He was already looking at criminality. Is there a gene for criminality, for football hooliganism, for football, for prostitution? There is for addiction but weirdly people with the gene don't necessarily get addicted. Nothing is that simple. In my life as a journalist I watched all these people grow from kids into managers then retire; men with sticks heading for the sun. Some would be accused of one form of abuse or another, each had their own secret and that was my job, like a Catholic priest, getting the confession one way or another. Hacking a phone, a sting operation, the justice of it was for all to see. They didn't have to fall for it, John Tao with the girl, or Augustine Illumines with the boy, but they invariable did which made it so damn easy.

5

AVOIDING THE BEAST

'What time do you call this you slime-covered cock grovelling sand under the foreskin cunt of a cunt?'

'You said ten o'clock, didn't you, Governor? According to Greenwich that means I'm bang on the money?'

'Don't give me that, with your fancy pants talk. You fucking barmy are you, are you, a bit peanut butter, one olive short? None of that me-old China stuff either.'

What should have been a porcelain sky opening to a limitless infinity was a slate grey oppressive mass, burrowing into the players who were practising seven-a-side at a teddy bears' picnic. This was England, if it wasn't clear enough.

'Sorry John, yes I did, son, I know. What's up with you, you look as rough as a rough fuck. On a bender last night was we, was we Jonathan? Well, speak up, lad!'

'Me mother, she's died, guv.'

'Save me the fucking sob story, lad, I've heard them all. I wasn't born yesterday or even tomorrow.'

'No guv, she really has, me ma died, but I thought I better get in anyway and I honestly thought I was on time.'

The skies open and rain turns the glorious green to mud glorious mud. The governor is trying to take this all in, finding it hard to process, old floppy knob.

'Really John, I'm so sorry, Renee was a fine specimen of a woman, that one a living incarnation of sainthood.'

And off he goes, and that's the thing about death, people say all the things they should have said during life. Death brings you back to life. And you didn't need the resurrection to get that in physical form, did you, because if you got that then it defeated the point. He never really died, did he? They stuck the spear in, skewered it in with pleasure, and what not, and blood and wine flowed, and what not, but he was never really dead as a dodo, as he came back. Or he was never dead in the first place. Get out of jail free card. But coming in the flesh like that made it all real.

What's the fucking point of anything, people shopping, the arseholes; don't they know, the houses, the yachts, shooting pheasants, holidays in the Caribbean, the Aston Martins, Rollers, all rubbish, even the game, always the game–only it should bring him closer to the game, it should bring him more into the moment, into the exact moment where past and future have no hold. Or what we may perceive and why, because of the past does not matter, only what we perceive now creates the future–the game.

Like guiding the ball into the back of the net with your thoughts but he had the moment, it made him sick. All we've got is the past and future that's it and the future is the past, so be done with it. You can't be in the moment. It just doesn't exist. Get over the now. Moose knuckles, malatomy, camel toes, the beast within. We become a beast to avoid the pain of being human we all know that, not just Dr Johnson. And we become a human to avoid the pain of being a beast. You must find the difference.

'Mum's funeral's on Friday, so I'll miss training for three days.'

'Take all the time you need, son. I'm really sorry, John. She was such a lovely lady.'

Is that a salty tear slivering down his cheek or is it the bracing weather that dictates everything? The pictures might be all over the internet by now. Your silver Bentley swerves out the ground, a lust for life beyond you. You know you are what you drive, eat, do, think, and what thinks for you, your inner phantom. You know that. And you know you are more than that. You are what your mother thought of you. And that's gone now. But what you think she thought of you remains. You are the intentions of your previous relatives yet to be born, and part of your future relatives yet to be born, and already born. You feel good about that. You picture a time when you return to Elstree, and the Artichoke pub is full of people you knew and you're not sure if it's a dream but dribbling is as real as a tree waving.

6

THE ONLY MAN IN
THE VILLAGE

You are right, it's all about choice these days, isn't it? In Russia there is still only one sort of cola but we've got so many, like that fair trade one that sounds like an African god who creeps up on you every now and again. To say Russians are happier with no choice is oxymoronic, given the problem in the west is over levels of satisfaction. Are you really only a man if you choose to be a man? You make decisions but they are not really your decisions. You are born the way you are, aren't you? But if you're born a man you're not a real man, are you, as you make no decisions about it, it's not really your choice. You need to be turned into one, don't you? If it's all a social construct . . . And what is a man, a cock with two balls? Once they're off you can't sew them back on again. What if you're born without them? I was born without them. But I was born a man in a woman's body. Many men would like that, wouldn't they? To be able to caress their own breasts and vagina, any time?

You might be:

1) a man who wants to be woman and have a woman
2) a woman who wants to be man and have a woman
3) a man who wants to be a man and have a woman as a man
4) a man who wants to have a man as a woman without a cock
5) a man who wants to have a man as a woman with a cock
6) a woman who wants to have a man as a woman with a cock
7) a woman who wants to have a man as a woman without a cock
8) a hermaphrodite who is being forced to live as a girl and wants to be a girl and have a woman
9) or wants a woman as a man with or without a cock

39

10) or wants to be a man and have a man who wants to be a woman with or without a cock

11) or a hermaphrodite who wants to be a hermaphrodite or whatever combination you want, and what about those people who change into something different, more like an animal, or alien?

In great literature people pay to be sodomised by monkeys. In Germany it may not be illegal and on certain roads there is no speed limit, but you never see people in BMW ZXs fucking pigs, and going at two hundred miles an hour. Is that because we can't keep up? There are a nameless number who get moist over the brothels containing all manner of beasts, not just the number of the beast. We have read about the serial killer Fred West, who should have supported a football team instead. Of course all forms of rape are wrong, but what if consent is there when dogs start humping girls, to be a man you must what? Like football, grow hairs on your chest, balls, wherever. Pay for your round of drinks, on a regular basis and hang your shirts up correctly. That's only a certain type of man. But then in this game you shave your hair on your balls off again. I'm the only ex-woman playing in the football league, apparently.

Maybe there are others, but nobody is going to write about it, like a confession, are they, and it's not an issue, I've got the scars to prove I was once a woman, but now I'm a man with a cock. My clitoris is still there, below my cock, a mini me. I feel it all the more now with a cock. I get changed separately, that's OK. Nobody thinks it's weird. A lot of the blokes do that these days. We all need more privacy. They're told to do that if they're gay. I'm a bloke. Not making my mind up, transgender, or in transition. I'm a bloke that's it, full-stop; no period, not anymore, another relief not being on the rag. I noticed the changes rapidly once I started injecting testosterone. I found it hard to cry anymore, and I couldn't see the other person's point of view. I was always right. But that was good for me. If you're a professional sportsman you have to be mad. It's pathological, the focus, and if you see someone else's point of view, you're lost.

Totally–Brian Clough, the greatest manager that ever lived, England never had–it wasn't just he was a raving lunatic, stuck inside his own head, not always drunk, but permanently aggravated or aggravating. I loved him, he was my hero. To be human we need to see someone else's point of view, but if we bow down to that we lose our vision, so in this sense the greatest humans are not human. Power means not listening. I was in a transsexual club, and I heard a transitioning woman say while other people always wanted to be astronauts or a doctor, s/he had always wanted to be a woman. WOMAN, as the big sign on the road to the golf club said, just in case you fancied one, not becoming one. Is that an ambition, why be a woman? Because you were raised by a woman, and a woman attracts, so you want the attention. Go fuck yourself.

You can see the point? I wanted to be a man, to work in a man's world? Full stop and start period. I also, deep down, felt like I was a man. This is something beyond images, like guns and roses. Men go to these clubs because they want a chick with a dick. They're interested. Men will fuck anything kinky. But the transsexuals who are going to have the snip really don't want to meet a guy like this, do they, because they won't have a dick? The man hunting a chick with a dick then might fall in love and accept the man turning into a woman without a dick. That is something beautiful. But not as beautiful as the beautiful game, the green pitch, the slate sky and the moronic crowds, Bolton fans dancing with bellies out, shirts pulled up over their heads as the Watford fans carry on with their crosswords.

7

HACKED OFF

In bed, at five fifteen in the morning, listening to the birds, not the unborn chicken voices in her head, but the real tweets outside in the streets, that sit above the odd purr of a mechanical beast–watch the birdy! She has the picture, always about the picture. This would make a few quid. Why does she feel happy about that, evidence of a transgression? The extension needs paying for, of course, and she could do with a new Porsche. She needs it. Needs and wants, was there a difference? For Nietzsche to be is to do; for Kant to do is to be; but for Sinatra, do be, do be, do.

Don't mention she couldn't function without something warm in her mouth in the morning. In her study, her shrine to footballers possesses her. John Tao, with his floppy vein-ridden cock out, from that unfortunate match where a colleague had shoved his boot into his groin, dragging his foot down, ripping his pants, and they'd had to do an emergency operation on the pitch.

Then there's the human centipede photo–she wasn't able to get this one published anywhere worth anything. Seven International Bank of China League Division One players fucking each other in a circle, shuffling round and round, passing a football at the same time–pretty clever that one, and insisted on by the Greek coach to enhance bonding, so she was told: photos and video footage.

And so much better than the four cock anal shot.

While loads of papers had the press release insisting that England captain Harry Chimp be sacked, Wendy had her own headline in mind:

'Support players' rights to spit-roast models!' hankering for the simpler time when in those halcyon days of 1976 Malcolm Allison led Crystal Palace into the communal bath with porn star Fiona Richmond, or so she had read on a website on February the 2nd 2012, and I quote now, for legal reasons. Those were the days, my friend, we thought they'd never end. What was wrong with you, watching Crystal Palace beat Watford in the playoffs, like a martyr?

You can see Fiona now, tits bounding, smell all that mud and the dodgy soap made from boiled horses and cabbage, the floating congealed semen making surreal paisley patterns on the greasy grey tub, the bubbles from the farts. Spit-roasting may be cheaper than hiring two hookers, of course, and there was less trouble with one, so in these days of austerity, mitigation instead of litigation, clawing back at every corner, even for footballers on two million a month, this was inevitable. Not always. One player fucked her from behind, while the other fucked her in the mouth. And she became a large beast on a spit, roasting over the fire outside a pub in Elstree Village.

Everyone had the money-given right to do as they pleased, whenever they pleased, regardless, didn't they? Pounds, shillings and pence, still throwing spears. Forget it, if there was any substance, any soul, in the nature of things outside of us. That was how the world worked. You gained money through any means necessary, so you could do what the hell you liked. What the hell, interesting that. There's no freedom with observation. What money bought was privacy, being beyond the law; you became your own police force and God. OK, if it was in the total privacy of your own bedroom then so what, did it matter what you did but why was doing it in public any different after all? *Let's go outside* sang George Michael, perhaps, but only with privacy is there autonomy so George was actually looking to be caught and controlled by others. Punishment and control can be fun. And autonomy is removed through observation, for sure, of course. So shouldn't the public performance actually be better, more legitimate, less of an issue because autonomy is then removed. If you do it outside you are always going to be a conformist. In public there is no independence, everyone is one. And really, is anyone independent?

You could put a webcam in your house and broadcast everything to the world anyway. You might do that to someone you are sharing a room with, like that college kid in America who then jumped off a bridge. Shit happens, put a webcam in a toilet to reveal it, but don't we have the right to see what is going on, everywhere, a God-given right to be God. Even if we don't have a God-given right to know God, Deus cognitus Deus nullus, I always say. We pay taxes, some of us, and this is for our protection apparently, so let's watch what we're paying for. Well not really, as this camera was put in surreptitiously. But if people are fucking hard in public, then they shouldn't mind if we watch. And what about children, we don't want the children seeing people fucking now, do we? The line—draw it please.

The Pope had toured Latin America prior to the World Cup in Brazil, and there were outdoors confessionals, all being made public on one level, like portable toilets. In the confessional box all is hidden, then all is revealed, and forgiven but kept secret, uncovered and then sealed. When did we truly get away from the eyes of the other? If we believe in God never nothing is autonomous, nothing truly authentic, if by authentic we mean independent. And that's the point really, we are never independent. She begins by touching her two-and-a-half-inch-long, one-inch wide clitoris, lightly, relishing the autonomy of it, its independence, not thinking about anything or anyone, yet.

Nobody is watching, apparently. Part of her wants there to be, is desperate for there to be, that's why she has no curtains. It's her confession, and the confessional box is the universe. She's been a life model at Allum Hall Elstree, and wasn't ever invaded or penetrated by the eyes of others. Once she noticed John Tao watching her through the bay windows, but when she stared right at him he went beetroot. She'd enjoyed the way she had the control of others' visions, minds, hearts and desires through her body, even the student they called Road Kill, because that's all he could afford to eat—squashed badgers.

If people across the road want to they can stare straight into her room and see her masturbating, right now. Her fingers are slipping in. It's their choice. Their fingers are slipping in. They masturbate, synchronously, and someone watching them masturbates, and someone watching them. And a blind man, completely disinterested, asking what his wife is doing, records her moans, and a deaf woman spies the blind man's wife, and feels her pleasure, which pleasures her.

She couldn't see.

Jed has tied an orange blindfold on her. OK, she tied it on herself. She can't hear. He's put small earphones on her, *The Little Drummer Boy* by Bing Crosby and David Bowie blasting out at the highest volume, warp factor ten. He's plunging his tool deeper and deeper into her, deeper than ever before. What was he getting at and what was driving him on? Plumbing metaphors are so unsexy. And it was a plunger, as if he was trying to unblock her inner being, let out the genii that possessed him and free her. Sadly some might say, all we desire is our own desire, is that it, so we fuck our self for sure, and how happy we are when we realise nobody can satisfy our desire if we're an Eagletonian Lacanian. Sure he wanted her to cum, why not, yes he did, but it was up to her really, wasn't it? He wasn't going to get too worked up about it.

'I want to cum,' she bashed the bed with fists of meat.

He'd done the training, put in the time, gone through the teams of the divisions, every football club in every one of them, their first and second teams, even their youth sides and the women's teams, it was the journey not the destination, right?

She loved looking at herself with a mirror, checking herself out seeing if she was really there, the reflections counted, and she was counting anything else, the marks or signs, she was just trying to see the truth. Seeing what happened when she farted, fanny or otherwise, things like that, what we all want to know about. The answer is blowing in the wind. Observation was the key, and he found that odd, but knew it wasn't. Most people would like to see themselves.

It was actually her flesh and blood, but maybe it wasn't, more a gift from somewhere but she had to come and own it possess it and this was her way. If she didn't examine it with a mirror, get others to draw it and possess it and be possessed by it, then she wouldn't own it would she, but this wasn't all there was to her.

And it turned him on and around, that it turned her on John, it made it less work for him. Strange that it had become work. The phrase 'on the job' had got to him as well, in its accuracy. It had all become so God-damn capitalist, with the input and the pay off, even without the money shot. Where was the profit in it though? Wherever it happened there was an issue.

The machine nature of it, so why not fuck a machine? When people were fucking fake vaginas weren't they fucking a machine or the machine maker? We hate the machines and we love them; we want autonomy and independence but we loathe it, we need controlling, we can hand over responsibility to the all seeing-eye, the vagina, we can make God not in our own image but in God's image, which is? The image of what exactly, as God does not have an image, and all images are Satan's work, aren't they? All images are an attempt to distract us from the spiritual. When we made love were we making love to the divine or our own image of the divine which was Satan. Was the love of God the root of all evil?

Do we only desire our desire as in our desire for our desire? Machines were in the human before they existed post-human, or were to take over and govern humans, and on other planets they might have superseded human-type beings, so it wasn't such a big deal, was it? And once we were animals, so why should be going in that direction matter? It was wrong, and shameful, but everyone would want to watch, they would be fascinated, in awe, it would lead to transcendence, a mystical experience, like meditation. Amen, so be it. And the spit was turning, the hog roast burning as the punters cheer and jeer at his lonely lovely eyes.

8

DERBY DOGGERS

There's nothing like rolling countryside or a roll in the countryside for that matter. John Tao professional pig's bladder player pulled over, oblivious to the photographs of him, and saw that he was limp and she was now riding the gear stick instead of him. We had to forget a guy had set fire to his own family, killing six of his kids, and to get over the trauma said he had gone out dogging in Derby, that he needed the affirmation of the sex and the people watching, as if all was a performance. Now you see it, now you don't. And then the authenticity of the public private act was this sex in a car shocking; not unless we realise that it was made of dead pig, the gear knob. We weren't in Germany or in Greece. This was beautiful in a way, as if nothing is necessary of which the opposite is possible. At least the pig had died for a reason.

Evil to him who finds evil.

The pig initially died so someone could hustle about the streets in a dodgy canary yellow super-woofer motor and damage the planet. Now the pig, at least in this afterlife form, was giving someone heaven. It wasn't just swinging from the heaven of a van, waiting to be carved up, or to being sent into the sea, one of two thousand Gadarene swine, stuffed with demons from the healed man. Go to heaven by giving heaven—surely this was the best advertising slogan ever? The pig may not have entered heaven, and she screamed, not unlike a pig in the ear of her lover, who was called Nigel, of all names, and Nigel began to grow hard again—again.

The way I grew hard was something I am sure you will have to get used to. I know what you're thinking as you watch on. A pleasant surprise, a way beyond the inevitable; give me the highlighted truth of everything you know, the stuck-on eyebrows or moustache. Each pleasantry in the caravan picking them up, on the doorsteps of mental hospitals using them to pave driveways where people bury their families, everything in the present continuous of course. I never thought I'd see you at the window of the Derby Doggers lost in yourself.

The fortune if there is one lost in the forest, naked, the girls with their sweaty jugs and spicy thighs crushing the men, reading books about people reading books as they have sex in cars, watched by people reading books about people in cars being watched by people having sex, in a book in a car, the whole machine a pig made of paper, a moment of truth.

It is not necessary to know your black silk dress is a fortune from start to finish, including the hooves. Each time we repeat ourselves there is something different going on but hopefully in the same way it exists, leads to a greater depth, the ritual is a moment of eternity black and white magic show. The jaws of hell, the ministry of justice, it will happen any second now, the beauty of it all.

How come you said otherwise, a brief moment in the street when we seek to see each eventually and then she is there, unconscious of the fact, so she will freeze to death, in her cut downs, long legs, and her eyebrows that are just there, nowhere else but left there minus. There was the film, *Crash*, both of them, that involved sex in cars, and that soap star who was going around having a blow job on the A1. She was arrested but not charged, sorry Sarge.

She never liked to think of the past, where her parents were put in jail for failing to ensure that she attended school. That's what happened, a chart not plotting their growth, but their moods and dreams. I saw you in the shadow of your past. There is nothing wrong with a celebration of a school where the kids say you will be chopped up and eaten by maggots, if that is all you want. At the school there is a mystery around the music teachers who are bumped off, or at least do a rum-baba, a runner, they disappear, ripping up the music sheets as they go, the worst kind of Hansel and Gretel.

At school, Mark stood in the playground beaten by drugs and a drug addict, a ten-year prison sentence of sorts. I was given back my knives, confiscated on a school trip, so this made me realise that dreams were being made. The best time was reading *Roots* in the library. The teacher was a bit of an actor, and for some reason I get the feeling he dated my sister. There was a play of *The Wizard of Oz* and my sister went out with the tin-man. Being younger you felt a bit left out of it all, but that was also good, you did not have to be totally wrapped up in it all; nothing had to mean anything at all.

A prison camp was a good way to describe it. After a bottle of gin, and I don't like gin, I fucked Sarah all night long, in a house of a mate of hers in Pinner, in the back room next to the kitchen, on the floor. Best night of my life, by far. We often fucked on the floor and got sore knees. Like at the Blanks' house in Radlett. The twins, reminding us that our identity was not unique, and their cohort, would be in the kitchen skinning up putting hombrero in his little jacket. We would be in the posh front room, the one only for dinner parties, doing it behind the barely touched sofa on the floor. I always preferred alcohol to drugs, unlike those in the kitchen permanently stoned. So I fucked Sarah in her mate's house in Pinner. For some reason in my little red note book I have written: does it matter if she was there? That's a bit cruel of me, on myself, don't you think? There was something amazing about her mate or cousin, and the next day my black Capri broke down. Red and black, which team plays in red and black? Red equals black; what is the significance according to Lacan or Derrida? Colours always meant something, Gaddafi with his green book, Wittgenstein and Jung with their colouring books. John could not help himself be paralysed by the equation.

A professional footballer with a penchant for dogging; at least it is kept inside the car. He never took *his* car that would be stupid; the press had his private plate and were constantly looking for BE11 END and B9 APE. He always hired one, went down to the woods and fucked some fat old slapper until she squealed, with people watching, giving everyone what they wanted was a trait of his, some voodoo black magic.

Well it didn't really matter we were at a loss, but it was only the battery, the car came to life and our mood changed. For my eighteenth I'd fucked her on the stairs at Camden Palace and nobody but us there and with another girl we'd fucked on someone's front lawn as her friend was cutting the grass as the cars driven by gorillas rocked by.

On the way to our wedding, I looked up and saw the top floor of the double-decker, screamed at by the upper classes, full of goat-headed monkeys and masturbating priests. That was the norm. John was at the bar drinking champagne chatting up two girls that had been in the television show *Grange Hill*. I liked the brunette, he the blonde, and he'd even somehow believed she lived in South London. Then, of course, he went looking for her but he saw her every week at the Camden Palace and I don't know if he ever got the guts to speak with her. Why should he, why would anyone want to break the fantasy? We had stopped in a car park to skin up and saw John dogging, nothing new there, giving it the Brown Derby with the Dirty Sanchez. The saloon bar doors had already flipped back, there was no answer.

At the Artichoke he walks straight up to the rotating swine and pats it like an old pal, someone he used to know and he has banged them in a pig suit and roasted them for good measure, male and female, for all eternity. Whether it is a Barbie doll in frilly knickers or a bar-b with a grill, it gives someone a thrill, and it rotates, see, watch it moving from the top of the hill. A third of a mile away is a playground, with one rocking fish, a climbing frame, and a broken swing, fences smothered in glass, and two graveyards where the holocaust memorial day is held and the following took place, live from Golgotha, as Vidal put it.

Memorial Day

*A cemetery in North London on a crisp mid-January morning. Well-tended graves are matched with lovingly kept grass that spreads all about. The soft purr of traffic and bird song accentuates the peace that hangs, containing memories of those lost and those who mourn. Two local **Religious Leaders** and a **Council Representative** gather here for the annual Memorial Day.*

RELIGIOUS LEADER 1 IS IN HIS EARLY FORTIES, STRICT, CLEAN SHAVEN, STUBBORN, SLIGHTLY SHY AND SOMETIMES PRONE TO AGGRESSION.

RELIGIOUS LEADER 2 IS IN HIS LATE FIFTIES, BEARDED AND GARRULOUS, AND, AT HEART, A GENTLE, IF TROUBLED MAN.

COUNCIL REPRESENTATIVE, HARRY, IS IN HIS EARLY THIRTIES, COMMITTED TO HIS JOB AND EQUALITY, BUT HE IS UNSURE OF HIS OWN IDENTITY.

Act 1 Scene 1

Religious Leader 1: This is ridiculous. Absolutely ridiculous, a crime.

Religious Leader 2: I hold you personally responsible. On a day as sensitive and important as this, and this all you could provide. You should be ashamed of yourself.

Religious Leader 1: Ashamed.

Religious Leader 2: Stones. This all you bring for us. Stones.

Council Representative: What did you expect–gold, frankincense, myrrh? I was hoping you'd be aware of the religious significance, their profound significance.

Religious Leader 2: What do you know?

Religious Leader 1: He knows nothing.

Religious Leader 2: You're right, this is like an insult.

Religious Leader 1: It is an insult.

Religious Leader 2: Millions of our people are murdered and on the day that is supposed to commemorate their memory you get us to place stones. Of all things stones. Inert, lifeless objects, with no beauty. The point being exactly?

Council Representative: The point being just that, of course, nothing can truly represent the horror, so these are symbolic.

Religious Leader 1: Symbolic of nothing.

Council Representative: They represent the weight of the tragedy plus the souls of the dead and they are like an offering.

Religious Leader 1: Ha.

Council Representative: I'm sorry but you gave me nothing to go on and I've done my best here. I really have. I've thought of nothing else for weeks. I've done my research, I've seen what your graveyards are like and you use stones, but if you wanted something specific you should have said.

Religious Leader 2: You expect us to do your job for you, is that it now?

Religious Leader 1: He does. Sure, he does.

Council Representative: No, I don't. But I realise people's taste differ, obviously, so I needed a happy medium. Anything I do might be taken the wrong way, might offend, so even if I can't win I might as well fail and fail well.

Religious Leader 2: Did Beckett say that? It's all about taste to you, is it? Nothing to do with identity, memory or history or people? Aesthetics, taste. You are a joke, you know that.

Religious Leader 1: A joke. Yes, a joke.

Council Representative: Don't get offensive. OK, the positive here is that you two who are normally disagreeing on everything have found a common enemy in me. Sound familiar?

Religious Leader 2: What on God's blessed earth are you insinuating?

Council Representative: It's not an insinuation, but a fact. Religion always has a common enemy. Those outside it, the goats, and you're the sheep.

Religious Leader 2: You're an outrage, you know that.

Religious Leader 1: An outrage.

Religious Leader 2: I'll have you sacked, cast out.

Religious Leader 1: Sack him.

Religious Leader 2: There's a sack over there. (He points to the other side of the cemetery)

Act 1 Scene 2

The same cemetery in mid-January, now late morning, nearing noon.

MICHAEL THE GRAVEDIGGER, EARLY SIXTIES, SHORT AND STOCKY.

Michael is talking with the two Religious Leaders.

Michael: So where's Harry gone then? He's a good lad, that Harry.

Religious Leader 2: Harry, who's Harry?

Michael: Harry, you know, the lad you were chatting with. He's got a good job with the council, does a lot locally. Helps out with disabled kids. They love him. Plays cricket with unemployed Muslim lads. He likes a drink, mind, but there's nothing wrong with that, is there? You've got to enjoy yourself when you still have your health.

Religious Leader 1: He's gone.

Religious Leader 2: That's right. Said he had another function or meeting. You know these council workers, always something on, meetings, meetings, meetings, never standing still, doing good for the community.

Michael: Did you like what they'd done for you this year?

Religious Leader 2: Of course, it was very pleasant, very appropriate.

Michael: Funny, but from where I was it looked like you were having an argument.

Religious Leader 2: Heated discussion, that's all. He's a bit of a theologian is our Harry. He wanted us to really understand the symbolism of what he'd done. It was quite sweet really, very kind of him.

Michael: Odd though, he didn't come and say goodbye to me. Me and his dad were friends you see. His dad was my doctor for years. Whenever Harry comes here we have a brew together and a crafty smoke, if he hasn't given up again.

Religious Leader 2: Like I said, he's a busy man, and so are we, so we better be off.

Religious Leader 1: Yes, better be off, goodbye sir.

Michael: One more thing before you go fellers. I had a sack over here, but it's gone. You didn't see who took it, did you? Just as odd as Harry not coming to see me that is, a sack disappearing like that into thin air.

Religious Leader 2: Sorry no. Terrible, isn't it. You never can be too careful, even in a graveyard. Adieu.

Act 2 Scene 1

The same cemetery, noon. Only the Religious Leaders remain.

Religious Leader 2: Do you think we should say a prayer for him?

Religious Leader 1: No, that would be offensive to God and to him, he wasn't religious.

Religious Leader 2: But God causes it to rain on the good and the bad alike, ours is an unjust God. And we need to pray for our own people who were murdered, so slipping one in for him wouldn't be too much of an effort, would it?

Religious Leader 1: I'd rather not.

Religious Leader 2: But it's not really up to you, is it, what you'd rather do or not do. We're just the vessels; we are God's hands.

Religious Leader 1: If you want to pray for him, then do so.

Religious Leader 2: I can't pray on my own.

Religious Leader 1: It's not like sex, you know.

Religious Leader 2: Sure, but it does work better with two, surely.

Religious Leader 1: You're much more experienced than me, yet you still think prayer is some form of magic. It's not about us bending God's ear, or us loving Him, it's Him loving us.

Religious Leader 2: I was just asking for support, it's about the collective, community, that's why we're here today, to remember who we are, and where we came from. I get the feeling you see faith as just an individual thing, like a personal relationship and that's it, no history. You may as well forget the past, if that's the case.

Religious Leader 1: I'm not saying forget history, but all the prophets said you'd always have war. We've seen it here today. Yet another battle, so when will it ever end?

Religious Leader 2: You think if you were in your nice cosy box with God and nobody else you'd find it was all perfect? You have got a lot to learn. Hell isn't other people. Hell is yourself making you blind to God. In your own little world with God there are so many more demons.

Religious Leader 1: Do you think that gravedigger really suspected something? Here take this.

(He hands a large hipflask to Religious Leader 2, who drinks heartily.)

Religious Leader 2: No. We're lucky. People trust us, and our people.

Religious Leader 1: I'd say it was the opposite, people are paranoid about us.

Religious Leader 2: I'd feel better if we both prayed.

Religious Leader 1: Your point before. It sounds so damn woolly, so liberal, as if God is just a part of your psyche, and all things wrong are just the negative parts. Have you become completely relativistic? Can't God be outside of your head?

Religious Leader 2: I think God is what we love, what we fear, what we think, feel, what we create. If you want to believe God is something more or less than that, then I am not going to dictate to you. I'd therefore appreciate it if you don't dictate to me. We're all grownups. Religion gets a bad name because people batter each other over the head with it, but faith is something that grows quietly. When Rebecca died and I was left with our children to take care of I didn't ask God, where are you now, I didn't rant and rave against the sky. I had good friends and family around me to support me. To me that's the key to good religion. Religion needs to be inclusive otherwise it is worse than some ideology that gets rid of people it doesn't like, as it claims to be acting in the name of God.

Religious Leader 1: So why have God in the equation at all?

Religious Leader 2: God stops us from becoming too arrogant. While we are his hands and his eyes, we still need to trust in him continually, and rely on him. Do you think we were too harsh with that man from the council, what was his name?

Religious Leader 1: Harry.

Religious Leader 2: Yes him. Perhaps he had tried his best. He didn't really know our culture, but he was trying to make an effort. And look what became of him.

Act 2 Scene 2

The same cemetery in mid-January, evening. The Religious Leaders remain, interrupted by Michael.

Religious Leader 1: People get what they deserve.

Religious Leader 2: People probably said that about our people.

Religious Leader 1: How dare you talk about our people in the same breath?

Religious Leader 2: People are people, do you not see that. The essence of religion is to understand this. If we don't we are lost.

Michael: Sorry to interrupt your chat, but it's getting late. We're locking up soon. I've had the Council on the phone, the buggers. They've not heard from Harry, accused me of going off down the pub with him. Chance would be a fine thing. Strange he would vanish like that. I mean you said he was off to another meeting. Did he say where?

Religious Leader 1: No, not that I recall.

Michael: And do you recognise this at all?

(Michael holds up a glove.)

Michael: It's one of his, I know it is.

Religious Leader 2: What makes you so sure it is his? It could have belonged to anyone.

Michael: Are you saying it isn't?

Religious Leader 1: It's getting too cold to argue. I hope you find Harry, now I must be off.

Michael: Does it not remind you of something, all those articles of clothing at Ellis Island perhaps?

Religious Leader 2: I'm not sure what you're getting at. As if this cemetery is a passage to the New World. It's a good metaphor; the Egyptians would have liked it.

Religious Leader 1: You two have lost me. Now, I must be going.

Michael: I know what you've done.

Religious Leader 1: I don't know what you're talking about.

Michael: Don't lie now. He was a bit of a cunt to be honest. Probably deserved it. Just tell me where you've buried him, that's all. We don't want to be digging up a plot only to find him now, do we? I'll even help you bury him again.

Religious Leader 2: No need for that. He's probably just gone off somewhere, who knows. We've got nothing to do with it, that's for sure. I don't know how we're supposed to convince you.

Michael: Have him raised from the dead.

Religious Leader 1: What are you getting at? Harry was Jesus, and we were the Jewish authorities that killed him? And now we must perform a miracle? Christians often forget that Jesus was in fact Jewish.

Religious Leader 2: Part of today was about acknowledging tradition. Jesus did that. He said he had not come to do away with the Law but to fulfil it. Although as a child I remember our teacher and my father referring to the man as 'that man', people being unable to pronounce his name. He may have been a miracle worker for all I know but I'm certain I am not.

Michael: So, are you admitting something has happened to Harry?

Religious Leader 2: We're all just visitors. Something happens to all of us, hopefully, otherwise we're not alive.

Michael: You're not saying it doesn't matter what happens to us, it doesn't matter if it's good or bad, only that it happens. That would be really nonsensical.

Religious Leader 1: I've got to be going.

Religious Leader 2: You're not going anywhere. You got us into this mess, now you get us out of it.

Religious Leader 1: OK, I'll admit that we . . .

Act 3 Scene 1

The same cemetery in mid-January, night. The Religious Leaders are sitting tied up together by rope. Mass of St John The Baptist, Gregorian Chant, plays in the background.

Religious Leader 2: This wasn't really what I had in mind for memorial day. If we're left here long enough, we'll be the memorial, so that might be appropriate.

Religious Leader 1: I know you rarely think of God, but would you say all we can do now is pray?

Religious Leader 2: That's the final resort. We need to work out where the man puts his trophies. He must do this to a lot of visitors, just for kicks. He must have a shed where he keeps trophies, like the fingers of his victims.

Religious Leader 1: You mean Harry?

Religious Leader 2: I don't know. Maybe Harry's in on it, who knows. It seems a bit off though doesn't it? I mean to accuse us of doing something to Harry, just after Harry disappears, a bit fishy, like they were both in on it.

Religious Leader 1: But what would be the point?

Religious Leader 2: A theological point maybe. This could all be a metaphor. We are tied up together, as if we get tied up together in arguments about God. We pray in the night, as we may need to pray soon, for peace. Everything can be a metaphor for anything; the grass can have the rain running up or down. I want you to know that I don't mean anything I say and personally I don't have a problem with you.

Religious Leader 1: You're talking as if we won't get out of this.

Religious Leader 2: My wife will come looking for me, sooner or later, so I'm not worried about that. A man went to the doctor and said his wife had died. The doctor asked him how he knew. The man replied, well the sex is the same but the ironing is piling up. I wonder what a wife would say. What would she notice that was missing? She might notice that she was getting more sleep without the snoring, or that the house smelt nicer without all the farting. She might be much better off without him.

57

Religious Leader 1: Your wife perhaps, the way you leave your clothes all over the floor, and urinate on the toilet seat.

Religious Leader 2: How do you know that?

Religious Leader 1: You may as well know this now, seeing as we might be buried alive. I'm having an affair with Sarah. She wanted someone younger with a harder cock. I was happy to oblige, for the sake of married harmony, you see. I didn't want her running off with anyone. I know you have four children she needs to take care of.

Act 3 Scene 2

The same cemetery in mid-January, dawn the next morning.

Michael: I always knew we could come to some sort of agreement there. Your man, your horse, was some kind of fucker, to be sure. The world's a better place without him I know that and deep down so do you.

Religious Leader 2: And, while I'm sure he gave my wife a good time, he didn't have much to say, did he; he can't have been very good with his congregation, whispering words of wisdom or sweet nothings.

Michael: I've buried him over by the pear tree to the east of the cemetery. The sun will be on his back, which will help his joints. He'll be able to hear the sound of the trains rumbling by. Maybe it will help him sleep.

Religious Leader 2: And Harry, is he OK?

Michael: That's a long story. The long and winding road. Harry went out on the lash yesterday afternoon, a wee pub-crawl all around North London. It was the anniversary of his grandma's death. I'd forgotten. They were really close. I feel terrible about it. I should have been comforting him; instead he was drowning his sorrows.

Religious Leader 2: Don't blame yourself, he'll be alright?

Michael: Sure, he'll be more than alright. Harry met a Swedish girl and was banging her senseless all night long. Lead us not into temptation.

Religious Leader 2: Banging it, like the nails in the cross. Banging the girl; crucifying her.

Michael: Not exactly, and yes I know Jesus was a Jew. What are you going to do with your wife?

Religious Leader 2: We are taught to forgive seventy times seven.

Michael: Is that how often she did it with your religious colleague?

Religious Leader 2: Only the sad or neurotic count these things. Love is not a numbers game.

Michael: I nearly became a monk, but I preferred love of the fleshly kind.

Religious Leader 2: I have my four children to think of. They don't want to know theirmother is a slut.

Michael: Just because someone falls in love it doesn't mean they're a slut now, does it?

Religious Leader 2: Sorry, you're right, that was wrong of me. No, it doesn't make you a slut if you fall in love. But where do you draw the line between love and lust? Lust's when you think of yourself, and how to satisfy your desires. Love's when you think of the person you love, and how to satisfy them.

Michael: They're not mutually exclusive. We like to think we can control all of it, but it's not that simple.

Religious Leader 2: So, if it's not such a crime, why did you help me kill the guy?

Michael: He was an arse, pure and simple, and it had such a good logic to it, including the burial in the east, next to the pear tree. Whenever you or your wife wants to experience him you can pick those pears and make something from them.

Religious Leader 2: He can be reincarnated in those that consume him. I like that. He claimed to be a strict observer, and saw his way as the one true path. He'll hate to be associated with another religion.

Michael: Well, this can be the final lesson we teach him.

Act 3 Scene 3

The same cemetery in mid-January, dawn the next morning. The Mass of St John The Baptist, Gregorian Chant plays.

Religious Leader 2: We were arguing about the Memorial Day. We both thought Harry hadn't made an effort, that he didn't understand us. But there was really nothing he could do, I can see that now.

Michael: He tried his best, I know he did. We all try our best. Sometimes it works, sometimes it doesn't. Like you. You might try and forgive your wife, get back to normal, think of your kids as your own, help others, eat well.

Religious Leader 2: All we can do is to try whatever happens.

Michael: Whatever happens, yes, whatever happens.

(Religious Leader 2 holds his hand out to shake Michael's hand, but Michael holds his hands together as if in prayer and bows low towards him.)

Michael: Now, if you'll excuse me, I have a job of work to do.

(Religious Leader 2 falls to his knees and prays.)

9

THE LOLLYPOP LAD

After that, we drove around at night wondering where she lived, fantasising over what she did when the children slept. Out of uniform, we thought she was just the same as any other woman with nothing to do, watching the soaps, knitting, stroking her pussy. We sped by the Artichoke, where creatures were spit-roasted. We were stalking her, the lady in white. Who else did you see dressed up like that? Maybe a butcher or a dentist, but none of them wandered around in the middle of the road holding up a stick with a big head on, stopping the traffic so kids could gambol safely across the road.

Our obsession with Mrs Turtle began when we found out it was her that had grassed us up. We used to sell kids a bit of blow, nothing too heavy mind. They wanted it, and we supplied it. They'd probably all be on heroin if it weren't for us! The only jobs going were in call centres, so this was one way of avoiding that nightmare. Would you really want one of us ringing you up, trying to flog you stuff?

Chris and Ray had chipped in for a classic Ford Escort Mexico, with bucket seats up front, and super-woofers in the rear. We had a right laugh cruising around, just going mental, blasting out music. Then, because of that old cow, the buisies began eyeing our every move. That's why we began watching her back, just to make sure she was paranoid.

It was easy really, in such a small town. Everyone knew each other's business. Turtle did duties at the school morning, dinner and home time, so we were always there. Why should we stop just because she held a stupid stick in her hand? It wasn't like she was a traffic light or anything. Given the law were watching us, getting us to move on and stop harassing her, we decided to find out where she lived. All the terraces were identical but her tiny front was as manicured and neat as they come.

I could hear the beats of *EastEnders* as my nose met her door. Through the letterbox, I spotted a large lollipop lolling against the wall like a skinny lover. I wanted one, thought it would come in handy if I ever needed to give someone a good hiding. But I realised it would be better if I did something obscene on it, or wrote: Please Run Me Over.

Mrs Turtle was moving to the kitchen, to make a cup of tea before *The Bill* came on. I didn't think it was odd that she was walking around the house in her white coat. As it dawned on me this was weird she caught me peeking.

'Kevin, how good to see you, come in, do come in, love!' she chirped, flinging open the door as if she was expecting me.

I shuffled into the hallway unsure of what to do next, noticing her wonderful perfume. Then it fell open. Her finely toned creamy body made me drool. It all seemed so natural, and I dribbled better than on the pitch.

'I know you and your pals have been stalking me. I can't think why, unless you want something. You do want something, don't you, John?'

She moved her right hand gracefully towards the top of her inner thigh, her rose painted fingernails caressing her milky skin. Before I could gulp, she yanked me by the hand upstairs, and into her bedroom. In the distance I thought I could hear a foghorn echoing.

'It's OK. I know what little boys like you like. Right. Drop your pants!'

I had never been spoken to like this before by a woman; so manly, so forcefully. To be honest, I loved it.

'Bend over,' and with this she spanked me like a demon with her large lollipop.

As she delivered whack after whack of almighty proportions my knuckles went white from gripping the bedposts. Around the bed sat a dozen different lollipops, some glowing silver, others onyx black. She used each one on me with relish and my backside went numb with pain, which I admit was pleasure.

'Enough!' I finally begged.

But she wasn't having it.

I lay slumped on her bed and she took a photograph of my raw derriere for what I thought was some kind of memento, to add to her collection.

'What you going to do with that?' I squeaked, a dissected mouse, all my life sucked into the lollipop.

'Never you mind, lad, never you mind. Just run along now and don't tell anyone, you hear me?'

As if I would.

As I stumbled out her front door I could sense the neighbours twitching their lace curtains. Chris and Ray were waiting for me, grinning like garden gnomes.

'Don't tell me you've been with the Turtle! No way man, no!' Chris prodded me in the ribs, dancing on the doorstep, my silence saying everything.

The next day Mrs Turtle was down by the school gates like usual. As she spotted us she spun the lollipop around. One side was covered with a giant photograph of my pimply behind.

'Do you think this will stop traffic?' she yelled, pouting her lips like a screen goddess. For a moment I wondered what it would have been like to have known her in the spiritual and mental sense, not purely in carnal.

'Now Ray, do it!' I yelled.

'Put your fucking foot down!'

But Ray was too stoned and shocked to do a thing.

'Kiss it!' I shouted back at her, punching Ray in the arm as hard as I could.

Mrs Turtle moved the lollipop towards her lips and gave it a long luscious lick. I felt a yearning swell up inside me like a tsunami.

They say my therapy helps, but I'm not so sure. No one here wears white coats. I've put on about five stone. I can't stop eating lollipops. You know, those traffic light ones, chocolate on the outside, green, yellow then red in the centre. I don't mind being fat. It's better than being like the others in here, the anorexics.

They're as thin as lollipops most of them with big heads and funny sticking out jaws. I get on well with one of them, Emma.

They try and stop her from using her phone all the time but she just screams back, 'Dial Emma, dilemma, it is all a huge dilemma, don't you think?'

We've all got our catchphrases, something to hold onto, like 'Jesus loves me!' Or, 'People like me because I've got lots of money'. Does it matter if they're true or not?

They're only words like STOP CHILDREN!

But they usually seem to work.

10

THE JOSEPH EQUATION

Men might have a problem with the word Mary depending on their obsession with seed. There was a lot you could do about them, under the vermillion sky, the essence of truth is that a woman became pregnant without man being part of this, sexual liberation of a sort. Joseph was much older, and someone else came first, of course, and found this is the way we feel about things, said U.A. Fanthorpe. There is always a hint of ego and disgust, at every turn of the fork in your eye. The way Doctorow can describe a Bunuel film. You feel terrible if you are not filling in a spreadsheet, as if you are not part of the network. It takes your soul then leaves you thinking it is your soul so if you are not connected to it you have no soul. At least you think you are and you need to express this, with a far more vocal need, or alimentary canal, without engaging with the psyche. Nobody likes someone with feelings. This is purely human. We like someone to switch off their essence because it gets in the way of our essence. And look what appeared to Adam Laing, not even recognised by his own father.

The children of R.D. Laing, there were ten of them. Dad was sport mad, played everything and in one fantasy united Glasgow Rangers and Celtic playing for both clubs, and Scotland. One lived on a Spanish island, and I am not sure his father recognised him ever as his own. He drank like the sea, and was a sailor who had crossed the Atlantic eleven times. The sea was wild and could contain him to a degree, the big drink, and once it is written it appears as if it was planned, the way he moved into a tent, and then was found dead, about my age. This all makes perfect sense.

His father's poetry kept me going, a net of knots that contained me from the sea, kept me healthy. There was nothing elliptical about this. The horizons and tides moved without us thinking about them and kids played football with Anthony Gormley statues on the beach. Time without money, there was everything we wanted to do about this, as when they came alive, or the man I was pushing around the Wirral coast of life got out of his chair and walked. If you do not take out their legs, they will take you for a ride. Every beach really does have these statues, if you look close enough, and we celebrate their lives–Dudas Andronicus, Super Baby.

Who lives in the basement, your other self, or the other basement of that basement; I had a huge girl on my face, sorry, I meant to say grin, as I manage to leave myself on both sides of the door, an own goal. The dying of the light, looked at me like I just pissed on his chips, her lips, she wishes. My boyfriend is feeding the rabbit (the rabbit?) in the library, and it is making me hungry, and the world is supposed to end today, so they are saying in the life.

John turns off TV.

Maybe it will, if there is no shift. Fay Weldon, a short story: woman talking to a shrink–we don't hear him, just her answers and no inverted commas; the one and only, a son for all, the need. The pen, and the need, for the rest, a metaphor such as Ginsberg, hello, fucking himself me, my step-father, stairway to heaven, so there is a novel about a woman who doesn't know her boyfriend is her step-brother and he is only allowed to inherit money if he has never committed a crime, but she has seen him kill someone after a football match, with laughter mind you, not lager, that would be obscene, come to think of it.

The Mayan calendar clicking, letting us all know, the world ends today, it never began, it is all in your head, Highgate Woods, painting pictures distributed around the globe, the essence of the elemental, up the stairs at the party in Oxford with the reefer, you know the one, running and arguing about how many can do a Korean disco dance on the head of a safety pin. There is a house falling into the sea, all of England covered, fallen, Albion, the end of civilisations, covered by the sea, the jungle, and the oak tree in Knebworth the tree of trees, Lisa Tebbs' flower shop raised up into the sky. The Barmy B-Wood Army marching, there is nothing superfluous about anything, and in each death, meant to say breath, God walks in Eden.

Our estrangement from nature, encapsulated in the Judaeo-Christian mythology as the 'fall', our transgression necessary for culture and identity, indicates nature cannot be tamed and, paradoxically, is the essence of culture. Perversely, the delusions of progress are our get-out clause that allows us to go beyond the imposition of the limit of thought.

They had made a device where you could read all the messages about you, all the time and places, all the plants in the zone next to the house, ambition is just a cave in which to hide. A light, stowed away, that suspects and condemns everything and everyone, a perfect example of illusion and humanity, crawling along the ley-lines.

In the bath, Jim Morrison's face Paris-oblivion, an end of the word freedom, life is living as if each day is the end of the world on an island talking to a football, a soccer head. When the first people on earth saw you, they wanted to know who they were. A tide with blue in the electric city mechanical clockwork city, phased with the unphrased, the first grave and the ashes spread over your eyes. The death of Lady Penelope, a zombie in the back of Thunderbird 1, me lady–Parker kills her, the 1970s were full of colour, the 1980s just red, the 1990s were full of yellow, and the new millennium white, like the dome, and this decade: needs a colour, needs a way forward, with the first was some truth, each man taken from the boat, and dropped the elaborate birth of Ulysses, heal the ball, the first light across the field a scarecrow within a human, so give us our day our Daily Bread, and let us know, who it is who we really know, who knows us deep down.

He knitted you together in your mother's womb, and you gave her money to get her to tell you to bury a picture of yourself in the woods, Highgate Woods, where your great-grandfather had owned the shops at the bottom of the hill going up to Muswell Hill, and your great aunty owned a house by the train station and the summer before you painted pictures in the centre, on the bench, oblivious to the naked folk around you and the sound of willow on leather, kids screaming about nothing and parents having tantrums, let you be rest assured if sharks only sleep by swimming, how about you, the truth of the matter, life is a fundamental equation, nothing but maths, the man who did the accounts for the nuns, now remember him, he had cracked it, we saw him preaching at speakers' corner, and he believed he had reversed the ageing process, well he had a degree in maths, who hasn't, the fundamental equation lost like a living liberty, are we allowed to say this, standing there in the first equivalent, all in your head, the truth of the matter, a label, that is all you are, a sell by date, don't dwell on it though, like that mysterious wind in the desert that drives you mad, and then human, all too human, the crucifixion in a glass box, with a shark, that is where you should be. I like to watch a thousand times, and make a shrine for you, elementary processes.

John Tao's towel the Turin shroud, Clough's face, the sacred power of absolutely nothing. The fortuitous Popol Vuh, a punk band or a mythology of time, you take your pick, but we couldn't tell how the aggressive nature was innate, as some had suggested, bonobos cannot form fists, just donut shapes, for example and there are others. Our punch therefore is part of our evolution; this has left us in our place, at the top of the kingdom yet alienated and alone, and the bonobo eating the donuts with a closed hand, the flat palm without the power, and the first thoughts were illustrious, a bark from God backwards, the cost of Sanskrit, and the creation of all we can create. The house left, still occupied, as the war still rages around it in Syria. A perfect choice, a syncopated reconstruction and a metaphor without knowing who is on the horizon, who told us that there was an inimical element to anything, and the girl who went on stage to be spanked, and all the knives in his warehouse, the spanker, and the sex line. She mentioned that she worked on this line in London and her friend's brother was put through to her and she couldn't really do anything about it other than go along with it, and the opportunity and the safety, and the fall out, always the fall out.

An artist on the boat, a man who never dies, every miracle is offered, come follow me, through fields of tulips of purple sand, of fields of rape seed, of poppies, of vines, the one true vine, Jesus, in your heart, head and soul, torn from limb to limb, smothering every tree and bush and shrub you've ever known. We know where we come from where we shall return and the sun turned into your face, ineluctably. You know when you die you were told before you were born they have got your number. The genetic coding, handed down, the first gift from your parents, unwrap it.

There is a café in Thailand full of ex-military who still desire to take over the East, and still believe the war is raging, and it is in their minds. They have their Thai brides, and their shit food, like over-grilled chicken in something like breadcrumbs, but it is sawdust, like chewing cardboard, and they still have their lost lives, stuffed full of memories of people being maimed, and the dirty sheets, they may have killed or fucked some they have forgotten, crucified them, X the Greek sign for Christ, my son said Christ as I wrote it, and it was not the language but the sign, the cross, His cross.

The nation state in one, on one, the inner ear, shaped like a face, hearing it and losing it, so the clue is in the meaning of the elaboration of the celebration, each OK, so, why you here, the first and last message that is appropriate from the shrink, the man looks to the heavens, a syrup of figs, the wig, the beauty of age, liar. He had purchased a kidney from a China man, and had died then they were after his family, who had put a bet on that John would score three before half time, so a number of lives, bodies, now depended on his foot, or head.

There was nothing that could be done about Sandy. Upstairs in the Artichoke tied to the bed, Lee Spawn beat her with a rotten leak. It was the Welsh in her. She had thigh length boots and nothing else. She'd read somewhere about a girl who liked to go to parties and have twenty to forty men masturbate over her. This wasn't her. She felt the hand of God out the window, the widow maker, the winnower, the cruel subtext of Lee's tattoo of a marijuana leaf. He was a jerk off, but he wasn't jerking off.

'Look what you missed out on,' she taunted, slipping out of the Range Rover, missing a banana skin, collapsing on the hog roast.

'I bet you'd like to spin me around like that, just to watch your pals fuck me in the mouth.'

He wouldn't. He wished he had invited her around his house when his nana was still alive. She'd have washed her mouth out with soap. Not just a kiss and a promise. Rammed the whole fucking bar in, until soap bubbles sprung from her arse and she floated up to paradise singing Bohemian Rhapsody.

11
TODD'S TRIP HOME

The crowd went ballistic and morphed into a squirming mass, as John Tao dribbled, positioning himself in a paradoxical angle, then swerved another banana shot into the net, and don't manipulate the severed penis sown on your head. This was continental football at its best, swallowed hard after grinding up a copy of the collected seminars of Lacan and boiling the remnants with Derrida's pipe to make a mind blowing infusion.

We could all follow Todd on the screen with the ghost of Augustine Illumines. Todd, who had been following John, switched off the screen, his yellow fingers giving the game away. Now the fag end of February, snow and dirty rain had left patterns of decayed leaves on the inner quadrant. Art students, like seventeenth-century sorcerers, sketched these designs, as if God had played a part in their symmetrical shaping. Todd felt sick. Ever since the beginning of talk about war in Iraq, Todd felt not that his country needed him, but he needed his country. He'd been in England since the Falland the past five months had been the longest in his life, despite seeing his life-time football hero John Tao train on the university pitch every day.

England itself wasn't that bad, honestly. He'd loved football since he was a younger than he could remember and worshipped them all from Gazza, to Beckham, through to Bale and Tao. John Tao had visited the university, signed some shirts; that was enough for him. Some of his fellow students were amusing, and the Artichoke boozer had become a home from home. Foreigners never truly understand the English boozer, where you went in with thirty quid but left with nothing, other than a feeling you were going to vomit and the gift of a headache the next day.

Generally he liked his courses, particularly filmmaking. But deep down in his stomach he felt an ache, a silent scream that yelled 'take me home, momma'. It made concentrating on anything twice as difficult.

'Sorry, I haven't done the essay,' became Todd's mantra. However hard he tried, reading every film book in the library, he just couldn't get it together. February moved into Easter, then the call came that would change everything.

'Toddy boy. Sorry to be the one to hit you with it, but it's your grandpa, the old boy's in hospital. We're pretty certain he won't make it. He wants to see you now. Yeah, I'll tell Sally Carol, it will all be OK, believe me, boy. It will be great to see you, missing you like mad.'

Grandpa had been a general in the US army retiring less than ten years after Vietnam to run a hardware store in Alabama. Sally Carol was the girl Todd had been dating at college in Kentucky before he opted for a year abroad in the UK. Jesus H. Christ, he must have been nuts! Sally Carol was a natural blonde with Scandinavian blood, five foot eleven plus, super svelte, and so damn sexy she left boys gasping.

Todd had been the only one bold enough to ask her out on a date. No way could he count on his so-called pals keeping their hands off. The evening after pa called he made his flight arrangements over the Internet and went for a beer at the union. The place was tiny, but had a weird edge to it, with an Indie music feel that Todd had grown to like.

'So you're off back to the land of the brave, the home of the free, Yankee doodle keep it up, Yankee doodle dandy,' sang Gorman, a peculiarly over-weight nu-metal fan, with an unhealthy interest in porn, Nietzsche and Scientology.

'Tell Dr Sarah I'll have to get the essay for film in late, will you?'

'It must be because you're American; you just do what the hell you like. You've got her wrapped around your little toe,' said Diane.

'I think you mean finger, anyway, I've got to go back, my grandpa's had a stroke. He might not make it. It's bad man . . . we're quite close, dudes.'

The group went quiet. They wondered what it would be like for them, studying in a foreign country, where everyone hated you because of what your country was doing, and now this. Would you go straight back and risk your grades? Would you stay put and risk not being able to see your grandpa one last time?

'You know I don't hate you little Englanders, but really, the world is not like you think. You need to wake up. Fuck that David Beckham. You know that phrase, 'shock and awe', well maybe you need a bit of that, maybe that will help in the long run,' Todd said, gulping the dregs of his sixth pint of snake-bite, and feeling triumphant.

'See you in a couple of weeks,' he yelled, heading for the union door, 'and keep the home fires burning!'

The airport was unusually packed, and Todd found it hard to manoeuvre his beast of a suitcase around the creatures sprawled everywhere. He had booked the most expensive standard ticket with British Airways, but there was a strike on.

Like an animal finding a spot to die, he sat on the floor in the airport lounge, scoffed a burger, and supped two diet-cokes, while reading Viz and *FHM*.

'Going to lovely America, are we?' asked an Arab guy in a white suit, peering at Todd as if he was a specimen in the end of a very long test tube, as John Tao dribbled on the screen.

'Maybe, what's it to you?' he felt like saying, but just nodded, vaguely, 'Hey isn't that the footballer John Tao, holding hands with a man,' he let out.

'That's most excellent. Forgive me . . . if I am so forward as to introduce myself. My name is Ali Rowan Van Richtenstein. A strange concoction I know. My mother was Dutch Jewish, my father Dutch Muslim, and don't ask about the rest,' continued the man, chuckling, offering his hand to Todd.

Todd took the hand, squeezed it manfully, then, jamming his chin into his neck, went back to his magazine, but the animated white suit continued.

'You see, the problem is I have too much hand luggage, a common occurrence I know, caused by lack of foresight, maybe some greed. I wondered whether you would be so kind as to take some on for me.'

With this Ali Rowan pointed to a metre long leather attaché case, with gold gothic letters embossed on the side.

'Sure, and blow up the whole fucking plane, you fucking arsehole terrorist,' thought Todd, wondering how to get rid of the guy.

Who wears white suits, unless they're porn-film directors, pimps, or independent MPs? Green letters on the screen declared his flight was currently delayed three hours, but it was creeping up, like gas in the trenches.

'Sorry pal, my mother told me to never to talk to strangers, let alone take things on planes for them . . . no can do,' he offered, in the most neutral voice manageable, pulling his Yankees cap down.

71

'Look, pal,' Ali replied imitating Todd, 'either you take this bag on the plane, or I'm going to slit your red neck, do you hear me?'

Todd felt the sharp point of a blade skewering the back of his neck, the pressure unbearable.

'OK, cut it out man, Jesus, dude, let's talk about this first, Christ, man, get that knife out of my neck,' Todd wined.

The man slipped the knife back up his broad white sleeve, and stood next to Todd, nonchalantly pondering the departure screen.

'You know many people die in airports, and of course the authorities put it down as accidents. They don't like the attention–get it? Airports are a lawless zone.'

'Whatever. How am I supposed to get away with carrying that beast on, those aren't my initials?'

The man laughed outrageously, his white suit moving up and down on his shoulders as if he were riding a stallion.

'Hey you kill me, you ignorant Yanks kill me every time, Allah be praised. It is not this bag I need you to take onto the plane, but this one here, over here, look.'

Todd felt relieved. Maybe he could do it, if it meant he kept his red neck, but hang on. What if it meant he died in the process, along with three hundred other innocent travellers, exploding, their fragmented bodies cremated, and receiving an unasked for burial at sea? What if?

'Don't worry, my friend. It is not a bomb, I assure you. We are not all killers, despite your propaganda. I have just come back from Holland, yes. In this bag are the most amazing pornographic films ever made starring that famous footballer, John Tao; I am taking them to America to make my fortune. When played on a normal video system they are just tapes of television programmes, old favourites like *The Good Life*. I love that Penelope Keith, her bottom so beautiful, don't you think? You need special equipment to access the porn films, so nobody will ever know. I will let you keep your life, and give you one thousand dollars as well. You cannot resist such a capitalist endeavour, it is not within your make up, yes?'

'Look, I'm not in a good mood right now. I've had a pretty shit time in this shit country. I've been waiting for my plane for over three hours, my grandpa is dying, and if I don't get there soon I won't be able to say goodbye to him. But I could do with some extra cash right now. Give me the money now, and you've got a deal dude, but don't put that knife back in my neck again. You think you know something about my country. All you know is your own propaganda.'

'And what they taught me at Yale Graduate School. Follow me,' ordered Ali, and Todd marched to the toilets, like a dog after a bone.

The two men entered one cubicle, the toilet blocked, full of indescribable matter.

'Look in here, Mr America,' ordered Ali, and opened the bag for Todd's inspection, 'I know it looks suspicious, but you can say you're a filmmaker.'

Todd stared at Ali, not liking such coincidences, and not wanting to tell the man that he was in fact an aspiring filmmaker, with three short films under his belt. Carrying all these tapes into a country paranoid about security was another matter.

'So show me the money,' he whispered, aware of movement all around them, the sound of gushing urine, bowels shifting, toilet paper posted within the underground veins of outer London, the rush of water, the heavy breathing of the amorous and addicted.

'Not so fast, my humble American pie. You now swear on your grandpa's life that you'll do this for me, on the American flag?'

Todd looked at the sausage shaped bag, and nodded ever so slightly. He felt a total fool, but also knew he didn't have a choice in the matter. As he nodded the man placed ten faces of Benjamin Franklin in his hand, slowly, one by one.

They exited the toilet separately. Todd now held the bag. He felt nervous, as if a hundred pairs of eyes were upon him. As he finally found a clear floor spot to crash out, his mobile rang.

'Toddy boy, it's a miracle, the old man has come out of it, no side effects or nothing. Seriously, we thought he was a gonner there! Sorry to worry you like this. You've got the ticket, so you could come back for a little holiday. I know the term ends in a few months, so you might want to hang on? I spoke with the airline and they said they'd refund the ticket or re-schedule it, it's up to you, son.'

Todd felt Ali's eye upon him, and gripped the bag tightly. If these videos were so precious, maybe he could take them onto campus and get Jed the technician to play them, and then make a killing.

At least it would mean his time in England wouldn't be wasted, then with the money he could buy a vehicle back in the States, and impress Sally Carol, and then plough the rest into making his own movies.

'Pa, you're right, I think I'll stay put till the end of term, finish my studies, if you're sure grandpa is OK.'

Todd pegged it, praying to his god.

Outside a taxi was about to leave, but seeing Todd scurry along it stopped, reversing to pick him up.

'Watford, and put your foot on it,' yelled Todd, watching, as Ali glared around the airport exit.

With the traffic the usual nightmare, it took three hours to reach the Watford campus, and everything, typically, was shut.

And then he saw his saviour–Jed the hippy. Throwing two hundred dollar bills at the driver, Todd jumped out the taxi with the bag, and raced up to the audio-visual technician.

'Jed, I've got some tapes here, it's real important you try to get the stuff that's on them off; they could be worth a fortune.'

'Sure Todd, and my name's Bill Gates, pull the other one,' said the old hippy, 'and anyway, it's Friday and I'm off for a pint of Twiddle Fiddler at The Fighting Cocks. Come in early Monday, if you like, and we'll have a look.'

'No man, I have to see what's on them now! Please! Come on dude, I'm desperate.'

Jed just glared at the American. Despite, or because he was an old hippy, he had a repressed dissatisfaction with life, and a deep anger that came out when people treated him like their servant.

'Jed, I'm sorry for shouting. Look, I'll give you three hundred dollars if you help me. You can't believe what a day I've had, somebody tried to . . . well it doesn't matter now. Still, look here, three hundred dollars, all for you, think how many pints of Piddle Diddler you can have out of that.'

'You sure play up to the stereotype, Todd: rich, loud, obnoxious and badly dressed. I wonder, do you practise in front of the mirror in the morning?'

How much of this crap did he have to take from these little Englanders? They just couldn't take it that they no longer ruled the world and if it weren't for the Yanks they'd be speaking German. Todd felt like hitting the old hippy, but instead began counting out the hundred dollar bills in the palm of his hand, slapping them down.

'This is just another example, Todd. You Americans presume that we will just love to take your currency, bend over backwards to be shafted by your swanky Yankee dollar, well I'm sorry, Todd, but it's good old sterling or nothing. Offer me two fifty cash in English and we may have a deal.'

'Wait there, Jed, just don't go away, don't go away,' commanded Todd, shouting, as if giving orders in Vietnam, and he raced off to the cash point.

'Here, what did I tell you? Don't you know American's always keep their word? Now listen, there is something really valuable on those tapes. They look like typical British TV shows but they're not, believe me, they're not.'

Jed just nodded, and led the way to the audio-visual section of the small library. He shoved in the first tape Todd handed him, the machine gulping down the plastic, and they both watched the black eye of the monitor manifest its dream content. The opening music for *Dad's Army* blasted from the speakers.

'I can't understand why people like this rubbish. Nostalgia I suppose. Now tell me, what am I supposed to be looking for, a break in the matrix perhaps, a black hole to another world, a lost Beatles track, a recording of Hitler making love to a British Royal, or the answer to everything maybe? Oh no, sorry, Todd, I forgot—you have the answer to everything.'

'Just do your job, Jed, and quit the witty commentary. If you can get what I want within an hour, I'll double your money.'

'Hang on, what's this here,' said Jed, spinning the dial back, splitting the ratio, and juxtaposing the line in with the realization input codes, the divided images colliding, pausing and then rushing in a reversed direction, 'this is sick stuff, Todd, where'd you get it?'

A loud thudding sound and wailing poured from the speakers above their heads. An American soldier was beating a woman, an iron bar in his hand descending on her back mercilessly, repeatedly, the resonant sound getting louder, and louder, her screams unbearable.

'This can't be for real,' whispered Todd, 'tell me this is just a movie, Jed.'

'Todd, where the hell did you get this stuff? Someone might kill us if they know we've got our hands on it.'

'I was going back to the States, and there were these massive delays. This Arabic guy in a white suit threatened to kill me, if I didn't take them on the plane, but I managed to escape and thought you could help.'

'Jesus Christ, Todd, a guy in a white suit? Nobody wears a white suit! I think we should go to the police, honestly, get real, this is deep shit.'

Jed scratched his mangy red and grey goatee, and tightened the purple band throttling his ponytail. Sweat was pouring off his neck, drenching his decaying Dark Side Of The Moon t-shirt.

'No, they'll only take them off us, and it will be like they never existed. Put another one in. Let's see what else is here.'

A man, a chain wrapped around his feet, was suspended from the ceiling. Three American soldiers urinated on him then began stabbing him randomly with broken glass. Laughter echoed around the room. A young Arabic child, barely in her teens, was being forced to eat her own excrement. Pinned to her head was a page from the Koran, and two American soldiers threw darts at her. Three women were having their heads shoved in latrines; by the end of the five-minute tape, two were dead.

'What's this, student snuff movies? Come on, Jed, time to go; going down The Fighting Cocks tonight?' asked Sid the security guard, peering into the room.

'Ah yeah, right, of course. You know Todd here, Sid, one of our American friends, budding filmmaker,' replied Jed, switching off the monitor.

While Todd chatted to Sid about the Grand Canyon and 'Red Indians', Jed placed the videos back in the bag, switched off the machinery, and locked up. It was obvious that the man Todd had met at the airport had a contact in America and was going to somehow do an exposé.

'I think I'll give the pub a miss tonight, Sid, have a good one!' shouted Jed, as they sauntered together through the car park, trying to remain cool.

'We need to do something with these, but you're right man. We can't tell the police, they'll just confiscate them and make out they never existed.'

Back at Jed's they went through all the tapes, becoming numb to the images. The supermarket clock struck two before they decided what to do.

'I've got a pal in San Francisco, another video nerd like me. I could transfer this stuff, download it to him, and he could show it to people. He's got friends in high places, I'm not joking, Todd.'

'You must be. It was probably people in high places who ordered this.

No, we need to find a journalist we can trust with powerful connections here. I'm not interested in the money. Once we tell the authorities they might have us killed. Don't tell me I've seen too many movies. This is the way it works. Right, who do you know?'

They sat in silence for three minutes, the sound of Hertfordshire at night closing in on them, the odd screech of a bird like a warning, Jed's t-shirt now soaked through.

'Well, there was a girl I went to school with, I had a bit of a thing with her, until my best mate's brother Richard made her cheat on me. Now she's a sub-editor on *The Blob*, works on the women's page. But this kind of scoop might make her career. I'm not sure whether she's sold out. I haven't spoken to her for ages, but I've still got her number.'

Todd nodded, gritting his teeth. He was pleased his grandpa was well, but felt like he wanted to go home, just to see familiar faces, to not have to deal with this.

'I know it's three in the morning, but I thought you'd just be back from clubbing. I've got something really important. It could be the story of the century!'

The phone went silent. Jed looked at the phone, at Todd, and then back at the phone, as if he had suddenly forgotten what the thing was used for, as if he or the phone had gone dead.

'Jed, I've got someone with me at the moment. Can't it wait till morning?'

'No, sorry, it can't. I don't want to say any more over the phone. I know this sounds paranoid and no, I haven't smoked any bad weed lately, if there is such a thing, but if you see what we've got it will blow your mind more than any weed on earth.'

At Sandra's Todd took in the photographs from Germany in the hallway, Sandra explaining her family had been in the holocaust. After the images cut from *The Good Life* to the scenes of torture, Sandra broke down.

'God, this is like something from Nazi Germany. Are you sure these are real, Jed, you not just pulling my leg, after I dumped you for Richard?'

The two men just nodded. They sat in silence, Sandra pondering how she would break this story, how John, on the politics desk and the war in the Middle East, would run this, how she would get an award, maybe journalist of the year, how she would get a promotion, be editor before she was forty, how women would be saved from further torture, how the American government would be brought down, how the smarmy British Prime Minister would be forced to resign. She saw her name in the history books. This was the real reason she had entered journalism, not to write about the latest frock for sale, fad diet, or what some z-list celebrity was or was not wearing.

A loud crack on the door brought her back to earth.

'Police, open up, you've got ten seconds, then we break the door down.'

'Quick, Todd, out the back window,' whispered Sandra, gathering up the tapes, 'take them to Canary Wharf, floor six, ask for John Harrison, politics desk, and say Sandra Cohen sent you, go!'

Todd dived out the back window, and waited in the bushes until the flashing blue lights had vanished. His cash supply having dwindled, despite the risk, he decided the only thing for it was to hitch, and walked to the motorway down Elstree Hill. Todd didn't have to wait long before he found himself in a comfy small leather seat on the way to the City, humming 'LA Woman'.

'So, you're American, are you?' confirmed the driver in her fifties, wearing a purple velvet dress two sizes too small.

Todd waited for the tirade of anti-American comments. Yes, I am the devil, he felt like saying, yes I am the cause of all the suffering and pain in the entire world. Shoot me now!

'I've heard you Americans, in fact I know you Americans, are really hot in the sack,' and with this, the woman took her hand from the silver knobbed gear stick and cupped Todd's scrotum.

'A good package, I would say,' she laughed, her calf muscle in her right foot bulging as she took the car up to ninety.

Lights appeared from nowhere, sirens wailing.

'Lady, please, I've got to get to Canary Wharf, a matter of life or death.'

'Urgent, hey? What, something to do with that bag you've got there, is it? Tell me, boy, what's in that bag that is so precious?' she asked.

Seeing the lights she drove faster, and Todd spied the speedometer rise from one hundred, flicking up to one hundred and forty.

The Porsche charged on, speeding through the lights at Golders Green, on towards the centre of the Metropolis. There was a screech and, spinning back, he viewed the police car twirling out of control.

'Todd, I can't take you anywhere unless you make love to me, passionately, right now. I find that making love in a car with a young handsome

American boy in the middle of the night is the only reason I can keep on living in this miserable corrupt world. You will make love to me, won't you Todd, won't you?'

Todd looked at the woman. She wasn't unattractive. Dyed thick black hair sat on a pale-moon taught face, the lipstick on her bulging manufactured lips matching her dress and shoes, her body chunky, but not fat.

'I'll think about it, OK? But first I need to get to Canary Wharf. Lives may depend upon it.'

Amanda laughed crazily, with her head back at this comment, and lit up a Gitanes, drawing deeply, and blowing the smoke through her flared nostrils straight into Todd's face.

'Lighten up, boy. How many offers have you had lately? A bit of free sex may help you. It looks like you need to de-stress a bit; come here.'

As she began to find Todd's prevaricating cock, a shadow moved along the window, what looked like an old drunk searching for the remains of bottles to neck back before the pinstripes were about and the police hosed them all off the pavement.

'Thanks for the offer, I'm really busy though, my heart wouldn't be in it right now, not that you're unattractive,' said Todd, trying to open the locked doors.

Todd realised he was talking to a man. Glancing on the back seat he spotted the tub of lard, gaffer tape, and sex toys.

'Now wait a minute, boy, a favour for a favour. I've given you a free lift, and there's nothing for free in this world, sonny Jim.'

A scuffle in the street caught their attention, one tramp scrapping with another over an inch of whiskey in a discarded bottle. Todd's phone rang.

'Are you sitting down? I won't mince my words, son, he wouldn't have liked that; grandpa, he's died, son. Christ boy, I'm sorry. They said sometimes people get a bit better before they go. Don't worry, Todd, he died happily, he wanted you to know he loves you, and he'll always be with you. OK, son?'

Todd drew a long breath, and held back the tears. He didn't want Mandy the randy transsexual to see his vulnerability, and perhaps be turned on by it. He thought about telling his dad about the tapes, about his current predicament, but then thought better of it.

'And the airline strike's been called off. I've booked you on a flight, the nine o'clock from Gatwick. Todd, are you there?'

One of the tramps had smashed the window, and was now dancing about the street with Todd's phone, while the American nursed his bleeding lip, and the other tramp had the bag of tapes.

'Todd, see you in a few hours then, I'll pick you up from the airport. Keep strong son, keep strong.'

The tramp laughed back down the phone, but before he could swear at the prattling man, Todd had football-tackled him, and was wrestling him to the ground. He grabbed his phone back and then kicked the other tramp with the bag, snatched it, and ran.

Outside Canary Wharf was still quiet, but by the time Todd reached the desk of John Harrison the workers were starting to file in for the early shift.

A man with jug ears spiked gelled hair and thick Red or Dead glasses sat forward in a swivel chair adjusting a toy dinosaur on top of his screen. A large hand entered his vision.

'Todd, Todd Coder. A colleague of yours, Sandra Cohen, said you would be interested in these tapes. Can I talk to you somewhere more private?' asked Todd, glancing around the open plan offices, two hundred computers, about a third being used, glaring back at him, their faces like accusations.

'Sure Todd, I got a call from Sandra telling me a bit about it all, what is it you've got there? I don't mean to be rude, but you could do with a bit of a clean-up, do you want to take a shower? That's not a proposition, by the way.'

'I don't have time to clean up, I've got to catch a flight at nine. John, I'll be brief. These videos contain images of American soldiers torturing innocent people. I hoped they weren't real but listen I'm no traitor and these are so real they're sick. People have got to know, only don't include me in your article, John, I don't want any flack from the CIA or FBI. My grandpa was high up in the US Army and he's just died. I don't want to spoil his memory. Honest to God, a man threatened to kill me if I didn't take these back to the US. He still might.'

John was the kind of person Todd could trust.

The news in the bar at Gatwick revealed John had done a good job. Arriving in the States, Todd imagined a sea of people waiting to interrogate him until he cracked.

'Confess, you Arab loving scum, who put you up to making these fake movies?'

'Grandpa's left you something in his will, Todd, something you can be really proud of.'

Todd didn't ask what it was but he felt he already knew. Whatever his know-nothing friends back in merry old England said, for once in his life, he felt no shame. Out the corner of his eye he could see naked photos of someone he knew on a screen, a footballer who everyone knew, but that didn't matter so much now.

12

MISSING CHILD
TRAIN JOURNEY

There is a sensation, livid, amongst the trees. We took her to school, sorry, I, I took her to school, and then she never came out, I mean I was standing in the playground feeling like a lemon, I always feel like a lemon, all the children came out and Sophie wasn't one of them.

'Excuse me, where is Sophie, has she been naughty?' I asked.

They just stared at me blankly with their corrupted computer screen faces like I was some kind of idiot, or worse, like I didn't exist, never had done, nor did Sophie.

'We thought it was odd when Mrs Grace didn't ring to let us know she wasn't coming in today.'

'But you saw me this morning, I brought her in, we said hello, you saw me, I came in here and put her bag up, spoke to Isabel. There were three kids with Tao on their back.'

They can say what they like about who has a baby, and who does not, the rivers are full of the bones of baby horses, comfortable, going around and around illuminated, illustrious, they need to be part of the chosen community, which percentile, now have you led yourself, or was it God, I can feel him behind me now, the power of his birth, and so we get led by the leash.

He left the tube to gain attention. A blind Chinaman bumping into you, with a bag of Chinese food, so you imagine. Fisting bonobo, there is a couple asking dumb questions.

'Would your parents eat fish?'

'Cod in batter, sausage rolls, must have them.'

She is slightly overweight, OK looking, about twenty eight, probably did English and sociology at university somewhere in the Midlands, like Loughborough. He is tall, skinny and spotty, probably about thirty, with

John Lennon glasses, a bored smirk and a ponytail. Probably dropped out of some computer course and anyone, apart from her, can tell that he thinks he is too good for her, when blatantly it is the other way around. This is the first Christmas when the kids are cooking the meal for their parents who by the looks of things have never met, so it is going to be hell on earth.

There's that old idea, the one you got from listening to that Julian Barnes' story 'Pulse', about whether we ever really know our parents. The narrator meets a girl called Janice at his running club. She loves his huge sweaty frame, calls his cock the beast, and he loves her. But she gets him to question the notion of his parents and how he sees them. Her point is because we don't really know our parents before they had us we don't really know them at all as they will be always hiding things from us. For example, I only found out the other day that when my dad was visiting his family up north he used to sit in front of the television talking to his family and brush my mother's hair all evening like she was some kind of doll, cat or Egyptian goddess, and he was a beer swilling, motorbike driving, rugby playing plumber who then moved down south, trained as an engineer and made a mint then learnt to speak every language under the sun. Weird what you don't know. In the case of my parents, when I mentioned this at their golden wedding anniversary he claimed it didn't even happen at all; my whole speech was about the two of them, but he only could see me talking, not the content. He thought I was taking his limelight, when I was shining the light on them. The point of the Julian Barnes story is that Janice is probably wrong, but what if she is right, and not just about your parents, but about everyone?

A huge list of food, these two on the train make a huge list of food; they are acting like parents of their parents already. He's probably not into football, she might be. Her dad will be, so they might have got him a DVD of best goals, including some by John.

While John is stuck in some hotel, worrying about what the media are going to do with the latest set of photographs of him, his cock a flag pole, something now banned in the suburbs, so everyone is raising the Union Jack with pictures of their babies on, running about the large suite of rooms, fretting, his lovely long legs gliding along like a dream, and don't say luscious lollypops, people will be watching his legs on television.

'Let's have an obscene amount of potatoes,' she roars above the sound of another train.

This is all sexualised, but proof of what exactly? Of abundance, or fertility, or adulthood but as I say she is already there, with her big boobs, a stud in her nose, pretty face, and limp hair and her plumpness. I can see the baby, teenager, mother, grandmother, corpse in her, and it all feels right, like a goal by John just before half time, just to shut those West Ham fuckers up. But I can't stand looking at him, with his long ginger hair, his *Pulp Fiction* Uma Thurman t-shirt, his pink plastic watch, the Hawaiian type watch, but not as cool as this might sound. He is trying to be nonchalant, but it is no secret that he is stricter about the food than she is. She puts in the grander suggestions and more interesting menu, and he knocks it back, like a king. It is meant to last forever, they are feeding the five thousand, but three million die every year of obesity, double the number of those who starve. She gives, gives, gives, sausage roll. Do you have a sausage roll, do you?

He does not care, as another fat businessman falls over at Potters Bar, someone out of a Sarah Daniels play, and is then bundled on the train by a girl. Will she rape him, hoping his seed will be her ticket out of here? I get one more glance at her tits, before sitting next to a urinated-on bag of chips. The first shall be last, the last shall be first, no phone calls on the Sabbath. Illustrious conversions, make head way to the pure Moslem, they drank from the semen that made them, sutra this and sutra that. Keep us at one with the Beast that lies within, the spaceman on the horizon. The back pages shout at everyone, about goals and conflicts and the selling of human flesh.

'The cure is in the disease, for ease is death,' barked in German, the waves that lap inside empty sea, the indestructibility, each couple stretching out on the beach, but for eternity, keep us at bay, tease us with the horizon.

The Artichoke is yet to be turned into a synagogue, but fate dictates. In its loins are the bones of the mistress of the Earl of Sandwich, a highway man, and a tramp who thought he was the messiah. They've been using the wood from trees growing in these very carcasses, biting off more than they can chew, with the mayonnaise on the roast something else. The mayonnaise is being thickened as we speak, as John tries to tear himself away from the pages of naked pictures of himself. And let's not forget the forgotten poet.

13

THE STONE ROSES

Thousands of years ago this substance was worshipped in Afghanistan; now some have a copy of it as a toothbrush holder. *The Kiss* by Gustav Klint was the last word on love, or the last word on gold. The worship of the sun and gold with the Egyptian sun gods, and the Byzantine and the Renaissance golden artefacts, so when the priest raises-up the wafer to the heavens what do people see, other than the sun? The so-sacred object is money, backed by gold, but not backed by anything and it has lost its shine, Norman Harrison doing the crime of the century, and he did it for what, exactly?

What about Elkington's Fools Gold, many fell for it. Grandfather works his entire life post-World War II in the vault, under the Swiss bank in London, replacing a significant chunk of it with the stuff, you understand, perfect copies of the substance, worshipped all over the globe, rotating in this expanding universe. If it is finite, it collapses in on itself with gravity, and it can't be infinite, can it?

'The act of war is just when it is necessary,' chimed Machiavelli, but when is it necessary–always? He had studied art, but then joined the army. After that he sold books, watching *Ripping Yarns* grow, and you can be certain he loved that but, back to competition, people always try to top your stories, they've always been there before, haven't they, always experienced something more, thinking one step ahead. They think that is the nature of everything, and this is in their nature.

That is how you survive.

Grandfather was never really that interested in money or sex, the two things that got everyone else going and prevent humans from under-standing. No, he wanted to just play a trick on the system. The thing is people think they are into what they are into, but it's the other way around, the thing they are into to, is into them, be it drugs, football, sex, money and any other distraction.

Don't preach at me, but they cannot bear to meet their own demon, their inner self. What they believe frees them traps them, of course, let's not preach, but it's a merry-go-round, with very little chance of getting off.

What would he do with the real gold, bury it in the garden? Give it to charity? Send it to someone, an old love, the one he really wanted? How about hanging on to it until you retire, and giving it back to your boss at your leaving do! Like an elaborate joke. A kind of *up yours*, but a gracious one, proving that you are honest, more than honest Iago, but also that you can beat the system; how amazing would this be? They would think it was fake anyway. They chuck it away, and the fake stuff then gets stolen and people get sent down for decades because of it, or the people try and sell it on, to find out that the stuff isn't the real deal, isn't kosher, and start chopping peoples' hands off.

The gladiators in the stadium, the two tribes at war in Wembley for the trophy, or the shield, women compete on the level sometimes of the look, although you are going to say that that gaze is male-dominated. I find myself realising that they need to write more on the process than anything else, so do we need a special place to write, possibly not and we need to get into the habit of writing absolutely anywhere. Imagine you are on your deathbed, or your mother is about to croak it.

'Hang on, have you got a pen and paper,' and you quickly scribble something, anything, like 'once upon a time', so one life is ending, and the other life is beginning, somewhere. 'Have I ever told you,' or, 'it was all a game.'

Or, you are using their skin as a manuscript. After the war, only one in twelve were cremated, and soon that rose to one in two, so the manuscript was burnt up. Strange, how we believe in words and we seek lost words, so they will tell us something from somewhere, and during the last Oasis gig ever at Wembley I was there, with John, John with the dong, we liked to call him, or the magic schlong, and everyone knew about it, from the photos in the papers, and on the net, from those shorts when he ran around the pitch, but my grandmother died the morning after.

My cousin protects girls from themselves, working in a half-way house, where they often go on the internet to find older men, who come down and rape them, and nature is Satan's church. Some have a sliver of liver between their legs, others Satan's brush. But how about taking Sycorax from *The Tempest* and thinking about this in Neapolitan, using a different word for the witch, more in tune with a local myth of witches. Not everyone would allow for Shakespeare to be re-written, but when she tries to screw you in the graveyard, opposite his church, and you refuse, either she is nuts or you are. Death of course has no plan, because it is the plan, and we all need to be taught how to be cooperative.

'I'm in love with a German film star.'

We were on the bed, and I had my thumb inside her, when someone jumped out at her from a hedge in Barcelona.

'Can we use toys?' she kept texting, 'I want you to cum in all my holes,' she declared, weird choice of phrases, and then, 'I was in the toilet at the gallery, and imagined you fucking me from behind.'

Big bounding breasts that bounced weightily, universes in themselves that controlled universes, as she moved up and down on me, filling in the gaps, her hand seeking my balls to cup, nice touch, the sweat pouring, and in the film script, instead of going to Lourdes, I end up taking her to Las Vegas and we get married just as it is noticeable, like a teacher in a tight grey dress where you are not sure, but the baby is still-born, and we bury it in the desert, watching as a bird carries it off, into the heart of the sun, after pecking it to pieces. Everyone should wear this type of bird on their head. Repeat, just getting missed, just getting out of someone alive.

I took Mary Lou to the bus stop and waited in my usual spot, with my blue badge. A man in an executive Jaguar got out, and started jumping up and down like a gorilla.

'What you looking at, you fucking pair of cunts?'

'Is he on drugs?'

I had to watch it. Last week in Barnet, a woman with her ten year old daughter tried to manoeuvre out of a car-park of a pub. Let's not say she was drunk, someone was in her way, she sounded her horn, nothing, got out to have a word, and then the woman in the other car hit the accelerator, knocked her down, and then ran her over, repeatedly, in broad daylight and sped off. Nobody got the plate. But the echoes of the fans at Underhill bounced about, the Barnet stadium having moved to Harrow, all geography collapsing, a psycho traversing London, round and around, re-enacting the ellipsis of Europa, the moon of Jupiter containing enough water to keep us going.

What was happening to all these people who thought having a dishwasher was a luxury, even though it was saving water? Did they think that of a hair dryer, or curling tongs, or a TV, or a toaster? How far did it go? Daddy, Daddy, Daddy, she called, Daddy, please kill me, sucking my used-car thumb. What could I do, I mean should you do as you're told in these circumstances? Would you turn on a David Lynch film, where some LA hood retches into his handkerchief after drinking an espresso, and this reminds you to give her a call, because you remember her going to the sink after bringing you off, to coin a phrase. You know love sucks, true love swallows. Amen to that. So what is it you like? Gagging, that's what.

There was this geezer, who worked at Kodak back in the day, splicing together pictures, a montage in his head, and he opens the machine, ruining all the holiday snaps, they all come running out, so the holiday never happened. A holiday where a girl falls in love with a man, who pretends he has a brain tumour, and she sleeps with him, and then he does the same with the next girl who appears in the holiday camp, and the next. The white adobe walls make the white skin roast, Los Abrigos is required, and on the horizon is the insubordinate clause, the lonely chateau, where they record their album. Those factories and shops are a thing of the past, a digital archive abandoned due to lack of hardware, but the things that were seen remain, the photographs of the act. We can't speak about it in French, about how we hung around warehouses in Paris, until a man with a dog approached us.

'What are you doing here?' he asked, startled that anyone should be in this totally disused and abandoned area.

'Looking for Jim Morrison,' I felt like saying, but of course I meant Baudelaire, not Beckham, or Tao.

I want to cover my face with the moon, carving my face on the moon, carve out your face like the moon, carve out moon animals like the madman in the harbour, and make your moon into a face. She was a presenter on local TV, and had pictures of herself everywhere, smothering every surface, as if she was stalking herself, or was setting herself up, like Jill Dando without a dildo, so the Russian mafia would take care of her. I don't know if she kept a diary that documented all their activities, or whether she just invented anything, fabricated a more exciting life.

He tied her up. Fucked her, ate her, not all the children were his, he didn't care. He'd read that book, *Happy like Murderers* about Fred and

Rosemary, and he'd watched the matches, the incessant matches, and the banter and the beer. It had really stayed with him. How could a father, a mother, do that to their children; don't think about it. In the thirteenth century they blamed it on bestiality. Now they blamed it on the media, homosexuality, immigrants, fast food, intellectuals, microwaves, mobile phones, Jimmy Savile, or some other celebrity.

But crime was going down, and he blamed that on access to pornography, so he banned pornography to keep the police in jobs. And, at the football, they let their aggression out, shouting at the ref, and the opposition, who were always a bunch of actors. There was a man in the doorway that appeared from nowhere, with swastika eyes. Then there was a girl at the park with the same peepers. How can people ever live in such a small town? She kissed my face, and said life means nothing at all. You touch your skin, your own skin, or was it sin? You have never felt it before. You don't even dream that there is a white cat sitting in your freezer, and you may have accidently shut the door. You don't even dream that she is looking after the alcoholic friend of a friend of yours, because you don't even want to think about it at all.

'Pig'–the word you chose when you read her mind, one you selected from the four hundred thousand possibilities, although she probably only used between ten and twenty, and there was no way this was a co-incidence. This was proof of telepathy, if you needed it. You know you're left in the garden of the Artichoke with a fork, the garden of forking paths. They are turning the spit with their hearts and minds, hog roasting in the flames, turning and churning and burning, her head, or his head, the hog with an apple in your eye, and in its mouth. Cider is flowing down the necks of the fifty plus people present to greet the fiftieth year of John, returning from Tenerife, the isle of plenty, the horn of plenty. The fields are as dry as her fanny, twice as sweet, dapper from your napper to your feet, white horses and faun trotting to the beat of redemption songs blasting from the DJ's unit. The heat makes every movement hell.

'Don't you just love it!' yells Sandy Tarzy, clopping from one of four slimy shiny black Range Rovers, followed by ten gentleman in black.

14
MEOW, MEOW

John Tao's three rows back, off work with a strained ligament, the ghost in the machine, Augustine Illumines, working tricks through his scrying glass. She coaxes me on stage, forces me to lift her leg up and spin her around. We are one, but a neo-Nazi knows a Jew knows a Scientologist, knows everyone knows. She receives a bow and arrow for Christmas, on an island she finds the pig, slits its throat, with babies tossed in the air, sliced through by blind men, feeling for brail in the sand. In the blender, penises prefer to have that cut off, than lose your phone or hand it over, hand over fist, penis over penis, life in the mainstream, in the elongated tube, you knew what you would become.

The Egyptian, what goes on there, a flight into the Ibis bird's path, between us a celebration of righteousness, all is calm, as we predicted the truth of the matter is? You got a sports scholarship, and you are just going back to your old room at Cryfield, to barricade yourself in, and play football against the walls of your cell, and come out when you are sixty, listening to all those people fucking around you, was she meaning to get pregnant, did it mean anything, the sex that led to it, the meaning we read into it, and we loved to know who it was, and did it mean anything to itself.

Then the hair of the wave, the ball-headed fiction, the Japanese depiction, the act, sticking the flower, here, there, you really have on there, a guess, unless, she was trying to ascertain the latest picture of judgement, of competition that worked, for if you were first, the rest would die at your feet, like an Australian graveyard, by a river, with her grandfather's name hovering over the park, a light mist, the sun burning through, echoes of kookaburras.

At the moment you thought all he needed was a woman, a man on the bongos and tambourine was playing *no woman no cry*. Everyone unhappy writing books about how to be happy, how to do something, instead of incoherently incarnating it. Macmillan publishers on writing, on the nature of handwriting, keep it up, brother.

They ask her to be part of a swingers group, on Brighton beach, as she watches people whizzing around the helter-skelter, and the waves crashing, throwing up stone after stone, and memories of a small lifeboat hitting the head of George Pocock on bank holiday, circa 1984, knocking him under until he was a gonner. And you realised there was pampas grass outside your parents' house–hello–and then what? They get locked in a room, an interesting idea, but does it have legs, possibly.

You're living in a state where all festivals are banned, and there is a secret cult where it is happening, where it is all happening, the beauty of it all. The tattoo on the neck of red lips, and on the hand, the heart broken apart, and the story of the woman who goes to the states to make it in films, and she gets tied up, and so on, delete that. The course case, the trouble with Girls Aloud and all the bands, kidnapped. The days were accomplished, she should be delivered.

Holy Spirit breathes in me now, lest my words be dust. Every year we get the same Emperor's New Clothes, so what is the gift we have been given at Christmas? Angels are everywhere and what about men being raped, think of Oscar and Lucinda for example, or the Last Station. In truth, let us reach out to the others, and what is Mike doing in his flat in Camden. The little child is God, and treasures us forever, but vice versa? Forsake your pride. On this day God forsook his majesty. In 800 years all your treasure will be dust, except the love you give and receive.

The swan swans across, an oar broke, protesting against, Fenton ran across the park and the internet hummed with it all, the van went about the local town, picking up fruit pickers and prostitutes, nobody would know, or was supposed to know, don't you know. The weeds, the fish, the underwater vibe, a great protest, big sweaty boobs on the cricket pitch, praise the Lord, let me have them, here and now. There's a lot to be said for going to prison for what you believe in, but everyone is their own prison, wearing those goddamn jeans, not through choice, and they do very little about getting out of it. A very odd way of putting it: he had fucked the cox, and one of the others had, unbeknownst to them, seen and heard it all, in the rowing club pavilion, one balmy night where the moon follows and penetrates all.

Jumpers, hats, all the clobber, and sponsors; labels and casuals gone mad, down Soho, squeezing your feet into a pair of blue-suede Diadora, they don't fit of course, but you must have them, for fifty quid in the early eighties, they go with the Sergio tops. And when they die, we told you so. The inconsolable, that is you all over, like a man on top of a hill rotating, believing he not only is the only person that exists, but the only person that should exist. Each day the claims get more extreme: not only did she work for *Marvel*, her friend went to live in New York and set up a comic, just about her, she is the star character in one of them. Hello! One pound of fish, sing a song of sixpence, any old iron.

A kind place nobody does not notice a stranger; Shuffles in Edinburgh, where you first heard Northern Soul, that kind of place where the light on the sea speaks to you. Many are called but few are chosen, heart break guaranteed. There was a man from Nantucket, who had such a large cock he could suck it. He looked in the glass, saw his own arse, and killed himself trying to fuck it. All the people run over by trams, Nicole's ex, and Jacquie Connolly's Dad. I used to see him every day, the road linking to theirs opposite the alleyway next to my mum's. What about the threesome? I was lying on a girl's bed, Louise just remembered, fingering her while Jacquie wanked me off, Louise was too pissed. She was always too pissed, fat and lovely and pissed, calling me up while totally wrecked.

A motel room in Las Vegas, the fountains pumping, orgasms squirting, with a girl who spoke hardly any American, hookers dying, then coming alive again, the Jesus hooker, I am a doctor, I will be your doctor, speaking no other language, other than through a glass of bourbon, the bed is bigger than your desires, than a football pitch in your dreams, than your derriere, my kind of dream. Every wall in each room is a screen full of porn broadcasting what is happening in the room next door, all the people you know, you know you know, the gulls are the people, and she is the bird, and there is a pool, do not forget the pool. There is a fridge, but it is empty, apart from the heads of hearts of everyone you have ever known, and the one lonely beer. You reach for it and it explodes in your face and you love that foamy beard on your chin, it is so beautiful.

I need to know whether we are in a pool, where there is no water, only empty beer cans, and blown around trash, or if the desert is the pool, we travelled across Arizona, through Death Valley, we prayed hard, with no gas for eternity, but we still arrived in Las Vegas, something, everything must have been driving us, across all horizons, not Jim Morrison, or Aldous Huxley, or any sense of a hangover. I wasn't sure what I'd find there, inside the motel room, inside your closet, inside your heart, or what you would find in mine, everything or nothing, I hoped. Let me know, OK, what you want to do, no, you let me know. There's very little we can do, otherwise.

The point being, driving at a million miles an hour to get to Walton, and the cover of the book looks great, and there are words inside too! A burnt patch on their lawn, burning effigies of themselves, and all the porn gone, all the stashes, all the connections, and nothing on the internet, and Disneyland rewriting history.

Then it happened. They took a baseball bat to every toy and smashed everything. Each house was now Jewish. They asked you to cut part of your dick off if you were walking down a certain road. It is about a girl who falls in love with a Jew, gives birth to a black boy, or gives birth to a man with just a foreskin, or gives birth to a foreskin, or gives birth to the . . . well never mind.

Don't ever listen to what doctors tell you in hospitals, they do not believe in medicine, God, or anything else.

The way slander took place, all about reputation, they didn't gain any financial reward but the state and the church did. But the numbers of illegitimate children went down. Each child that was born was given a phone and a watch. It didn't matter if these were fake or not; they were perfect for what they needed.

She had one of those hats which had the ears of a cat on, a pink nose, big black eyes and whiskers grey Doc Martens with roses on, although clothing means nothing to me, or her, obviously. Some cunt was barking in Paki into his mobile, probably just raped and beaten his wife, or molested a load of underage white girls with his mate. Some other girl looked like she was from Babe-station of course, ranting at a phone, begging for someone to call or to buy photos.

He wanted to write a ten thousand page novel about three academics, two men and a woman, who were fucking each other, while they were writing about the life of one of the greatest living writers, but he knew it wouldn't sell; just like in 1502 Queen Isabella had burnt one million books in Arabic and other languages. A couple in Derby had burnt to death six of their children, and had done a rehearsal three weeks before, like a play.

Pregnant women riding an ass right on down the high street, and I can't say for sure, to be sure, that the ass has headphones on, and is listening to Boney M, but who knows. Like all stories that have passed into legend, there's an issue around fact, but not around truth. Worry about interpretation, will you; I mean it, what kind of spin are you putting on it. A rubber lung going up and down in a jar your granddad lying there, dying, with a mask on his face, the state on occasion handed out free cigarettes, poppers, ecstasy pills, the beauty of it all.

Mini revolutions, James, who he loved the most, was it more than spiritual, wanted to ban any written versions of the message, interesting; it was all about the power of the verbal, get it, give me the oral. He could see how it worked. And anyway, how could they compete with all the other suits that were being spewed out. From birth you received contacts that had all you needed. School was unnecessary. Then there were implants in the brain. You could pay to have these removed, at a price.

And the chip plant declares the world is the way it should be, she was no God, there is this way. A balance of chips, a surgeon in France removes them then these people have to disappear, and come back?

He had some mad plan to steal ancient Aztec treasure from the British Museum, now someone who worked there said there had been cuts. How was I to know it was not bullshit, given I had been there once for an interview to work on the indigenous American exhibit and they lead me down endless corridors, like someone's brain, and through secret doors in walls, and someone whispered what if earth is another world's hell, and I replied what if it is another world's heaven. They always say that kind of stolen gear is worthless, as you cannot flog it on, but he already had a punter, a Mexican politician who said it should never be in Britain in the first place. Some king of Spain had given it as a gift. The Mexican was desperate for it to be returned. The museum could be broken into. But how to get out and how simple was it? The money came from drugs and everything else. Picture it now, severed heads on sticks, minus their tongues, cocks cut off and stuffed in mouths, vaginas crammed with the heads of chickens.

Then she broke off and ran towards the motorway and tried to hurl herself at the traffic. They held her back once more. He fucked her in the toilet. The Derby Doggers. The new website and app, tells you where the action is. Don't ever forget about it. Can I combine this with . . .? The thing is, I was standing outside some service station on the M1, they all look the same, and having a smoke and this black woman kept on breaking away from about four people and trying to run on the motorway. Two years later I was watching a documentary about two Swedish twins who were picked up doing the same thing, one really damaging her arm. The other went off with two men, who claimed all sweet and innocence and next thing you know she has beaten one of them to death with a hammer. And here is the thing. His mate knew she was bit of a fruit because she was saying her cigarettes were poisoned and after passing them around started desperately to try and get them back again. At some point a single pubic hair was put in a letter and if this was returned with the hair missing then it was proof that this letter had been opened, like some kind of fictitious council tax claim.

They were all damaged goods; they could not really say what they wanted; they were in love with the idea of love. And an old couple had a map they were given when they purchased a house which had the Latin name of all the plants in the garden. Save me from dust and small objects and collectables and car boot sales, but not from sex in cars, she cried. It told you, the map, what to do with all these plants, and you followed it like the Dead Sea Scrolls. They also had one for all the people they knew. A map that told you what to do, and a cat with a map for a face and the map was the size of all the places it depicted, as big as the world, meow meow.

The head of the hog fell open, piñata style, and out popped the Damian Hurst socks of a vine-swinging dude. Who knows what he had been doing with the socks. The hog was spinning in the late afternoon sun, an ontological necessity, make me fulfilled, I can't get enough, don't make me beg for it, spitting and being spat at by the body of the Artichoke that had already fallen on their knees like fellaheen. They whipped themselves up with cream cheese and assortments from the buffet, the cider and beer never enough, because too much never is.

'Take your tampon out!'

'I don't like the fact you think you can spin the hog, smoke a stoke, and drink beer and tell everyone they are queer, when it is general knowledge the only person you have made love to is an alien.'

Sandy was in fine form, accusing Jack Scott of nothing but virginity. To some this would be a complement. The will power would be magnificent, like walking into a boozer and ordering a soft drink. John was in the background, moving the furniture around, as nana used to say when there were rumblings in the sky but no rain. Patchwork fields, quilts made over the centuries, an army of dolls moving towards the zone, getting with the programme, spinning in the sun and a church spire in Elstree.

15
GRANDFATHER'S BUSINESS

John Tao was researching his grandfather's job working for the Swiss Bank, and discovered that a lot of the gold came from the Nazis. His grandfather smoked a bit, not that much. The empty golden packets, not tickets, were collected up by his daughter, my mother, and given to the children where she worked. Her job was at the Royal National Orthopaedic Hospital, a behemoth of a place, like a town with cafés and shops, and everything. I wanted to track down the family of these people he had worked with. He said he hated his job, and yet was heavily into the Masons and it seemed to the rest of us that he was always with them. He clearly took pleasure in putting my grandmother down and thought she was bit thick.

He liked to drink, but he clearly loved my grandma, I can see that now. He was old school; he didn't like talking about the war. The one story I remember, he was on the coast somewhere, Italy or maybe France. There were about seven thousand troops. They marched up to the front, and then were told to go left or right. He went left, I think. Once he was on the ship he heard an almighty explosion, the other ship had been torpedoed. Then they watched in horror as thousands drowned in front of them. I suppose they must have had some form of identification. With the Americans you always think of dog-tags. With the islanders off Scotland you think of the jumpers that their elders have knitted. That I think is the only story he told me about the war.

I heard that his brother, my Great Uncle Harold, was on stage during the war with Frankie Howard. And Harold's wife, my Great Aunty Doreen, was a code breaker at Bletchley. Did she win the war? The government today use the war and nostalgia to keep everyone in their place. No one can change class really, it doesn't matter how much money you have. I mean, when you're listing to The Jam, you are either part of the scene or you're not, get what I mean? My dad once ran an engineering firm. He was on a train and bumped into an old school friend and gave him a job, there and then. Those were the days when interviews, psychometric tests, CRB checks, were for idiots. The new employee had an Asian wife and had sent his son to an expensive school, to change his class no doubt, both my dad and the guy before the poor north of England, and see the fruit of his loins not have to face the class discrimination he had experienced. The son rejected his dad, thought he was too common. That's what happens if you try and help people. They reject you. And because the guy felt rejected he took to drink and my dad had to sack him, no choice in it, but he didn't do it himself. My dad had his brother do it, as he was the office manager.

He topped himself.

This is what happens if you try and cross boundaries in this country, remember. It just is not possible. You know that story of that top Tory minister allegedly calling a policeman a fucking pleb? It was the *p* word that mattered, not the *f* or the *c*. It doesn't matter what you say, it was what people hear. I get it all the time with women. Nobody listens to each other. It's like Britain and Argentina. Nobody likes to admit the other may have a point.

There was the woman with blonde ringlets, and the man with the three quarters of his face burnt brown, the other quite light. That trip to Paris. And you remember, clearly of course, the empty swimming pool, by the chateau, she will not come out in the sun, just lounges naked under an umbrella, smoking, drinking warm red wine, writing her memoirs.

We did it all, vulnerable, how much so, how strong. More people on earth than there ever was, with the sheep demanding the shepherd. Malcolm X explained that there is the house Negro and the field Negro, and the house Negroes love their master more than themselves. All quiet on the western front, and don't talk about her behind, or which front. I, of course, followed in his footsteps, into the bank, after they sold the cherry orchard, in the name of the father, lend us a fiver, he enjoyed it. I mean I did. And was not sure why.

And another disaster, I wasn't certain how to react, anyone can be a cunt if they want to be, but why be a total cunt to your own son? My father had spent his whole life competing with other people. Was this his own fault, given it was in the genes, and it was a matter of being frightened some other fucker was going to rip the food from your mouth, the shoes from your feet. Equality meant nothing to him at all. He always had to feel above people or below, seeing a certain hierarchy of being. Don't you think we all do this, one way or another? The way you see her now, unchaining her bike, and you think you should have spoken to her about her writing, about Hungary and bear cub trousers, those unfashionable things like tracksuit bottoms that everyone wore in the days of Soviet Russia. But you're too shy.

Why did he feel the need to put others down? It was like Samir. He always felt the need to work harder. I never felt that the penetration of women was the same as colonial conquest, or that celibacy related to post-colonial theory. But I knew that some had analysed the camps of missionaries in Latin America, and seen how their designs had resembled vaginas, *vagina dentata* no less, and so the more you denied desire the more it became manifest. Neither my father nor Samir truly accepted themselves, they only accepted through their work, through beating the other, through competition not cooperation. I was like that in the context of love, sitting on a train to Brighton with a mini-bar bottle of gin and the competition for her affection all around me. But, overall, it made me consider that if they both got off on playing fascist arseholes so much then why was I spending so much time with them. Was I a fascist arsehole, perhaps?

We had this idea for a TV show; let the public vote for the biggest twat–Jeremy Clarkson, David Starky, Jeremy Kyle, Piers Morgan, the list was endless. And that's just the blokes, surely Jordan is high up there, and Kay Burley. What you do is get everyone to vote, then burn them, in the flesh on top of a pile of books, something by Tolkien of course, who just loved people slaughtering each other, as some kind of romantic, like the *Aeneid* or something Greek. As long as he is in charge then that is fine; it alleviates his anxiety, don't you get it? Perhaps someone did something bad to him? I will have to investigate this. Go to where he grew up and investigate. And I did just that, and this is what it brought up.

16
FOUR OF A KIND

John knew there were four kinds of truth, and though he doubted truth to be a liar he never doubted love. Switch on the TV, and see what went on fifty years ago with Raymond, Uncle Raymond. The raw Yorkshire sun thawed his naked shoulders, as he pulled the roller rhythmically across the cricket square. Raymond Lee knew this was one moment to hold onto, like the beggar on the street with his last can. Later on in life he would tell people he used to bowl to Geoffrey Boycott, not as the brag as most people could not stand Boycott, just as away of positioning himself in time and space.

Inside people were drinking in the coronation of the young Elizabeth, but young Raymond focused on heaving the roller, back and forth, doing his duty. He was in charge, unlike on the actual day of the match when, at the Captain's decision, six large lads would pull the giant roller. Uncle Raymond loved all sport, more than anything in life, revelling in the chance to show what he was made of, to go beyond. Older boys resented his talents, and tried to put him down, but this only made him stronger.

'What you trying to prove, Lee?' asked Freddy Harrison, three years his senior, who'd appeared with two other lads, as he was enjoying this moment.

Raymond said nothing, knowing any response would be shot down. Freddy Harrison hated school, but loved the attention he got through bullying.

'Look Freddy, the big bugger's ignoring you! Thump him, go on. Give him one he won't forget!' coaxed Richard Wade, a barrel of a boy, who was bright but dedicated to stirring trouble.

'Look, he's even walking away from you! Now, that's just pure, unadulterated, insolence,' yelled Wade, parroting the words verbatim of their Latin master.

All four boys were at Stavely Grammar, and, despite being below them, Raymond Lee knew the teacher, and got the joke. He realised the banter of Harrison and Wade was nothing compared to the quiet strength of Robert Dyer, who was standing back from the other two fools, observing. He'd seen Dyer deck boys for nought. Despite his youth, Raymond had made it into the rugby first fifteen, with Dyer his main competitor. They were the same weight and height, but Dyer had that confidence, and was so much more aggressive in the scrum. He'd broken the legs of an opponent like twigs, and was worshipped amongst the lads. Raymond didn't need any trouble, for his dad would strap him blind.

'Let him go,' said Dyer, squinting in the sun, 'he's worse than shite on your shoe.'

So Raymond continued pulling the roller, getting up the momentum, and was forty yards from the three lads before he turned back.

'Simple' Wendy Smith, the butcher's daughter, was stumbling down the lane beside the pitch, with Harrison and Wade following, Dyer hanging back, watching. Wendy was running now, as Harrison and Wade chased her down an alleyway, Dyer at walking pace. Silence. Muffled screams floating across the cricket pitch, or was it the cry of crows?

Raymond took out his monogrammed handkerchief that his granny had given him for this thirteenth last month, and mopped his brow, the RL letters turning a brighter blue with the sweat. He felt himself becoming like Dyer, the watcher. He thought about Mary, the girl who lived two doors down, who he had spied on in her garden, but never really spoken to. Four minutes on, Wendy burst from the alleyway, her clothes torn and soiled, her face already swollen from the beating, weeping. Her hands were moving up and down, like a puppet, reaching out to him desperately, despite the distance. Raymond thought he'd called out to her, but he wasn't sure whether this was just in his head. The sun was driving down on him, making him sluggish.

'You say anything and you'll never walk again, you hear, shit head!' shouted Harrison, his boot pressing into Raymond's throat, 'now go home, and forget what you've seen.'

One of the boys had managed to rugby tackle him to the ground, while he was in the moment of indecision. If this was a real match that would never have happened.

Raymond's parents didn't have a television, but the radio was on in the background, as his father sat smoking a Woodbine, reading *The*

Mirror and drinking tea, while his mother ironed. His sisters, Anne and Kathleen, were at the neighbours watching the grand ceremony.

'Done the pitch then, Ray? Beautiful day for it.'

Raymond, ignoring his dad, washed his face and hands, trying to hold back the tsunami engulfing him, his legs shaking.

Five decades on, as he sat with his grandson on the couch, both nibbling Pringles, he watched Harrison conduct another celebrity interview.

'You went to school with that guy, didn't you, dad?' asked his son Jake, coming in from the kitchen with the coffees.

'Sure, and Harrison never liked it. I heard him on the radio droning on. Said he never got anything from school. Is that really the example he wants to give kids? He's got to be the least interesting chat show host there is. And he's made his living as a Yorkshire man but turned his back on Yorkshire. You know they hate him up there.'

Raymond Lee's life had gone well with the force. Married peacefully to Mary, the kindest person in the world, his only difficulties had been with his daughter, Amanda, who'd had an abortion as a teenager and was still struggling nearly twenty years on. She studied as an actor but still hadn't had a break, and now was desperate to get a job, any job.

'Do you want to go for a quick one?' Harrison asked his guest at the end of the show.

'Shag you mean? Ah, sure why not, just a wee one.'

The BBC bar was empty, everyone tucked up in bed with their millions, but these two celebrities were ready to rock and roll.

'I heard you've been made Chancellor of the University of West Yorkshire. Pretty funny that, for someone who didn't even like school and hates the place!' laughed his comedian friend, draining his malt.

He was only a few years younger than Harrison, but with his purple beard and orange striped trousers they were years apart, and it was strange how they were genuine friends.

'And, it's even weirder, because my old pal from way back then, Wade, he's now Vice Chancellor of a place down the road. A brain, mind you, he deserves it.'

'Your lot are taking over, must be that old boys' network kicking in! It's just like that in LA. But you need to be related to someone, all in the genes, not the old school tie. The class system's even worse over there, whatever they say.'

'That's why you love it, I suppose! You always were a total snob, pal. How's that beautiful wife of yours?'

'Still rolling in lovely dollars, giving sex therapy to the rich and famous. I'm pretty sure she doesn't do demonstrations, but you never know, she's a sixties child.'

Dyer was also watching the interview that night, but not really taking it in. The medication meant he found it hard to concentrate on anything for more than a few moments. But, like Raymond Lee, he'd been very aware of Harrison's rise to fame. After Dyer had broken his neck during trials for the national team he'd been hospitalised for what seemed a lifetime. The best part of four decades passed by in a blur: thrown off various regional papers as a sportswriter; a few breweries drunk dry; one disastrous marriage; a daughter that never spoke to him, who now had kids of her own that he'd never seen; four, or was it five, admissions to a psychiatric ward; and now a damp bed-sit in Muswell Hill, with a small grey view of North London.

Dyer switched the television off, remembering that vivid June day when he'd watched Harrison and Wade attack Wendy Smith, his silence the deep stamp of approval. Before the accident, before the drink, he'd been somebody. Those two had really made it, but what had happened to Raymond Lee? Dyer had secretly admired the younger boy's fierce dedication, the way he dared to compete with the older lads. He'd never heard anything, so perhaps, like a billion other people Raymond Lee was living an ordinary life, in an ordinary town, invisible. Was that true success, to slip away and become so at one with your environment nobody notices you and you never notice time slipping away?

He'd seen the invite on his hotmail account from Friends Reunited to a school reunion, and vaguely remembered being bladdered on whiskey when he'd originally signed up. He knew it would be too much, that he'd have to confess about what a mess he'd made of his life. Harrison, the superstar, wouldn't show, but Wade just might, bragging of course that success didn't really mean anything, that the titles and the money were meaningless, that it was all about serving people, enabling others to achieve. You could say that, of course, once you'd made it. Even Raymond Lee might show. Maybe Lee would be sympathetic, and not judge him. And what about Wendy Smith? Had she been scarred for life, or just forgotten about it, and moved on? He slumped back once again unable to get the energy to go to bed, but not letting the dreams of others keep him from sleep.

'Bob,' whispered the breaking voice on the phone, 'it's Sheila.'

Dyer reluctantly absorbed Alexandra Palace in the dawn where they'd broadcast the first television images before the war.

'Mam, our Mam, she's gone Bobby, gone, passed on at four this morning.'

Dyer knew it would be heartless to say that, to be honest, he was shocked she'd lived this long. So he gave some comforting words to his little sister, inwardly shuddering at the thought of returning back to his place of origin. His mind was blank the whole train journey up north, churning over nothing, a cow chewing grass that is no longer there.

Next to him at this mother's graveside stood John Tao, his nephew the professional footballer, always in and out of the papers for his various in and out behaviour, Wendy Smith, one of the carers who had nursed Mrs Dyer through the final stages. Dyer, not talkative at the best of times, kept himself to himself, averted eye contact, and prayed in silence for the day to cease, so he could escape back to his flat, his memories, and his view.

'Did you see Freddy on the telly last night?'

Despite his best efforts, back at the house Dyer couldn't ignore her now.

'Sort of, I was falling asleep. I'm not one for telly really. These dodgy celebrities, they always say the same things, just talk about themselves. Why should we be interested in that rubbish, what makes them so important?'

'But it's so exciting, don't you think, all that glamour?'

'Whatever clicks your switch, I've never been into the lives of the rich and famous. I'm sure he's not short of a bob or two, so maybe I'm just jealous. He's certainly done well, and that other one, his mate from then, Wade.'

Wendy paused for a second. She was mixing mayonnaise into a potato salad, and had already been criticised by one so-called expert for over doing it.

'You know, he couldn't do it, that's why he beat me so bad that day.'

'Who, Harrison or Wade?'

'Harrison. His little friend wouldn't work. Wade just stood there laughing like a hyena. He thought it was hysterical. Wade had the time of his life, like he was watching a show. The little pervert.'

Wendy carried on mixing the potato salad as if she was talking about a recipe she'd read in *Woman's Weekly*. Despite the mayonnaise jar being empty, she kept scraping the contents like an archaeologist.

'Would you like some potato salad?' she offered Dyer, who was staring at her in amazement.

'I should have done something, I know. I really should have. I'm so sorry.'

'Pardon. Sorry, I didn't catch that, Bob.'

'I said, Wendy, I should have done something. I knew what they were like. I just hung back and didn't stop them. I'm as much to blame, maybe more. I was the tough guy back then, everyone was scared of me, and they did what I told them. They would have listened to me. I was the leader.'

'That goody two shoes Raymond Lee, he didn't help either. When I came out of the alleyway I was in total shock and screamed for help. He was the only one about, but he just stood there like a lemon on the cricket pitch.'

'He was scared, and he was younger than us. We threatened him not to tell anyone.'

'And he's done pretty well for himself I heard, moved down south years ago, not sure whereabouts, mind you, but I heard he retired in his early fifties.'

'Good for him, he was a decent sort, I should have been mates with him rather than the others.'

'You think so?'

'He was dedicated, Raymond, that's for sure, and people respected that. He was young but just as tough as us. I know he didn't help you, but I was the one to blame really.'

And so it continued, and before Dyer knew it he was on his ninth can of John Smith's, listening to Wendy Smith's gossip about village life. But soon she was back onto the main topic.

'It would be a great story for the papers–"chat show host raped young special needs woman", or "Vice Chancellor raped girl", what do you reckon?'

Dyer choked on his beer. He'd been waiting for this for years, dreamt about it in fact during his long years as a journalist. Every time Freddy Harrison came on the television he'd prayed for this moment.

'But he didn't rape you, did he?'

'Even better, he's a failed rapist, not even a real man. Perhaps I wasn't the only one? I mean, if he tried it on with me then think of what he might have done since then, to lots of nice girls, with all that money and fame. We're suckers for that kind of thing. You know, after that day I spent years in and out of mental hospitals. I'm lucky to be here now, the things I went through. I've only recently got my life back together. Your mother, she helped me so much when I was her carer. Not in obvious ways.'

Dyer knew this was his cue to mention his own similar experiences, but he said nothing. He didn't want to get that close to Wendy Smith even now when he knew they shared something in common.

'But you're OK now, I mean you seem OK. You look good, healthy.'

'Yes, I'm OK I suppose. I liked looking after your mum, it did me good, she was kind, but she had a wicked streak, really funny. I loved that. Where's all that in you, Bob? You seem to have lost something deep down inside. You're deader than she is, or maybe you were never alive?'

Dyer didn't like these type of conversations, he hadn't had that many of them, and didn't want to start one now.

'It's my mum's funeral. Do you think I should be a bundle of laughs?'

He could see John, his younger cousin, now a superstar celebrity footballer watching on.

'She was old. I know what you're thinking. She had a long life. Maybe it's the shock of seeing me again, the guilt,' Wendy chuckled.

They both stared at each other, deeply. They wondered about Harrison, Wade and Lee. How come Harrison and Wade had got away with it, and whatever else, and the two of them were left now with nothing.

'I couldn't prove anything against them, it's such a long time ago,' said Wendy, sipping another sherry.

'Raymond, he saw everything from the pitch, he knows what happened.'

'He just saw me afterwards, not during, so he's not a witness. And everyone thought I was simple. That's why I never told anyone. You never did back then. Even now nobody believes you.'

That night Dyer forgot to take his medication, and in the morning felt better than he had done in years, more alive. The train journey was like a meditation, the fields out the window caressing his eyes, the movement soothing. Maybe Wendy had been right, they could go to the papers, or go to Harrison first and blackmail him. But he'd have some hardnosed celebrity lawyer who always won, and then Dyer would be back to square one. His mother had left him nothing, apart from some bad furniture, worthless knickknacks, and her ashtray collection. So, did he have any other choice?

The following week he got the bus up to Barnet, and then the 107 round to Elstree, and sat outside the council offices, across the road from the film studios, waiting for Harrison to show up for an awards ceremony. He hadn't mentioned anything to Wendy, other than he was glad to have met her again, which he knew sounded so trite and unbelievably false, but he meant every word of it. A brand new Jaguar Z7, number plate FH 1, drove straight into the studios, without stopping. But Dyer could wait. He'd spent his whole life waiting. As he sat on a bench pondering whether to go for some sandwiches and cans, or find a television shop to watch the ceremony through the window, a loud queue was forming outside the studios. These were the *Big Brother* fans that gathered every Friday to chant and jeer at the evicted. Maybe he should go in the house himself, get on telly like Harrison? Then his phone rang.

'Bob, I found out about Raymond Lee,' chirped Wendy, 'His sister Kathleen's now working in the post-office. He's living in Elstree, here's his number.'

Dyer couldn't believe his luck. He'd heard that Lee was a retired copper, living down south. Maybe there were more women like Wendy, who'd been attacked over the years by Harrison, the ladies man. This was it. After talking to Lee his suspicions turned out to be true. Despite it being confidential, Lee mentioned a number of other cases where they'd had more than enough evidence, but couldn't go to court for complex legal reasons.

'People like him are beyond the Law,' said Lee, just as Dyer heard screaming.

Saying goodbye to Lee, Dyer ran across the road to the *Big Brother* queue to find out what was going on.

'It's that chat show host, you know the old one, face like a turnip, can't remember his name,' shouted Tracey from Romford, wearing a lime-green boob tube.

'He's just about to go in the house. Look, he's getting out the limo!'

So they drive in using their own car, and then go about two hundred yards in a limo? Saves on petrol I suppose, thought Dyer.

'I thought he was supposed to be presenting something tonight?'

'That's just a decoy, so nobody knows who the contestants are. The press usually spill the beans before they go in anyway.'

'And who are the other housemates?'

'There's probably some loud feminist, an ethnic, a gay, you know, the usual people.'

'If it's always the same, why do you bother?'

'It's exciting, being out here, seeing celebrities, we're part of something special, and it's free! We might even get spotted to be on something. Why are you here?'

'I used to go to school with that old guy Harrison, he was a ladies man back then as well, an animal really.'

'Really! You should do an interview, they love all that stuff, speak to *The News of the World*. It's all about sex, isn't it?'

Dyer had already thought of that, and then noticed Tracey was considerably older than she had first appeared. She was dressed like a teenager, but was probably around forty-five, old enough to know better.

'Day fifteen in the *Big Brother* house, nine forty five pm,' came the emphatic Geordie accent.

'Freddy and Susan are in the lounge, having just finished three bottles of wine. The other housemates are in the garden, playing Twister.'

Wendy was glued to the box, quivering. Freddy Harrison, and the feminist writer and broadcast Susana Buckingham, were sitting, or, more accurately put, canoodling, on the enormous purple sofa that dominated the BB lounge, neither aware of yesterday's headline in *The News of the World*–'Freddy The Dirty Dog'. One prudish executive had actually had the audacity to suggest removing Freddy from the house, now the chat show host was accused of rape. But the other programme makers realised this would boost the limp ratings sky-high.

'I love you, Susana,' whispered televised Freddy, slipping his hand up her thigh.

The executives were praying for the money shot. Dyer bent round and kissed Wendy, feeling something inside him for the first time in a decade. They were sitting on his sofa, watching the telly.

'We've got him now, look, live on TV, this is proof. The old dog.'

'What do you mean, the feminist's leading him on!' replied Wendy.

One year later, Harrison, wearing a deep tan, was on the sofa of the sex therapist wife of his close friend. The waves of the Pacific Ocean lapped outside the windows, gently filtering into their discussion, like smoke. For all Harrison knew, this was being broadcast.

'Liz, I'm nearly broke, what with all these women trying to sue me. Brenda got both the houses, the clever cow, and eleven million cash, plus three hundred and fifty thousand a year for life. Did you get that cheque from Wade?'

'Why is Wade paying your bills, Freddy? What have you two been up to over the years? He's a respectable Vice Chancellor of a burgeoning new university, so you shouldn't drag him down with you.'

'We're from that generation where you look out for each other, that's all. Call it Yorkshire pride, or pudding. We respect each other.'

'You're not going to like this, Freddy, but we've had your other school friend, Raymond Lee, uncle to that top footballer, on the phone. You know, words whispered through bars lose their power.'

Harrison went decidedly pale. Hitting seventy, his past was flooding back, not the usual nostalgia, but bodily, and with the body being the soul, Raymond Lee haunted him physically, the mere mention of his name making him sick.

'He's been telling us a lot about your past, Freddy, but part of my job is to help people see that these are stories we tell for certain purposes. We're not interested in the facts, but we are interested in the way they are processed, and how people make sense of them now.'

Harrison was stunned. Did this mean he was off the hook? What about all the money Wade had lent him?

'There's a way you can pay Wade back if you want to, we could make a show for my series on satellite, a special, just you and me. How would it feel being interviewed for once, rather than the other way around? I wouldn't force anything out of you, but it would really boost your popularity. You could write a few books. That's what people do. I've done it, and it really worked.'

Back across the Atlantic, Raymond Lee was on the phone again to the usually laconic Robert Dyer. But Dyer was now ranting about how they needed to bring Harrison and Wade down, how they had witnessed the attack, and how Wendy was prepared to testify. Lee wasn't so sure. He knew that in cases like this, even if they were contemporary, it was difficult to get the evidence to stick, so this was nigh on impossible.

'Dyer, I know you've had your problems, but you've got to move on. Getting back at those two won't help you. Remember, they were actually your pals. You can't blame them for what went wrong in your life, just try and make something of it now.'

Dyer wanted to get nostalgic. This was all to do with age, with getting on, and trying to put the phases of life in perspective. Whatever achievements Harrison and Wade had had, and whatever he hadn't had, and however comfortable and normal Lee's life was, what difference did it make in the long run? They all had to deal with things separately, despite their united origins. That day back then, when he stood back and did nothing, and listened to Wade's annoying laughter, was now only a memory. Wendy was damaged by it, and there were the other girls, but was it up to him to seek retribution? He wasn't certain.

Dyer met Wade, Harrison and Lee in The Mitre Inn in Barnet High Street, the best pub in North London within a five mile radius, particularly for men of their seniority, the Eastern European barmaids brightening things up.

'Do you remember old McNally the English teacher, that day he threw my American novel out the window, telling me what I was reading was trash? What did he know? They were so stuck in the past.'

Harrison held forth on subjects old and new, while the others supped. He bragged about his businesses in Portugal, until Wade gave him a kick. Wade wasn't the alcoholic ladies man some made him out to be. He was a businessman, turned academic, and, after propping up Harrison's schemes, was desperate for his money back. He wasn't going to cook the books forever. He was in total control of the university's finances, but there were hotshots around him, sniffing for anything unseemly.

'Aren't you Freddy Harrison?' asked a sexy woman in her fifties, 'Is it true, all I've been reading about you?'

'Read my book that's coming out soon, duck, now that's all true. I'm the only one who really knows me, all the other stuff people write is just pure jealousy.'

She gave him her number, and sauntered off, aware of the eyes upon her.

'You're a lucky guy, Harrison, a very lucky guy,' chipped in Lee, deep down wanting to be at home with his family watching his nephew score a hat-trick on Sky, only there for the sake of Dyer.

After four beers they got onto the real subject.

'To be honest I thought she was easy pickings. I was only doing it for a laugh. Things were different back then, no such thing as women's rights. Blokes did as we pleased, and nobody cared, just as long as you brought home the bacon. Now, if you just look at a woman you're done for assault. It's bloody ridiculous, all this political correctness.'

They talked long into the evening about that afternoon, and all of them realised it was strange that how, as you got older, distant memories became stronger, but often you couldn't remember what you'd done or said five minutes ago. After Harrison and Wade got their taxis, Lee pulled out his digital recorder, and played it all back to Dyer. They had everything, each fine detail of the confession, plus the so-called justifications and reasons why it was fine back then, on the second of June 1953. The sky was perfectly clear above North London, the stars closer, everything more real.

'We could make a few quid selling this to some rubbish tabloid, or tell our side of the story, write a full book about it, ask Wendy to give her side,' offered Dyer, thinking for once with unusual clarity.

'Well you're the journalist, this should be right up your street.'

He got to work that night, like a man possessed. For the next nine months Wendy and Dyer pulled together all the evidence about that day, and about Harrison in general, poring over his files, spending lengthy days at the newspaper library at Colindale, and up in Yorkshire. He'd never felt so strongly about anything.

Harrison was alone, nursing a double and a pint in The Mitre, when Lee strolled in, trying to look casual.

'So, you'll stop Dyer publishing his book if I find your Amanda some job on the telly, eh? Am I hearing you correctly Lee, or is it old age?'

Lee went through it all again. Harrison's life had gone down the pan, but Dyer's book could really be the final nail in the coffin. Harrison was no messiah. There'd be no resurrection. Nobody would glance at him. Harrison was stuffed. This was the only way out.

'I still have a few showbiz friends, I'll see what I can do, pal.'

Watching his daughter presenting Football Today and discussing John Tao's new tattoos he remembered that afternoon half a century ago, when his sisters were out watching the coronation and all they had at home was the radio. He hadn't heard from Dyer since the day Lee had told the publisher that Dyer was a schizophrenic and that it was all a pack of lies, that he'd fabricated evidence just to get revenge. Plus Lee had helped Harrison over his debts by getting Wade to shut up completely, threatening to reveal about Wade embezzling money from the university to fund Harrison's dealings.

After listening to the closing comments, pleased with how his lovely daughter was doing Lee moved into the kitchen for another cup of tea, whistling the theme tune to the show whose ratings were phenomenal since Mandy had joined. The image of John Tao was with him as he mixed the tea-bags in the pot, an old Yorkshire habit, the orange light blanketing the garden.

17

THE REVOLUTION

We are in the eye of the hog spinning in the spit, waiting for each member of the Artichoke to take their turn at spinning and being spun. Before I can see the continent of Africa revolving on your sandal, not a scandal, I need to look at my foot resting in dust formed before continents were formed. All leaps forward in knowledge come through an absolute rejection of authority. What does he mean by the two-fold gaze; it is easy really. Seeing distant things close-up and vice versa, *The Way of the Samurai*. The five rings sounds like a sexual perversion, a kind of freak show in a carnival in the American Deep South.

'Roll up roll up, come and see the girl with the five rings; feel for yourself,' like some kind of Jesus.

And a big hall full of suits, many with ball heads, listening to what exactly? Women way too fat, always the same, squeezed into tight suits. That morning they've been reading magazines about grannies at it, thirty times a week, or day, losing weight. People that know nothing more or less, really less than zero. I flew to a hot country instead, and so people droned on, stood up and asked stupid questions as if they were clever, making themselves noticed, putting themselves about a bit, flopping it out so to speak. Other places are worse, the final message, so does it make it any better. For the love of God! James Joyce locked in the attic, a dissertation on him or his sister, or mother, or daughter, I forget. Ginsberg signed the document for his mother to be lobotomised, Arthur Miller never knew his kid with Down's syndrome, a different age, could have done it differently, he said he was proud of his father, just like her mother sharing a bed with Gary Glitter, a different time. But when time and space have no relation to matter we become immoral or immortal, same thing.

'John, John, I know you travelled a bit when you retired from the game, but listen to this.'

As she rowed down the river, the 400 Baht note sat neatly tucked in her back pocket. She could hear his voice, inside her head, muttering about hairline fractures, his boss, and how his mother would take him to Sunday school. At church, soft felt disciples would fall from the green board, into the sticky orange juice spilt on the floor. All the children would stamp on Peter, James and John, and the rest of them, pretending they were their enemies. They were oblivious to the demon eyes of Pastor Gordon, watching them from the door. They tried to remain oblivious when we turned their backsides red raw.

The river was full of letters to loved ones, for it was the feast of the seventh moon. Each time her oar plunged in, it returned covered in the wet words of a wet dream. She shuddered to think that behind every curtain, in every apartment, house and hotel room, men were composing more and more words of love that nobody except the water goddess would read. Did they find it useful, writing to an imaginary self, or was it part of the process of gaining the strength to write to a real person?

She was out far from the bank now and felt the dampness in her armpits. Along the bank she could see the monks perched in the trees, some obviously asleep. What if she flashed her breasts at them? They all thought they were superior. The moon was so bright it made her eyes ache. The trail of love balloons flowing up into the heavens was a ladder to the moon. If only she had not gone with him, then she would be fine. She could return to her studies. Her studies! She cursed herself for getting into such a stupid mess. She had her final exam tomorrow.

To hell with it!

She watched the oar go down again and surface this time covered by an obscene drawing. Men!

Why was everyone so repressed? She felt the semi-shut eyes of the monks penetrate and judge her. She had had enough. Slowly she peeled off her brown t-shirt, theatrically placed her hands around her back, undid her bra and threw it in the water. The warm night air felt good on her chest. Gaining confidence, letting the boat drift, she kicked off her old white trainers, lay back and unbuttoned her jeans, pulling them down swiftly, along with her panties. The freedom was exhilarating. As far as she could see, there was nobody on the river.

She felt fresh, as if that old firang, the owner of 'The Funky Butt', had not touched her at all. The fat man with his white dreadlocks and straw hat, who did he think he was? She had told him to put on a condom but he wouldn't listen. He had forced himself on her. She was not going to have an American child, she was certain about that.

Rowing powerfully now, building up a sweat, she was proud of her body. But part of her still felt fear. She tried to squeeze out the image of her father and brothers appearing in a boat behind her then beating her till she could not move for a week. She knew they would like her to disappear, to just go. But hadn't she only joined up so they could buy a new television and other gadgets they were so desperate for and couldn't live without?

Why didn't they defend her? Had they never loved her? She was gliding through the water with speed, men and boys shouting and whistling from the bank, her mind full of plans. She would leave, got to Europe or Australia and forget everything, start her own bar, forget the fact that she had a family.

Fireworks were exploding everywhere. She was a queen; this was all meant for her. Then she dived. The river was warmer than she expected and in the womb of the water she felt safe. The lanterns people had lit for their love bobbed randomly. She managed to brush them out of the way, but was careful to not disturb the flame that burnt inside them. She still believed in it all, this ceremony and all the others. She knew that to walk through the streets naked would be a grave sin in the eyes of the elders. But what would Buddha have said? He probably would just laugh and praise her for her boldness.

The boat was too far off now and the bank was approaching. Maybe she should swim on and find a more secluded spot to climb out. Then she recognised him—sitting on the wall next to the bank, rolling a cigarette with Drum tobacco. He had not been to see her in months, but hadn't changed. The same grey Singha Beer t-shirt and tracksuit bottoms with the holes.

'John!' she shouted, but he was too busy rolling his cigarette.

She was breathing heavily, but was excited now.

'John, hey it's me, Kamolthip.'

Her voice sounded confidant, full of strength.

He glanced up and stared all about him in a daze. He looked drunk, a half-bottle of local whiskey sloshing in his pocket.

'John, you idiot, look,' and with that, he turned in her direction to view her step up out of the water and onto the bank.

Her body shivered and glistened in the night air. John immediately took off his t-shirt and once Kamolthip had it on it came down to her knees. Nobody, other than an old man, chewing his bloody gums, had seen a thing.

'I've been meaning to come and see you, but I ran out of money about two months ago. I had to sell everything, even my Rolex.'

'That was a fake, wasn't it?'

Now she regretted not stealing it when she had the chance.

'I won't ask how you landed up in there. Ours is not to reason why.'

She then remembered why she found John so annoying. He was always quoting things from someone like Oscar Wilde or The Bible.

'Can we go somewhere, I could do with a drink and I'm really hungry?'

He thrust the bottle in her direction. The golden brown fluid caught the moonlight and looked like it was alive. His hand shifted to her thigh but she swatted it away.

'John, you are such a loser, such a loser.'

'And you, Kamolthip, you're a winner?'

They sat and watched the love lanterns on the water, the flickering balloons drifting in a crooked line up to the moon.

The money, her jeans, her exam, her ticket somewhere, drifted down the river. But the liquid felt good at the back of her throat.

There is a café in Thailand where American men think the Second World War, or Vietnam, or something, is still raging. They sit with sweat dripping down their uniforms, down the walls, with young girls, eating fried chicken, drinking beer, listening to the Beach Boys, heaven and hell. Maybe it's where you end up. Astronauts saw the curvature of the moon, and they saw the curvature of their minds, and they had ten seconds of fuel left during that first real landing. They had to override the computer. The first three men up there on the moon were very different, and did you know the first rocket to the moon blew up, all died in a fire?

What can you do about it, you are bored, someone is still asking a question, and a decade has gone by, explaining what he thinks about the future, so now it is the past. You want to ask who is worth it, you can't even say here, in fiction, whether there really is anyone. You think of that film where the guy jerks off in the office toilet. Then a plot comes together.

How is it we know someone is looking at us, when we cannot see them? Words are painted fire, a book is fire itself, Mark Twain, dead behind the eyes, you walk through dead man's views of hills and streets littered with cartons with your face on, a lost man, a wanted man, a hunted kitten, a head on a pike, paraded around the town. The crops are dying, more must be sacrificed. There is a blank email, it is the equivalent of heavy breathing, with one hundred and thirty thousand children shipped to Australia to build children's homes, and to populate the barren land, and to shows us that the children of whores need punishing. For which whore do we mean here, going back to find yourself at Warwick, doing what you can, the challenge, it isn't you, you can do everything and nothing, life in an incinerator, stay put and keep things as they are, do not trespass, or pass go, my lad, keep off the grass, freedom only exists on the head of half dog human in a pyramid. The temptation to exist could be too much, and whatever we have seen, we shall believe. Let all we know of you begin at the moment I knit you together in your mother's womb, or before. God really does love you and wants you, and loves all. We are all precious and equal in his eyes.

Rufus Sewell, Harold Pinter play, swapping the parts of the women, flip a coin, matinee and evening, women friends in a house from twenty five years ago, Rufus' husband of one, then confused memories, on for twelve weeks or years or minutes or seconds, or twelve wives, or husbands, or cigars. Some Macdonald's in Chicago, a boy eats a used condom in the play area. We cross-breed with Chimpanzees 40,000 years ago, from the genes, bacteria, plants, humans, all the same; information technology like all other, that is it, natural selection, random, and in Islam Adam is unique, created in a human form, created out of clay, breathe into him, fashioned from clay and mind. Darwinian man, though, is well behaved, is nothing but a monkey shaved, said Gilbert and Sullivan. The Koran says I have created you in stages, like a plant; Darwin states what happened, not what we should do, but adding God to the equation makes no difference to the science. It seems a shame that in the US you cannot have religion in schools, and Darwin is really anti-progress, and in natural selection we are not special or unique. There must be a better way to be moral than the authority of others. Look up the Koranic verses, the point is that 750 verses concern reflection, and 250 are laws, and yet it is seen as a law-based religion. The ragheads and boneheads giving head to each other on the boner bone head of Buddha Alan, sleeping his printed vestments, a cock of crosses, a cross made of cocks, did they kill Jesus because he was part of a gay cult?

Did Jesus tell Luke what he said to Pilate, about the truth, a great idea that, truth I believe a favourite, of course, and so beneath the waves of officialdom there were oceans of evidence; truth can penetrate the hard, said William Blake. David Morley compared his work to that, and then Will Self compared it to Foucault. She made my balls tingle, why become a Church of England vicar, become Christ, it is the only way and to say that means; no one comes to the father except through me. The Father, exactly.

Policemen have a target, including how many arrests, and does one ticket inspectors? They are all raising money, like speed cameras, and spirits exists if you want them to, or webcams in every room. People only want to watch if they think nobody knows they are watching, on one level. Of course, people have been having sex outdoors for centuries and nobody cares; we always find what we are looking for, see Tabitha on Heidegger.

Go to church, make a difference or go to work on an egg, all the same to me, become a vicar at forty five and go to lots of parties. Get rid of clichés for a living, people always bitch. There was a t-shirt, the girl was saying, which read 'occupy me', another that read 'my body is an amusement park'. What were they really saying? A man, look at him now, at Potters Bar station, his eyes are so crossed he looks like he is putting it on, the cross. Think of it, Jesus crucified on a cross made of eyes, de Sade's eyes, they let us know.

Remember that boy who shared a room at university in America. His roommate recording him having sex with another boy and shared it on the internet and he committed suicide, jumped over a bridge. Remember that? Just one example, and the conversation with the woman who sells coffee, a barista, was it you who resurrected it all, was that spurious, all the material about chromes disease, the operation had taken place, yeah, she has to wash her own clothes, you just carry on don't you. In her job you have to wear a silly hat, but they make you wash it yourself, and then there was something about the soap power, like a TS Eliot poem, that made her head come out in a rash. Do not let her be anything other than you, and the chap doing some PhD in physics, he puts in his thesis 'if you have read until the end, my friend, you can have a bottle of whiskey', and he takes out a bottle of whiskey at his viva, and none of them take it.

Let us write a report on the number of viva past today and in the past. Is it all so easy now, extenuating this that and the other. She wanted

118

me, in a tight leather jacket, me or her, I tried horses of fire. Let us see how many Mercedes crash into your pussy the mugwump sex tribe unleashed the feast of your benevolence. So road the concupiscence, those beat poets, they were there and they were in love with love, they never beat the typewriter so much, the fever of the past was full of bombs going off, the steps to oblivion, Vietnam, Thomas Pynchon, a box in your face, a blanket dream, the height of your soul, this is as circumspect as your behaviour that lives within our necessary and deliberate mastery of our behaviour, who was it that lost the first born, on the radio, they put her in hospital, left her there, an abandoned whale. I drank the elevated perspective to my tree and found time only reverses if Emerson sits beside your possession harmony.

So I choke on the electricity that takes me to the mountain, the shack where he sits, he cannot return to the centre, the life threatening disease, the doggers are to the east, footballers to the west, or is it the opposite or the same? They wear masks of former lives, friends, but not the famous. And they address each other with their real names, not a Derridean construct. The planes of Africa exist, as does infinity, within a known space, and they looked into infinity and realised all was connected, planetary consciousness. I love the performance, the past is here, and so The Intended is the delivered one, who sprinkles the celebrated focus, and in the tube train delivery, the first shall be the last, who is the way forward, and in the heart of my mind, the box, within which sits infinity, and the stolen area, a subdued park with rain clouds swirling the shape of gryphons carrying medieval kings high into the sky and ancient Chinese emperors.

The short story, the long story, inside the chosen story, the life from the horoscope, meant to say horizon, Chinese boxes, and in the relatively recent past, the relative was all we could find. Dancing with angels on pinheads, her friend said if he read the theology of the archbishop four times then you would get it, but really it is nonsense, so much nonsense, like the Enlightenment itself. We found a small white feather in the garden and knew we had been visited by an angel. The bridge is the bridge where they met in San Francisco, where Sal Paradise and Dean drove naked across states, with a woman between them, doing whatever she pleased. And the drugs store, or the stories are The Intended, the benevolent fund, kept on the shore, with the typewriter. That, if you are asking, I know you did, sorry it was the thought in the head of the woman in the novel behind me, who was reading a book that contained a writer working on an old Olivetti. The typewriter writes the world, but no one is typing on it, the only instructions are deliver this accurately, there are no deviations that we can see, other than an e that is missing from the keyboard, no moments of inaccuracy, and so the divine typewriter, without the typist is banging away night and day, dictate, dictate, speech acts, sex acts, verbal equations, life sensitive libations, the first is the last and the second is the first.

Keep it hidden from time going back they all visited me, in Berlin, although I'd never been myself. Her petal tongue languishes in my ear, a severed trophy, the ear languishing with her tongue within her eye, the centre of the universe, her anus, and us, an us, incurable incunabula, the favourite circumference, the blurred deliverance, keep us from the capricious, following on from fucking, killing and eating my parents, I met that celebrated nun nuance, that one *Moll Flanders*, sixteen years a whore, loving it all, married five times, twice to her brother, Elizabeth Taylor in an endless flat in New York, too large for anyone to find her. That face she wears, the first smell of rain, or summer, the same as my face. Which face isn't?

She lies there is summer, there she is now, I can see her through the net curtains, listening to the sound of the world. Is she really asking, do I have a place in this, can I not exist? One boyfriend took her to the clinic, another picked her up.

'Thank God they take Visa,' the potential grandmother remarked, and there was nothing that could be done about this.

Has she learnt anything? Probably not, because rather than the baby (I know it's a sin to call it that, but anyway), or the men or herself for that matter, she only truly remembers sitting in the large white room with lots of other women in large towelling robes banging the heads of boiled eggs. I have always thought this would make a great painting. Perhaps there is a vista outside, similar to the Priory hospital where a friend of mine's staying, along with a famous singer who died from an eating disorder.

In essence she was at a large country house in Richmond, and in the morning she had a boiled egg, an abortion, with a group of women, twenty in all, the eggs the eyes of their children, painted on the egg and the Chinese were coming, the government said, why pull down the red flag. I lived with the man who had been in the square when the government opened fire and drove tanks over them, does anyone want to stand up to anything, the left eye always watching the right. Then at the Olympics so many homes were removed for some bird nest soup, they parked the car fucking like dogs. She turned the last page of *A History of Dogging*, and still asked what it was all about, sex in public, given sex in private was now so well publicised, with everyone having a webcam in their room, that sex in public was now the only private way to do anything. If something happened in public you had to turn a blind eye, gouge it out like Christ or Oedipus.

If all is public then there is no identity, we see that we cease to exist. She let it slip, her slip in her bum ditch, the first world war, in her bed, the trench, the hysterical beach, the life time of finding them fucking in a toilet. The relentless fucking, like rain, it disturbed you as you threw the washing up into a ditch in California in the dark. How were you to know the big yellow plastic tub full of dirty duds contained yet more plates and cutlery? The public nature of it you loathed, going around California on a Green Tortoise, she did not mind her man was fucking another man; she might have, if it was her brother, her dad, or her son, the legions of allegiances. Escape before it is too late, into the sparkling cave, into the throbbing gristle, into the night, when she lived for only herself, abuse the endless, the relevance, equipped with sources that try and take us to their only familiar birth, on a hill, in the cave, worship, Charles and the rest. The family, do not forget the family the strip can echo of the preliminary through, pre-language, the reality a wound to filter out truth.

And the hog roast was turning, and the landscape was drawn up into a white chalk drawing of a man with a penis raised above one head, which she hugged, until white vans ejaculated from the end full of copies of religious texts that could only be deciphered if you ripped your eyes out and read them with burnt finger tips, after tasting the flesh of the hog.

18
DISTASTEFUL ABILITY

Something beyond the established norm was threatening, so she always smiled with no legs, and she was always meticulous with eating other people. The birth of her behaviour was the estimation of her contribution, and far from essential. The result keeps coming back to me. They didn't know, the twins were fucking their own mother in the same hole, or each other, watching as their father did her up the dirty, Dirty Sanchez a kiss we all preferred. Spread with bliss, she had kissed the mirror and left lipstick and I wanted to kiss those mirror lips in red, wherever they belonged, Liverpool kisses.

Man is as man as that which makes him mad, so man confirmed previously by the word, but who was man to confirm this? Chekhov had remarked to someone in a novel that to say what life is is to try and say what a carrot is; you can't. But Chekhov, the point was, is wrong in a way, because you of course can try and have a go, like trying to play like the Nottingham Forrest team of 1979 that won the European Cup and Clough always got players to have a few drinks before to calm their nerves. If we ever stopped having a go, that would be the end of it all, but there was nothing preventing us from trying, like when we crawled into the Torriano poets base camp, throwing grenades, waving rifles, stinking of drink and the trenches, with the rain licking our sex like a demented pig on heat.

He was the ginger heir who had ginger hair pinned to his arse, how cute, but he felt he had to show a picture of it, and his hair, now cut, and the story was delicately arranged on the table, a piece of skin here another over there telling everything. They had swum around the cove in Thailand. He had met the girl, nothing like a gnome instead of Juliet, Heidegger always looming and proving a ludicrous teleological tautology.

He loves to bang on the window of himself and find the helix, the DNA, and the time was right for the words to drop from the heaven of your dream that was inside the memory of your future. She was a non-person, lapped up anything, but was she in reality? In bed with a bag of oysters and a one-eyed cat. The Wicker Boy–he had watched the film fifty times and was in love with the girl. His mother abused him and he tries to get the girl and cannot get erections. Correction, he cannot get a connection on his mobile when the girl's mother rapes him, aged fourteen, forcing him to chew her pussy until she bleeds. And don't say you were bleeding anyway, I don't believe you. That's different. And it wasn't a nose bleed, or a bleeding heart, or bleeding hell. You know how he expected him coming back; I saw those teeth he got you. And you weren't really that grateful, were you?

So he believes if he takes the woman's daughter and puts her in the wicker man and burns her, this will bring him back to life. His seed he believes is linked to the original Lord Summer Isle's. She saves her daughter but gets trapped and she burns to death and she is a Jehovah's Witness. And so is he, a reformed alcoholic, an artist who has been part of an experimental mental health group. He needs a blood transfusion but cannot get one for her or him. The thing is, he starts a relationship with the daughter, but ultimately he is just a project for her, and then she burns him alive. The trees in the distance come alive and keep us at their point of elevation, a fixed tree that knows the difference and can circumnavigate the world. Do not hesitate to tell us about Auschwitz in a shoe box, men playing football with one another over the trenches, a kind of material that burns into my heart, like the pages from a B.S. Johnson novel, lost in the wind, then reassembled by monks who have resurrected lost alphabets to decipher texts that construct ladders, stairways, and spiral paths to football violence, you know about Gazza? Gaza? No, Gazza, the one with the sixty lines and four bottles of whiskey habit.

He was crying because he missed a kick. Remember, Gazza, turned up as a mate of Raul Moat's, or just to get on television again, no one was sure, but it created press interest, sold papers, and that's what matters. This man was a figure in the narrative, known as 'I kill coppers', previously fictional but now true, not I spit on your grave, but spit roast.

Before dawn they shall see the doggers on the football pitch, the launch at The Rams' stadium, Pride Park, the head of the ram or sheep through the pub window, the elevation, and so the point of collaboration and celebration, the chosen one, keep us still. Amen.

They slept through Christmas, sent presents to those Jehovah's Witnesses, they never thought otherwise. She pretended to be a bit thick with his parents, so they would think he was clever. Then it worked, and he really did think she was stupid. They went into the kitchen, and when they came out she was herself and they thought he had just taught her to be clever in the kitchen, so they thought even more of him. After all these shenanigans, and lack of sex, they admitted they weren't his parents anyway, so there really was no one to impress, like there never really is.

'Never be haughty with the humble or humble with the haughty,' the wind whispered, before dying, the funeral for the wind not a state affair, just a derelict square up a hillside in a Spanish town, with graffiti saying: three wise men, come off it, I don't know any! Unicorns are nicer than horses because if they do fall off it can make people better with its horn. The head of her tail, the essence of the script, fabulous baker and butcher boys, nestling on the bottom shelf, she dragged it out, the person on the bottom rung, and so she felt there was a movement, four in the morning, that created some waves of energy all around the world, the windswept patterns, now owl faces, but the quintessential element of the owl face, the dwarf dancing on the table, and the animatronics of the spider, the essential pickled creatures in the jar, leading to competition, usually twins in the jar, Siamese pigs, the foetus in the jar at school, foetus of the school, and so the teacher, his brother, played for QPR, and we saw the astro-turf, as we played in Lancaster, a great story that, evolving from a mouse into a man with a tail, she prayed and prayed, the detail was essential, the cat returning unaided, the ball between the apple trees, what were the words you sang when you played, there at Harvesters football clubs, and Wilson the ball on the island.

So you are on the Southbank inside a tank fucking a bloke, and you can see people and they can't see you, but they can take a peek, and when they do they see themselves fucking you. And so the time came to take part, and no longer be part of the audience. Contact is forbidden on the chosen planet removed from birth, and there is the castle where we live beyond life. Each memory is forgiven, until it is rethought, and so we found the elongation of the proportion, the time is right.

They can place the data, ones and zeros, in genes, so all the data in the world can be put in the back of a lorry, and then shipped off. To where? The illusion of the illuminate, on a hill in Spain, Peniscola to be exact, a ruck in a nightclub, plant pots flying, a foot being cut off and fed to the fans, a woman cut up and found in a washing machine, round and round it goes, and the feet of players going into the pies they consume.

They were doing it for art, of course, and they found tables that were giving it some, the birth of a new age. I can't remember, when I first kicked a ball, can you, odd that, isn't it? Nobody can remember. I went to an American school. The heroes went to the States and played American football. We had matches, fights against other schools. I liked the showers. My grandfather had a friend called Frank in the war. At the office party when he was leaving, Frank got drunk and got into bed with him. Grandpa was disgusted. They found it an issue. There were elements of everyone in everyone's faces, nobody was unique, but everyone was alone. Everyone wanted to pretend to be more than isolated to make them even more than unique, not part of the group, the herd, the mass, Amen.

The final birth and breathing, the skin that covers the larynx, delectable shots of first transferences, give me the scope and this is the menagerie of the minories, the true purpose of our first development, and if we ever could fulfil our mission, this was true. A library with all the books in that are notified of our deliverance, so the hills full of the living spew lines of eyes that spin around the universe, the endless limitless universe.

The room writes the boy, who looks up, sees the woman fucking a tree, in a novel in Paris being written by him, as an older man when blind, tied up in a chair by language that exists on the walls of his skull.

19

LOVE IS THE DEVIL

John Tao went on holiday every year to the same French campsite, way down south, almost as far as St Tropez. Dad stuck a cassette on of Johnny Cash, sparked up a Rothman, and away they went in their big white whale.

'I spy with my little eye something beginning with *b*.'

After five guesses each from John and Margaret, Liz proclaimed the correct answer–'bum'.

Brown parched fields blurred past the windows of the Triumph 2500, along with the shells of barns.

'Just cut that out, Liz, or I'll give you a thick ear,' shouted Dad.

They had loved the ferry trip over and the start of the journey through France, but now they were tired and bored, kicking the seats and playing up.

Mum was snoozing, oblivious to his rage, dreaming of French men and their baguettes. They'd decided to take the scenic route, a right fucking mistake, thought dad, on their way to a holiday camp in Carnac where a large blue tent awaited them.

'That's right, blame me, why don't you? Can you tell him to stop pulling my hair!' whined Liz.

Kids, thought Dad, who needs them! Dad was an engineer, with plans of starting his own company, and he'd regretted having three kids. They should have stuck with just one. Margaret was sensible and well behaved. She always did as she was told.

The others were the proverbial pain in eye spy, beginning with D, not Dad, but derriere. Dad calculated that they still had five hours to go, and no way could he put up with this for that long.

'Why don't you all follow your mum's example and get some sleep?'

'Dad, I need a wee,' wined John, squirming in his seat.

Screeching to a halt, Dad looked for a suitable place to park. There'd been numerous stories about a species beginning with P, paedophile rings, so he didn't want to take any risks.

'That looks like a good spot,' shouted Dad, still with a cob on.

'Get a move on then, John', he barked, but he didn't move.

Dad then realised what had happened.

'Christ John, I only had this car cleaned last week. What do you expect me to do now? Are you going to sit in your own mess for the rest of the journey?'

'Oh, it stinks,' Liz rubbed it in.

Going to the boot, Dad took out an old golfing jacket and laid it on the offending spot.

'That's going to have to do,' he growled.

After this he had nothing to say too, and just remembered when he was on a journey to Cornwall and his dad collided with farm wall, and he vomited everywhere. Mum was awake and volunteered to take over the driving. She tried to put her foot down and off they went, swerving through the French countryside, the sun leaving a vermilion streak.

By the time they arrived John needed the toilet, but he now promised to hold on. Inside their tent, with their luggage unpacked, the three children quickly changed for bed.

'I'll take John to the toilet,' offered Liz, dragging her little brother by the hand.

The two children wondered off into the darkness, Dad blocking out any fears of abduction. It had been all over the media, with the disappearance of a girl in the Algarve.

Before they reached the toilet John had once more done his business, but this time it had been done neatly, the offending solid item slipping out the end of his pyjama trouser leg, an offering to the Gallic gods.

With the sun high and activities planned, the family forgot the nightmare journey and all set out to enjoy the holiday to the full.

On the first night Margaret met a boy in the bar who really fancied her. Tony was from Norfolk, working at the camp for the whole summer. Margaret was impressed. He was well tanned, had lovely muscles, and was so intelligent. This was the first time a boy a lot older than her had taken an interest in her, and she was totally smitten. Knowing how much Dad over-reacted to things she decided to keep it a secret from the rest of the family.

'Have a good time last night?' asked Mum, whisking up the eggs for an omelette.

Margaret was about to reveal all but then saw better of it.

'What's up with her?' Mum asked Dad, who just shrugged.

The delightful daughter was saved by her brother Sam, coming back from fishing.

'Look at these lovelies.'

Liz was sunbathing and John poured the contents onto her head; she went ape, running about topless, a young Barbara Windsor.

That night Margaret met up with Tony who was in the bar knocking back bottles of Stella.

'You should have a drink love, let yourself go,' offered Tony, now on his tenth.

Margaret loathed alcohol. Dad had a habit of getting roaring drunk, she'd find him in the alley near the house or on the doorstep and then she'd drag him to his bed before mum was back from work at the hospital. But Tony insisted and soon Margaret had downed four Stellas and found her head spinning.

'How about a kiss then?' asked Tony, 'Or do I have to ask permission from your Dad?'

She fell towards him, stumbling off her stool, giving him a peck on the cheek.

'Not like that, like this,' explained Tony.

A beery slug of a tongue lolled inside her mouth. The way he moved it around felt like he was trying to clean her teeth. When he tried to reach for her left breast, she knocked his hand away.

'Come on, girl, don't be like that,' Tony yelped, once more reaching for her breasts.

Out the corner of her eye she spotted Dad looking around the bar, and she pushed Tony back, the boy stumbling to the floor, Margaret running back to the tent and hopping into bed before her Dad spotted her.

The next evening she turned up to see Tony but insisted on not drinking. By the second week of the holiday most of the family were getting into the spirit of things but Dad was still following the story on the radio. She had been missing for three weeks now. Celebrities had all chipped into the reward fund.

There'd been fun runs and football matches all to raise awareness.

'They're not going to find her,' he muttered, turning up the radio, 'that little girl, she's not going to be found alive.'

'How do you know?' asked Liz.

'I just know, that's all.'

Margaret was now utterly in love with Tony. She hung on his every word, and adored his fit body. But, even so, she wasn't prepared to go that far with him. Unlike her mates at school, she wasn't going to sleep with a boy just because he wanted to. It had to be right; it had to be perfect.

Then Tony hit Margaret with a bombshell.

'There's something I have to tell you,' he said nonchalantly, knocking back the remains of a bottle and lighting up another.

'I've got a brain tumour. That's why I've been out here for six months. My family thought I may as well live life to the full, well, what I've got left of it.'

Margaret was devastated. Was there anything she could do? No. Nothing. He only had three months left to live. But perhaps she could make these months as wonderful as possible.

As Tony entered her, she tried to put on a brave face, but it hurt like hell. The next day she was bleeding and wondered whether she should go to the doctors. They hadn't used anything and she felt so sore it was unbearable. She couldn't tell anyone, least of all Liz, who would blurt it out to Mum straight away.

'They think they might have found one of the people involved,' offered Dad, turning up the radio.

'That poor girl! And just imagine what it must be like for her parents,' replied Mum.

Margaret sat at the table, glum faced, as Liz and Sam mucked about outside. She'd given Tony what he had wanted so badly and now she felt rotten. In a few months he would be dead, and then what? She imagined going to his funeral, a weeping widow dressed in black.

She was still feeling sore when that evening she went to see Tony in Amethyst, a soft rock outfit with a girl singer, who had purple hair and skin like a ghost. Tony was the drummer, modelling himself on Keith Moon. She didn't like the music, preferring soul, but she could tell they were good, and Tony was a demon on the drums. After the gig she tried to talk to Tony but he was ignoring her, drinking with his mates, his arm around the lead singer.

Back at the tent, Dad was the only one still awake, listening to the radio. Margaret thought about telling him everything but didn't want to spoil things. She was Dad's golden girl. She tried to put Tony out of her mind but it was impossible. Did he try it on with all the new girls at the campsite? She couldn't believe how stupid she'd been.

'Dad, I met a bloke but he's with someone else. It's broken my heart.'

She could tell Dad was also heartbroken.

'He told me he had a brain tumour and I fell for it. Perhaps he has, I don't know.'

'Where is this bloke?' asked Dad, wondering whether he should use a tent pole or a large spanner.

Margaret told him everything. She just wanted to be Dad's little girl again. Tony was in the bar when Dad arrived, the spanner hidden inside his jacket.

'You've been with my little girl. She's only thirteen!' screamed Dad.

'So what, she was more than willing, I can tell you.'

Dad brought the tool down hard on Tony's skull.

'I'll give you a brain tumour, you fucking little shit.'

Splintered skull and parts of brain splattered about the bar, while the drinkers continued supping, no one attempting to stop him.

It took the police just over two hours to find Dad, cowering in the showers. He'd hidden, while young people had merrily stripped, cleansing themselves of a musky forest primordial nature.

'But the boy raped my daughter,' he tried to explain, gesticulating wildly, the police just staring blankly.

'All I was doing was protecting my little girl.'

'I need an English solicitor,' he pleaded.

Margaret made it back to England, and had the child, who was beautiful—a little cherub with his father's angel eyes. One life had gone; another had been locked up with paedophiles, poets and presenters. Is this what was meant by mind your Ps and Qs? But here, in her lap, was a new little man, full of life, full of joy, and full of hope.

And the little man loves being thrown around as the hog keeps turning, burning, roasting, predicting the future, resurrecting the past, floating towards the source of the Nile. John would make this spawn one of his, if she wanted, or send it off down the river in a wicker-womb.

So many wanted fire, not just pieces of flesh. Upstairs at the Choke, Sandy was dripping with human blood, pig's blood, saffron, amber, musk, semen, the blood of cock, baying for more.

20

NORTHERN FLOTSAM
AND JETSAM

Johnson watching John run rings around the partially covered rings of men, spied the bonny Bolton fan, bouncing up and down sans top, in minus and below, a real heathen if ever such as beast were allowed below heaven above hell, larger than an airship, bounding into space, hairy gonads spinning, twisting and descending to the roar and applause of the crowd. He donned a humungous handle bar, ala Chopper, moustache, and it wasn't covered in humus. Nor was it a dirty Sanchez.

Tasty or fat, his gut heaved up and down, a barrel, he was a beast of a man, bald minus a shirt, minus five degrees, deep and crisp and uneven, a total utter peanut butter. The perfect stranger, a perfect stranger, under the bridge, one black one, one white one, chanting some Buddhist get-rich mantra. When time and place in relation to matter has no affinity we become immortal, for the love of God. You could have easily sold your sold sign to the moon. If all life is so competitive we actually get taught this, one tribe against another, as such, and we tend to think we rule forever, and a day.

It's never easy, with a tattoo above the bum ditch, cleavage reading– No Regrets–in spiral Gothic writing. Nick Cave spider crawling out of her crack, with a thick tool, stuffed with the blackest ink, to do the indelible job, creating an incredible manuscript that does not recognise failure ever, for that would be to recognise the human, at last a definition. I think the way they tied him up in the chair was magnificent and after cremation forget being shot into the air in fireworks, think more about being turned into a vinyl record or having your ashes fused with ink, and being injected into someone's skin.

They met in the alley, between their houses, which functioned like a cleavage. So what if the women fucked each other, which was common, and the men watched. They played football, in the refugee camp, and everyone applauded this.

After the rape of Harry the Hornet, the mascot at Watford, we go back in time to when football violence was the norm, to the lock-up where John Fashnu died. Forget those boys who recently got let off rape, again, he's swinging from a rope, soap on a rope. Not Guy Debord's look-alike. We see the Dadaist tears, on and on, the tiaras and the tantrums, the empty rooms, the missed opportunities, the bungs, the match fixing, the rants from the likes of Brian Clough, again. What were the ghosts they both saw and swore at, Hamlet the elder and the younger doing battle with their own inventions. Chopping the head off a referee in Brazil, nicely; three kids and their dad kicking to death a linesman because he disagrees with them; putting the head of a goalkeeper on a stick, and parading him around town to ward off goals and placate the spirits that infiltrate every orifice.

'Keep it to yourself, you fucking poof, otherwise no one will want to play with you, your career will be over, and you'll be worthless.'

So what did he do? He went to play in America, as do all shaved golden balls, looking for the American dream, moving west and then east, the football pitch a universe. We might know the rules, but we do not know the outcome, it does not help you to win. He knew nothing about it, bunged into it from afar, the love of Christ, born again, was it an own goal? Say Christ was crucified in the middle of a pitch, there are some men there, loyal supporters, but say he was the real deal, live from Golgotha. It was all twitching, the whole of life was out there, the remedial nature of it, he even beats me at Subbuteo, when he took a kick and I didn't know. He's got a fur-lined sheep skin jacket, quote, me pa says it cost a packet, quote, he thinks that I am a cabbage, quote, because I don't like University Challenge, quote–The Undertones.

Sitting cross legged keeps the men penned in, thinking about something stops the revolution, do you ever see the socialist worker signs outside the grounds, or in the back room of a pub in Ireland, which is really an airport lounge where people sit and draw each other, out? I didn't think see, so the stadium, is that it? A new Hitler figure, Newman and Baddiel had done it, David Ike had done it, Oasis had done it, and now the Pope was doing it. Filling stadiums with people, all roads lead to Auschwitz, or was it Rome, the stadium would lead people out and get them away, away from the thrill of the kill, take them to another place, harvest their organs. A world without organs, body without a world, inside with no inside, a mind with the realisation that all is mind, and they took them to Auschwitz. And afterwards a professor of French was only really worried about whether a dog there could smile; he spent his whole life thinking about it.

We gave them identities, sold them histories, and fed them tales of sea anemones. They crept between us, thrown in the lightening elements of the screaming queen, dragged by Nietzsche's moustache, whoever possessed you to behave in such a way? Those that had sex in secret were destroyed on the spot. The only channels left were porn channels on TV and on the radio people screaming orgasms. They say the best *petit mort* comes with death, upon strangulation. So the authentic records came from those who went to the camps. There was peace to be had, much peace, and love too, if you believed in such a thing. It was easy when you thought of it. The media was dominated by one man with a hair transplant, who liked to fuck underage girls because he had a small cock, all the empire-building part of the equation. So the truth is conscience is for cowards, Hamlet, only abide by your own law, they got the manager an Aston Martin if his team scored five in the first half. And he couldn't stop looking at it.

Everyone was invisible. They lived their lives invisible, translated in French. They are living their lives, invisibly, the roll of the dice, a flick of the coin, and they appear. Hitler lands plane on moon, Nazis have tribe in Latin America, an old man in Wood's Wine-bar makes a joke about the lottery numbers on the arm of someone and Jews in Israel today tattoo numbers on. I could worship from afar, or I could sense the inevitable, the feast of old puss, who is it who regulates your mind, the clocks in the process of their birth. I was there when the Pope visited Auschwitz, we were all there. Amen and he in the Hitler youth. Spreading AIDS in the showers, on the pitch, the bitch prancing and biting. I predicted it all. The bloody congeals with all the other fluids, a message from Satan, there is no need for shirts, they have their names carved on their backs.

A head on a stick, or a sniffing stick, a smile on a severed limb, a wayward sign that reports on this, given we believe in everything we see, we do not touch our sides. He gave his wife the head of her mother as a wedding present, hello. On the beach we see the horizon in your eyes, the beautiful swollen synapse, the information implanted in the

134

genome. The phallic birth, the play right playwright who wants the cult to end and in one they drive down in buses to Guyana and drink the juice, in another they cut their balls off, in another they place chemicals in the underground and retreat to a hilltop hideaway, praying for America to retaliate against China, even though this had nothing to do with China.

The fallopian envy, inside the ill-and well-conceived constructs with the voice of bravado all over. Each cum-splashed breast arising in the spoken dawn over the blessed horizon alphabet, echoing headless across the blessed cobbled streets; who is the first? A flock of birds appearing when you look, when we talk, the birds eyes revolving back within their heads, the elevation that keeps up with our approach, the voice of our cum, that spends its time seeping into the skin, and keeps it young. Inside, your birth, who was it that wept obliviously over your balls, wrenching them this way and that, keeping time and that kept us hidden from the patterns of herself, the man, the greatest lover, the shoes and the moustache, and all things, are you too big to kiss, I will bend you down, you can bend me down, for the love of God. And so the answer lay like the hut in the field near to us, at the top of the frog, with the condoms on, where all things went off and on, Blondie looking so rough, we were there, and security set their Alsatians on students we know, and in the queue my student tells me she had fucked four guys, tells me by telling someone else, instructions given to the directors and artists, fascists dictating from death, all the authors living with us, haunting our brains, possessing our every molecule. Shooting up in and out of every orifice, the follicles opening for sure, up and over and upon the goal, minus a goalkeeper, who just keeps on coming from the bench, is it John?

Inner reality is the space, or is the truth his meat because it hurts? The point is she coughed so much she broke her ribs, then her sister, no, mother-in-law, he or she, died through coughing, while before they made the Christmas dinner, hanging from a tree. He liked it when she laughed or coughed when he was inside her. And who else died, because it only happens if it has happened before but it has to be different, otherwise it is not happening. Nobody can tell you how it is, or how it is happening, otherwise it wouldn't be. Living is death, so they say death is sanity, I say. Keep us to the limit of sanity, and the rebirth leaves the team behind, and so the future cannot be maintained. Whatever he wrote

135

or thought or breathed was appearing on the screen, all are atoms and the empty space, and the rest are opinions, according to Democritus.

They travel back to their dream space, and how perfect this is in comparison. Brick squares on a screen that keeps us from deliverance. We've been through the desert on a horse with no name, a hippy chick dancing with beads outside the back of a daycentre.

'That was bollocks,' the response following ecstasy to hide the orgasm, hunt the cookie.

A little red rooster, who is comfortable at the football, the twenty five thousand people at the Celtic game, complete glee, like a bunch of puffs, jumping up and down and all around, crushing the manager to death with hugs, man hugs, boy hugs, queer hugs, the church maudlin and full of guilt and fear, and responsibility. The catechism torn out and pasted all over him, with semen, trying to preach, Billy Graham and miracle workers, healers, preying and praying on people. A footballer who has his career ended, the clever one, goes into religion and politics, spells it out for me, and is totally corrupt. Amazing, but a full life, Jesus in a cave or a cake? Inside the cave are pictures of the main man, inside Jonah's whale, inside the ark, inside the whale seeking the ark, and inside the astronaut the dream of finding Noah's ark, playing football inside the ark, on the moon, and playing the way a patient of Oliver Sachs gained the ability for three weeks to smell like a dog, so this is inherent in everyone, all of you. You go into space, and this is within the genes, again.

II
MÉNAGE À TROIS

21
STOLEN EDUCATION

The essential beauty of London comes through being aware of the contrast. Nothing would exist if there was not the monotony of houses and so we fly, the pack of us, not sure, a flock over Kew Gardens. We see the psychiatrist who fucks us over fucking, or is that a fantasy, fucking with other lives, Freud couldn't get it up. How many times do we do things when we're thinking about something else, so we don't really do them? All that is not resolved returns. When he asked me who I think about fucking at work, it is just a sexy question, he does not know, or does not believe I do not think about it. He wants me to turn him on by this. Then he says that swinging is fine. A group of men have to believe that no man has impregnated the holy woman, if they had, then she would be unclean, and, just like them, useless. They would have a reason to be jealous, if she had been touched, and then it was the experience of my life, to elevate my horizons beyond the birth. Two fixed entities.

Tale of two cities and in Salford she went to work, and in the other she had killed herself, and written a note blaming her boss, so the other one said. It was a joke, like saying a mother's love for a daughter is forever, ha ha ha. She didn't kill herself. Justin did. He was sick to laugh at that, and I don't mean sick in a good way. We translated this into the stadium, where there was the feeling, yes Democritus again was right, we are all atoms, and yes all else is opinion. But the unit of feeling and the unscripted nature of the ritual I then finally understood. Football is better than religion, but not as lovely as opium or sex.

There was nothing wrong with breaking into student rooms, as a rule. But the problem was most students didn't have anything worth stealing: a couple of packets of condoms, a few cans of lager, an eighth of hash, blow, gear, ganga, call it what you will, perhaps a pair of jeans worth taking. I'd once had my jeans stolen from a washing line in Coventry, but Salford was different, everyone knew that. You never walked around Salford on your own. Books were pretty worthless as sell on. In robbers' terms, it was handy though that the red brick Victorian houses backed onto the park.

Gary loved the park. It was as if his soul existed only in the park. Whatever time of year, whatever time of day, he found himself there. He'd lost his virginity to Tracey Harris in the park, got drunk the first time in the park, spent night after night setting fire to things in the park, played game after game of football here, but would Yasmine approve of all this? It worried him, to a degree. There were times, when out with the lads, they would all brag about all the dodgy things they had done but he was starting to grow up. All that seemed like years ago.

Mum had bought him lots of Body Shop stuff and he loved it, particularly the strawberry smelling things. The bubbles felt good on his scalp and the hot shower cleansed his skin. Gary, former street urchin, wanted to look good for Yasmine, look better than he'd ever looked in his life. She was the most beautiful woman he had ever seen and he couldn't believe how lucky he was to be going out with her.

'You want to know the score, I'll tell you the score–you are a sad old cow!'

Even with the power shower on full he could here Mum and the lovely Ray having a blazing row. Why the fuck doesn't he just leave? Ray had tried every stunt under the sun. They all knew he was sleeping with other women, anyone who wanted a cock, and just going with Mum so she would buy him fags and beer, even though he had money of his own and drove a shiny black Jag. But Mum was getting on, so she kept telling everyone. Ray loved her, so she kept trying to convince herself. He had a fit body, well so what. He had been in the army and thought he was special. What a hero! He'd tortured people in Iraq, sliced the heads off children, eaten their eyes in a curry. Was that something to brag about?

Gary stepped out and stumbled slightly on the mat. It was a bit odd that. Ever since he stopped playing football last May he'd felt like he couldn't balance properly. His cousin John had worshipped Justin Fashanu and had gone on to be a professional himself, moved on from making the tea and polishing boots, to polishing it off, one in the net, then raising the silver that someone had to polish afterwards, and breaking his legs in the process. Was it polish, or Polish?

He didn't want to tell anyone about his weird moments, because they would just think he was a hypochondriac, going on about himself all the time. Sometimes when he looked at himself in the mirror he wondered who he was. His other cousin Dave just sat in his room and smoked draw, and never came out. They were both the same age, had gone to the same school, and even went out with the same girls. But Dave had never been sociable, and had left school seven years ago and had not really been seen by anyone since, except his dealer. In another life he would be an international footballer, with all the money and girls, just like his cousin big John who'd ended up somewhere in the Canaries. He actually hadn't been that bad, before he got into smoking draw, or is that what they all say.

Gary had the ability to make people laugh and he wasn't scared to do daft things, just for the sake of it, a clever clown. The lads liked having Gary around and he was part of their history now, the loyalty of the lunatic.

As he stared at his face, wondering whether he should keep the stubble or lose it, the noise from downstairs got louder. He was certain Ray had never slapped Mum, but there was always a first time, and it seemed to be the way of the world, frustrated men beating up their women after swallowing the wife beater. Why couldn't people just get on? He dried himself down with a small gay towel and felt like he was back at school in the changing rooms. He checked his balls, religiously, pulled back his foreskin, looking for other signs of something, he knew not what, and then sprayed on enough deodorant to kill a man.

Shadows from the lamps felt like long people with arms outstretched, trying to reach him, strangle him, a sack of drowning babies. When he had popped his head in the lounge to say goodbye, Ray and Mum were kissing on the faded purple couch, Ray's hand on the journey, so he left them to it before he felt sick. He didn't want to imagine what they were doing now. Ray ran a gym in Bolton, and was thinking of starting one in Salford to get the low life off the streets, so he said. But Gary was no waster now, not now he had met Yasmine.

As he slipped into the park, Chris, Mark and Buzz were standing by the tree, a spot that had mythical connections for them. They didn't speak, giving him the silent treatment, again. What had he done this time to betray them? He was going out with a Paki, well so fucking what! How bloody stupid can you get? None of them were in the British National Party, English Defence League, or anything. Mark's dad used to be in the National Front, but that was years ago and it wasn't serious. He knew them all, what they thought, what their dreams were. They weren't thick. There must be something else.

'Haven't you heard?' said Chris, sparking up a fat joint, shuffling from one foot to the other, staring at the ground.

Of course he hadn't fucking heard. How could he have heard, his mobile had been stolen yesterday at the Arndale Centre.

'Mark's dad's been arrested. They searched his house and found all our stuff. He won't grass, but the pigs have it all, man. That's two years' worth of work gone, just like that, blown.'

Gary had told them not to keep the haul in one house, to spread it around. Mark's dad had been inside a couple of times before. The police were always watching him, hoping he would lead them to better things. Sighing, having stopped smoking three months ago, Gary took the joint and sucked hard. There was some rustling behind them. Must be a bird caught in the undergrowth. They were all completely lost for words, so they just stood there smoking, saying nothing, nursing their collective wound until the joint had burnt out.

'Sorry about your dad, Mark, see you at Fox's then. I'm off to meet Yasmine,' grinned Gary, expecting one of them to say the proverbial *give her one from me*.

He had a good buzz on right now. The strength of the weed had gone up exponentially since he'd last had a wee toke, and this latest batch of hardcore skunk just blew your napper right off. You could feel your skin tingling at the back of your brain, glowing, like being stroked or nibbled by weird creatures. Taking the third path across the park, he was dreaming about getting a flat with Yasmine and moving on and up, away from his childhood and his current nightmares, and the activities on the purple sofa. She still had a year of her science degree to finish, and he'd just started another apprentice scheme, but you had to have dreams, right?

The moon was fulsome and clear, the sky empty of cloud, sucked clean. Gangs of lads patrolled the park, but most knew Gary and they knew not to mess with him, given his mum's boyfriend's reputation, and his own. He still carried a knife, just in case, and he did boxing twice a week. He was capable of taking on anyone, so he liked to think. He could list the blokes he didn't want to fight on one hand. As he stumbled along the path he remembered the vision of his face and the loud voices from downstairs. That face. Was he still the same person he was as a teenager and would he still be this when he was sixty?

Perhaps he could leave his latest apprentice job, go and work for Ray, help him set up his new gym. He didn't like Ray and had been embarrassed a couple of times by the arse. Once, when he was with Yasmine, Ray came in to borrow a DVD and didn't even knock. Yasmine was on top of him, naked, her lovely cone tits exposed. They had only just started to have sex that week, after waiting six months which was torture. Gary went absolutely tonto, and Ray got the message.

Yasmine would never go round his house again.

Crossing the bridge over the stinking River Irwell, Gary spied Yasmine's student house now, with the green stained glass above the door sending out a message into the night. The door was open. Something deep inside him started to shift and churn and turned to panic. He ran, stopping every now and then to listen, to hear footsteps or a sign.

There was nothing.

'Jesus fucking Christ, man. Yasmine, Yamine!'

He was bellowing. Going in, he could see it had been fully ransacked. He pushed her door open. Yasmine was tied up, naked, in the corner of the room. Swastikas, in red paint, covered the walls. He felt the need to kill someone—anyone.

He untied Yasmine and tried to hug her but she just pulled away.

'Who did this, Yasmine, who the fuck did this, tell me which fuckers did this?'

But it was no good. She was a wreck. As Yasmine called the police Gary noticed an odd smell. They had smeared human shit along the corridor walls.

He would make them pay for this.

'Did you get a good look at them?' the female police officer with tight buns all over asked, but Yasmine wasn't talking.

Gary knew everyone, he would find out, even if the pigs couldn't. To the police this was an everyday occurrence. They hadn't raped Yasmine, just humiliated her. She had watched as one of them had pissed on her Koran, which another had torn out pages and turned them into a mask that he then stuck on the mask of a football manager. The police were relieved that they hadn't put all this on YouTube, not yet anyway. That night Gary spoke to Jay, her brother, and they swore they would hunt down the scum together. They also agreed not to tell her family, her father in particular, who had never wanted her to go university in the first place.

22
ENTERING THE REAL

What I didn't want to tell Gary was that Simon was making a film for part of his degree, and Gary walked into our film set. The police were just as convinced as him, and so was Jay, so the project worked. Simon had hidden some cameras around the house; it was amazing to watch their reactions. He'd wanted me to put on some liquid, like salad cream, to make it look like that had, you know, but I said that was going too far. And anyway, it wasn't the same, was it? I was impressed by the way Gary had gone mental and wanted to protect me, but this wasn't about me at all, but about him. It was like I was one of his possessions.

Living in Salford wasn't really any different from living in Pakistan. At least I could see that now. And this gave me an excuse to not get that close to Gary, to keep my distance and make out I was going through some kind of post-traumatic stress disorder.

'But you must have seen something, got a look at one of their faces?' Gary insisted in disbelief, rocking in his Adidas.

'I told you before Gary, listen this time! I was lying in bed with the lights off. They burst in, put something over my head, and then just trashed the place. If you don't want to believe me, then that's fine.'

I crossed my arms and slumped down in the corner of the room.

I realised that I had pretty good acting skills.

'It's not that I don't believe you, it's just I really need something to go on.'

The next day Gary went to the police station and they told him they had made no progress at all, which made him go mental. They knew he was linked in some way to the stolen goods at Mark's dad's house, so they really did not want to take him into their confidence but what could they have told him anyway?

It was funny the way Gary and I had met. I had been on a stall outside Top Man, popping into the changing rooms every now and again to pray. He'd come up and was amazed by what I was saying about how the government should be Moslem and that this was the problem with the country. His dad had been a socialist, and had taken him to some meetings before he died. I told him all politics was corrupt because they didn't follow God's law. We had had some juicy arguments, wrestling intimately with our minds. He was good looking, spiked blonde hair, fit. For both of us it was love at first sight.

Once he left, Simon said we had to tell him, but I wasn't sure. Gary would know he had been set up and might decide that was it. He was already on the edge, back to smoking weed and hanging out with his lads. I still loved him. I could sense Simon wanted to hurt Gary. Simon was from down south, he was posh and hated the way the locals hated him. This was partly about him taking revenge on the likes of Gary, class war. Stupidly, I thought it was about him getting a good mark for his film project.

'Are you sure you don't need some counselling?' asked WPC Fletcher the following evening.

'I mean, your boyfriend tells me you're just not speaking about it. Perhaps it might help to talk.'

I managed to explain to her that I come from a culture that is very private and we deal with things our own way. I told her I loved Gary but he was going about this the wrong way. She started to take notes. I could see her using this in some BME training course on 'race, diversity and crime'.

It was amazing how people were so gullible. She really thanked me as she left and then asked if I ever wanted to speak myself to victims of crime. I said I would think about it but I had a lot on, being in my final year. She didn't even ask me what I was studying, and probably thought I was doing religious studies, or maybe business. They always think we're doing business.

When Fletcher left I went to Simon's room, and told him what she'd said, and we both wet ourselves laughing. Simon was a good friend, and even though I knew he fancied me, our relationship went deeper than that. He liked telling me he was gay, which was rubbish.

'What about doing a film about you helping the police, we could show you getting ready, meeting the police and then giving a presentation and then film the question and answer session afterwards. Nobody would know it was a spoof.'

Again, I told him I would think about it. I had to concentrate on my work. I also had to try and get Gary to calm down. He had spoken to most of the gang leaders in Salford and was getting a reputation for someone about to lose it big time. People saw him as a liability. Just one minor thing and he could snap.

The 'break in' happened on Saturday, and by Wednesday things had moved on. Simon had convinced me doing the film with the police was a good idea.

23

COMMUNITY SERVICES

Anselm Road Community Centre was at the other end of the estate and for Gary and the gang it was going outside of their manor, a foreign country. They were full of bravado, mucking about like mad, just asking for someone to start on them. Gary was up on Buzz's shoulders, peering through the cracked windows at a couple of old ladies slurping tea and chomping Hob Knobs. There didn't seem to be anyone else about. Perhaps there were a few things worth stealing, perhaps not. Over the years the centre had become derelict, with various gangs using it to practice their firebombs and graffiti. Whenever the police held a meeting the young people would condemn them for harassment, for stealing their booze, and for there not being a place for them to go. The police would then mention Anselm Road. Then the youth would laugh and say the place was a dump, and the police would agree and point out that kids like them had turned it into a dump, wrecked the place with a vengeance.

Gary was still on Buzz's shoulders when Yasmine arrived with WPC Fletcher, or Mary as she preferred to be called, and the Lovely Simon. Gary always called Simon the Lovely Simon. He hoped, for his sake, that the guy was gay, but he wasn't, he was just posh and rich and up himself. It pissed Gary off that rich kids from the south, whose parents had had the money to pay for an education, could then swan into university, even if they were as thick as pig shit and even live with his girlfriend. Yasmine said the Lovely Simon was good with money and that he was the bursar of the house and they let him sort out their accounts and the budget for food and utilities. He had some shares, apparently, including some in United but not City. If anyone was worth robbing then it was Simon, with his two-year-old Ford Focus Zetec. And how did he get that, Daddy? Gary was wrong there. Simon had worked

148

in a bank before Salford and that's why he wanted to play at being a student more than someone straight from school.

The room was still pretty empty, but the Lovely Simon helped Yasmine set up her PowerPoint presentation, while WPC Fletcher, that is Mary, chatted to the old ladies. They had all been victims of crime, and their faces revealed it, bitter and twisted. They had seen things, things the rest of us could only imagine. Gary got Buzz to let him down and with Chris and Mark smoked another joint, making sure it was a weak one; he didn't want his eyes to turn red and get fits of laughter. His Mum, known to everyone except Gary as Sheila, and Ray, were supposed to be turning up to be supportive and Ray wanted to find out from the filth, as he put it, how much protection they could offer from yobs if he was going to set up a gym in the area.

'Good evening everyone. I'd like you all to meet Yasmine. She's been through a horrendous ordeal, but she has survived and, as they say, what doesn't kill you makes you stronger. I just want to say a few words before we begin. Yasmine is a dedicated student, who gained a scholarship to study biology at our university.'

A faint round of applause from the crowd interrupted Mary, leading her to reveal a crooked set of teeth, feeling like the thespian she always dreamt of being. She paused to allow others to find a seat, and get comfortable. Why were people always late? You couldn't say it was being fashionably late, because it wasn't fashionable coming to a place like this in the first place. A man in a trilby hat who came to everything sat down at the front and started clicking his teeth, while other stragglers found places quietly and tried to not be noticed.

'As you're well aware, we have a problem in this area with student crime; that is, crimes against students, not by students. The students are poor themselves, then vicious gangs take from them whatever they can find. Yasmine here was the victim of such a crime. Luckily, no real violence was involved. They tied her up, but did not attack her.'

There was a gasp, then a long pause. Gary, sitting at the back with the gang and playing with his Burberry cap, felt as if Mary was going into too much detail. Some people might be getting off on all this, here to hear lurid stories of abuse and at home at night fantasise about it.

'This is bloody boring, let's get out of here for a beer,' whispered Mark, desperate to be outside smoking another joint.

'We're here to support Yasmine, you twat, don't you care that she was attacked, you selfish shit?'

Gary whacked Mark in the shoulder and the rest of them laughed. Sheila turned around and gave Gary one of her looks, and then the WPC continued, giving some statistics, and whizzing through a high-tech presentation full of graphs and pie-charts, that gave the breakdown of the areas with the most break-ins and the spots with the most violent crime. She even mentioned a new app people could download. Things were starting to warm up. Even Buzz was pleased he came. Knowing which areas were the hotspots told you which areas would be the best ones to hang out in or avoid.

'So, as I say, the real nasty crimes are concentrated around Crescent Road, Chalfont Street, and the Huntsman Estate, as you probably know, and the north east side of the river. We've got officers with dogs that patrol the area and I am pleased to say unlike the Manchester constabulary less than two miles down the road we've not had any significant gun crime. Knives and other weapons yes, certainly, but no guns. I can assure you, we're doing our best to not let the situation get out of control, and things are actually getting better.'

With that, Mark let out a howl of laughter, which one of Sheila's looks put a stop to.

'What about the hold up at the post office in St Paul's Road the other day? They had guns, didn't they?' asked one of the old ladies.

'They were only replicas love, toy guns. They still managed to get away with it though. Now let me pass you on to Yasmine, who'll talk about her personal experience, Yasmine love.'

Yasmine stood up, smiled politely at the audience, and explained she was a second generation Pakistani Moslem who had always faced racism. They didn't seem to get it, or want to get it. She went on to talk about how she was born in Salford, how her boyfriend was a local boy, Gary.

'He's over at the back, there, the one with the daft hat on.'

The rest of the gang laughed. She went on to say she was studying science, and enjoyed films. Last Saturday, was the worst night of her life. The bastards had scrawled racist symbols on the walls of her house. Didn't they know she had had to live with this all her life?

She was clever, but she wasn't that emotionally strong, she admitted. She appealed to the audience to help them stop the crime together, to actually tell the police if they saw or knew something, and to pass this message on to their friends and family. As she finished everyone stood up and applauded loudly. There was a feeling of togetherness, and Mary beamed as she said closing remarks about how this was their community and they should let nobody ruin it.

'That was fucking fantastic, they loved you,' Gary purred in her ear.

As she turned and kissed him the Clint Eastwood man lit a cigarette and looked their way, as if he knew something but was too cool to say. Gary felt really proud of her. He always had done, but this was different. His family and friends had been watching. They had seen how clever she was and how way beyond any other girl intelligence wise, and what a star she was, a genuine performer. And she looked gorgeous.

Before now, they had all thought she was a bit of a geek. She had asked her family to come, but none of them did, not even her brother. It was strange, because she was starting to feel more at home amongst the white community. Gary meanwhile felt guilty for spending so much time with Chris and the lads, and for going back on the dope.

'Ray's offered me a job with him at his new gym, what do you think? My new job, apprentice mechanic with a bunch of sixteen year olds, is a nightmare, I can't stand it, Yaz.'

She wanted to tell him to stick it out, because she knew what Ray was really like. One night, when they had all been out down Fox's he had come on to her, rubbed his semi-erect cock on her at the bar, and he had turned nasty when she'd refused. She hadn't told Gary. Now she wished she had.

'Don't do it, Gary, you know what that bloke's like, he's a user. He'll get you to run the place, work you like a dog, and give you the minimum wage. Ray can't be trusted, you know that, or are you never going to learn!'

She was right, of course, she was always right. Sometimes he felt intimidated by her, as if, when it came down to it, she was too good for him. There was some doubt in him that she really loved him. Why should she? What had he got to offer her? A place in the white community, was that it? Yasmine turned down a lift from Simon, and as they walked back to her house Gary tried to tell her this, how he felt, what he hoped would happen. She liked his sincerity and said she hoped for the same things and she might do a medicine conversion course and become a doctor. Wouldn't that be great! She could be their local GP.

Back at his house, Gary checked his balls and penis for any signs. He felt slightly uncoordinated again. It couldn't be the dope, the effects of that must have warned off hours ago. Perhaps he should tell someone. Putting on his headphones, to block out the squeals of Sheila and Ray shagging, he crashed out on the bed and thought about Yasmine. He couldn't help thinking she was seeing Simon on the side. God, please God, no. He never prayed. His parents had split up for religious reasons. His dad thought he was God, but his mother didn't believe him. Gary had stopped believing in the real God years before his Dad left them, years before his grandma died. It must have been when he was around six.

He was playing in the road with Sarah, a girl who had gone to live in Australia. They had been kicking a filthy tennis ball about and he could see it now, as if it had happened this afternoon. A man came over and introduced himself as Sarah's Uncle Steve. Later he found out that Uncle Steve had been fucking Sarah, as well as her mother. It had gone on for years, until she was fourteen and had told her mum. At first her mum didn't want to believe her. That afternoon with the tennis ball was the first time Gary had met Uncle Steve. What made it so memorable was that Steve had told Gary not to play with girls because they corrupted you, and he believed him. Sarah had come knocking for him but he always said after that that he didn't want to play with her.

Gary had passed his test six months ago, but they hadn't been anywhere in a car and he was jealous of Simon. Listening to hip-hop, he smoked the last bit of puff Chris had given him and wondered whether Yasmine was right. Ray wasn't to be trusted. But he couldn't spend his life being a mechanic, listening to people moan about their motors. He really couldn't. As he let sleep overwhelm him at last, he felt that if he didn't do something soon he was going to be trapped for the rest of his life, like one of those birds they engage in a temple that people pay to release, only there would be nobody releasing him. He'd seen it happening in other peoples' lives and he wasn't going to let it happen in his; kids before you're twenty, on the dole, nothing to look forward to except fags and booze. What kind of life was that?

24
GAY LORDS

I always wondered about Simon. Not about whether he was gay or not, he didn't interest me like that, not my type at all. I need my men to be sensitive types. He was always on the phone to people and people were always knocking on our door. If he isn't a dealer then I don't know who is. Gary had told me about his mate who was a dealer. He got in debt and people came round and killed his mother by mistake. No joke. Tying me up for a student film was one thing, but actually dealing drugs? Perhaps he just knew a lot of people.

The talk went well, but I'm not going to do another. They were applauding like mad, as if I'd won an Oscar or something. What if they found out? Mary was trying to turn me into a missionary, but I've got too much on. Term starts in a week, and we were supposed to read all sorts of stuff and get a proposal together for our dissertation before September. Shit. I've got to get it done, just get on with it.

There was one guy there at the talk that really stood out, a kind of Clint Eastwood figure, all in black. He looked like he knew something we didn't. One of those old guys who has managed to keep his looks and just goes on getting better looking: silver hair, like Jacques Derrida, side burns that went down to the corners of his mouth, and his boots looked like they were made of onyx, silver tipped. I felt he could see right through me. Perhaps I've seen him somewhere else, on the street or in the supermarket, or even in a dream. There was something other-worldly about him, scary but enigmatic and attractive. Maybe he had come for another reason, to tell me something?

It was a shame Papa and Mama couldn't come. But what am I talking about! The whole thing was a con. I hope it's worth it. Simon got some footage. Said he was taping it so the police could use it again. Community awareness, race issues, all sorts of issues wherever you went. At the university it was ridiculous. On the first day we were given this handbook that had a list of all the words we weren't allowed to use. But what if we thought them? How are they going to police that? Perhaps they will, perhaps that's what the internet is all about. I'm glad we haven't got it at home. I'd be on it all the time. There's the door again. Perhaps I should get it.

'Yasmine, I want you to meet Tamar, she's my girlfriend from Holland I was telling you about.'

Simon stood in the doorway with a blonde hippy girl in some kind of crazy cardigan, someone straight out of a seventies pop group gone wrong.

I tried to remember when exactly he'd told me, but couldn't recall a thing.

'Don't worry, don't get up, only I've got some presents here for Simon you might like to enjoy, OK,' said Tamar over her enormous goofy teeth.

Tamar seemed really nice, but already she was annoying me with her loudness. Why couldn't I be more tolerant? It must be due to the lack of sleep.

'Welcome to Salford, Tamar, I must show you around tomorrow. I've got to get some sleep now, sorry. Good to meet you.'

Simon showed her out and then popped his head back in and winked. I wasn't sure whether this was a conspiratorial wink, as in 'we've fooled her', or a 'I'm going to get my oats now' kind of wink, but I didn't really care. Simon sometimes thought that I understood him when clearly I didn't have a clue. I'd read about telepathy and all that nonsense but had never felt I had any kind of supernatural powers. And anyway, I read somewhere that the supernatural is just the natural only the natural has been so damaged and wounded we think it is unnatural. Strange that, in biological terms; I dreamt that night that I was flying with Tamar between my talons, taking her across oceans, screeching with delight as she screamed. In the morning, the light shooting through my crappy blinds woke me up. The face of the man from the talk was still haunting me, as if he was questioning my very existence, who are you, what's the meaning of your existence, is it what you hold onto, or what holds onto you, do you have a choice about it?

Tamar was all loud hugs and kisses over breakfast, and it looked like she had nothing on under her crazy cardigan. I could smell her sex. It wasn't unpleasant. Simon was cooking everything: chicken, bacon, mozzarella, steak and kidney pies.

'I've decided we need to eat better in this house. I might put together a rota.'

'But there's only two of us,' I shot back, trying not to sound too aggressive in front of our guest.

'Sorry, I forget to tell you. Tamar's moving in with us, or should I say me. She's got a place at Manchester Met to study film.'

I couldn't believe what I was hearing. Why hadn't he said anything before now?! I didn't want to freak out or anything but then again I didn't want to give the impression that I would put up with this kind of shit, like I was some typical female doormat, this was just as much my house after all.

'Cool, I suppose we could do with some help with the rent,' I slipped out, clearing the crumbs from my plate into the bin.

I glanced back as I left the kitchen but they were so engrossed with each other neither looked at me. Simon had his tongue at the back of her mouth licking her tonsils, probably grating his tonsils on her ridiculous teeth. The bulge in his shorts wasn't that big, she could have him. It would be unkind for me to say he could have done better than that, or vice versa. Who knows, perhaps he was using her for something else. Was I just learning not to trust people, or was everyone a user?

25

MORE ABLUTIONS

In the shower he went over the attack on Yasmine, and he could see it all in his mind's eye. But somehow it didn't seem to fit. If Simon was in the room next door, why didn't he do something, try to stop them or anything? Was he there? Every time he thought of it another scenario occurred in his mind. The Body Shop strawberries made Gary's skin feel effervescently alive and the heat from the shower forced him to take deep, sharp, breathes. Sheila and Ray had gone out and Chris and Mark were coming over. Buzz was ill, probably a hang-over. It had been a rough night. He had dreamt that an owl had broken through his window, glass shattering everywhere, followed by a cat that had Ray's face. The cat had chased the trapped bird around and around the room, while Gary had frantically tried to get it out but it didn't work. He remembered the dream as he was drying himself, checking on the face that didn't seem right and trying not to stumble. He wasn't into analysing dreams, but it was obvious what it meant. When he was young he used to dream about flying. He would be running along Blackpool beach and then he would just take off. The dreams were wonderful, floating above the coats, watching the people in the waves below.

Even though he hated the thought of it perhaps it was time to cool it a bit with Yasmine, make her do the running. He had his mates and she had her work to get on with. He didn't want to get the blame if she didn't get the degree she wanted. Towelling his back he couldn't be bothered to check his balls again, even though the nurse had told him to regularly. In his bedroom, he yanked on the sky blue Fred Perry top he had bought yesterday and some old black Levis and tumbled down stairs, fingering gel in his hair as he went. Bills splattered the mat by the door and, for once, he decided to pick them up.

There was also a postcard: 'Time to wake up to the fact that your bird is a Paki and you're dead meat, arsehole.' On the front was a picture of Gary and Yasmine walking down the street. It was post-marked Salford and must have been sent yesterday but he didn't have time to worry about this. He had been kind of expecting this for some time and it only confirmed a lot of what had been happening. Shovelling down two pieces of burnt toast smothered in chocolate spread and some milky tea, Gary headed for work, the postcard in his back pocket.

Their street was quiet, but the noise from the traffic on distant main road blew him away. There was no point taking the bus, just to sit there for hours like a lemon, so he sparked up a fag, and began stomping, his mind getting into the tarmac and the walk. He had a knack of being able to ignore his wider surroundings and to let his mind concentrate on one specific point, like the bottom of his shoe.

'Need a lift?' barked Simon above the din of the traffic hurtling down the road that split the university in two.

For a second Gary didn't recognise him. Was he wearing eyeliner? He looked like that guy out of that eighties band, The Cure, Robert Smith, *that was it*, with lots of messy black hair and silver bracelets. Simon's ferret face looked up at him from his glimmering silver Ford Focus, beaming. Gary thought twice about it and then got in.

'This is Tamar, my lover from Holland. Gary's Yasmine's boyfriend, Tamar, the one I told you about. They've been together for quite a while, haven't you, Gary?'

Was this some form of interrogation? And who was this girl with the goofy teeth? Gary was regretting getting in the car already. The traffic was at a standstill.

'Don't worry, mate, we'll get you there on time. Galley Lane Autos, isn't it?' And with that, Simon overtook a Jeep on the inside, went down the hard shoulder, then cut back out, zigzagging through the traffic like a total nutter. Gary had to admire the guy's bottle. While this was happening, Tamar had got a huge spliff together and was puffing merrily away. The sweet smell of the strong stuff was going to Gary's head but he needed to stay sharp, there was a lot on today, what with Mrs Green's Mercedes, Barry Talbot's old BMW, and all the rest of them demanding their cars be serviced or whatever. When the smoke came his way he refused, apologetically.

'A bit early for me, I've got a busy day. Where you two off to so early? I thought students stayed in bed all day watching crap TV.'

'Don't believe the hype, Gary. We've got a nine o'clock seminar. It's Tamar's first time in the UK, and she doesn't want to be late. She's working on a digital film about vaginas.'

Well you're a cunt so that shouldn't be too difficult, thought Gary. She shouldn't be stuck for material. Did you have to audition? Was it a documentary with real footage? They were getting closer to his garage and he was starting to get slightly panicky and had to go out to get some air, if that's what you could call it with all the cars chugging out their exhaust into the Manchester atmosphere.

'Just here will do, mate.' He was using the mate term, as Simon had been, even though it didn't come naturally. Simon was a soft southerner, that was for sure, and he really didn't have a clue. Tamar seemed even more clueless, and her pink poncho and hair clips really were not cool, but he didn't have the heart to tell her. Anyway, what did he know, perhaps they were cool in Holland.

Getting out the car he noticed a minute fleck of red paint on Simon's shirt, the same colour red as the swastikas in their hallway the night of the break in. Not that unusual, he thought, as he ran down the road, patting the postcard in his back pocket. John, already under the Merc, gave Gary a bollocking for being twenty minutes late and he agreed to stay on after work or work part of his lunch hour. Gary didn't want to tell them it was his birthday, that today he was twenty-one, a real man, not with the other apprentices being so young.

Maybe he should take a year out, like a student, go and visit Australia and Thailand. He'd only ever been to the Isle of Man, not even France. Christ, why was he feeling so old and so hard done by? He took fifteen minutes for lunch and then was back at it, a fast learner, really going through the engines like a professional. By the end of the day John was dead impressed by Gary's progress. Not only did he apologise, but told him he knew he was getting frustrated being an apprentice and they might look into him being a real mechanic. He wanted to tell him about the shit he had been having with his bird, but John was a bloke's bloke, never said anything about his feelings just mentioned the football or what happened down the pub. Perhaps he could tell Ray, now he didn't have to rely on Ray's kindness as he was getting into being a mechanic. Walking back home he took a short cut through the park, just to see who was about.

'Gary long time no see me man, and what brings you over this way? I thought you were a snob, going out with a posh student, hanging about with southerners. You haven't gone all queer on us, have you pal?'

Spike passed him a can of Special Brew and they sat on the back of a bench and reminisced about school. Then Gary showed him the postcard.

'That's fucking bad, man, what sick fuck would do that? I know a few, mind you. The BNP have been round our house about five times in the last few months, hassling our Jacky. She's starting to get into it, the stupid cow. She was always so fucking thick.'

Gary pictured Jacky sitting on their couch munching crisps. She was thirty-two, but had done nothing except watch television and much on crisps since she left school at fifteen. Most of the other girls around the Crescent had got pregnant, been in trouble with the law, or got addicted to drugs. At least she was staying out of trouble, like a giant panda, the ones that just sit about chewing bamboo. Didn't they always have trouble mating them in captivity because the female was only on heat twice a year? Jacky was even worse. She'd gone out with Buzz for a week. He never got his cock anywhere near her. From what he said she wasn't interested in anything like that; it got in the way of the crisps and she might have missed something on the box.

'So what you going to do about this Gaza geezer? You can't just take this type of shit, let them win, you know. Yasmine's such a great woman, you're really lucky to have her, I wish I were in your shoes to be honest.'

Spike's first wife had left him for a German tourist and he hadn't really recovered from the betrayal. It was when United were playing Bayern Munich. A load of them had strayed over to Salford. Sue had started chatting to one and then she went back to Germany with him. The betrayal was more to do with football than with him loving her although he clearly missed her. He used to knock her about and now he had nobody to make himself feel powerful.

'I haven't told Yasmine yet, the term's just starting and I don't want to worry her. She's had shit like this before. Her brother got beaten up really badly, that's why he left Salford.'

'I know, Gary; you don't have to remind me. The police thought I was the guy who did it, remember?'

As Gary thought back, a girl who had been in Gary's class and now had four kids jogged passed and flashed them a smile. Kim still looked incredibly sexy, with a cropped top showing off the diamond stud in her belly button and her beautiful tan. For a minute Gary had to control his erection starring at her perfect buttocks.

'You are a fucking animal, Gary, you know that, an animal.'

'Ain't we all, Spike, ain't we all.'

26
DUTCH CAP

Tamar was in the bathroom, again, throwing up, again, like a right one. Morning sickness, was it? In the two weeks since she had moved in she had taken over completely, just eating and using everything, never doing any cleaning and never paying for a thing. I am no wilting violet, Simon had done me a favour letting me live in his house, moving in late in my second year when my parents asked me to leave, so I couldn't really grumble that she hogged basically everything, could I?

They had been working on another film together and Simon, making a song and dance about it, let me see the rushes. He had spliced together footage of the break-in and me, tied up naked in the corner of my room, with an expressionist piece Tamar had done in her first year at the University of Amsterdam. This involved lots of people running through woods, semi-naked, burying themselves in leaves and pretending to be animals. At least it wasn't porn. She was saving the vaginas for another project. It looked like a real mess to me, with no continuity, no plot, and jumpy cinematography and no sense of the visual. Not a *Blair Witch Project*.

At one point a Gothic looking guy, dead tall and cadaverous, who made Nick Cave look like Bambi, rises up from a grave and then nonchalantly rolls a cigarette. This was all supposed to be deep and meaningful and full of references to Godard, Tarkovsky, Jarmusch and Bergman, but it was painfully embarrassing. They didn't care though. Instead of using the latest equipment at the university Simon had all the gear in his room, purchased through dubious means no doubt. He himself, as well as director and writing, was dressed in bandages writhing up and down simulating anal sex. Why simulated it was the obvious question.

I tried ringing Gary a couple of times but he said he was busy, playing hard to get no doubt. I can read him like a book. When most people

161

need attention they seek it out but Gary does the opposite. There's no point getting all psychoanalytical about it but it must be to do with his dad leaving when he was four. One in three British men leave their children before they are two, so his dad beat the average right. Gary was a sensitive type and I loved him for it. He had taken this break-in quite hard. Perhaps I should tell him the truth but then what.

'Yasmine, do you mind if I borrow some knickers and a top from you today, mine are all dirty. I haven't had the time to go to the laundrette and don't really fancy it to be honest.'

The way she said 'to be honest' at the end of everything really grated as it sounded so fucking fake! She'd got that from a British realism film by Mike Leigh, as she said it in a slight Birmingham accent.

'I'll lend you a top but I don't have any spare knickers. Look in that wardrobe and see what you fancy.'

She selected the long purple velvet top I had bought at Glastonbury last year and had only worn once. Whipping off a t-shirt of Simon's, I could see her tell-tale bump was growing, protruding from her milky flesh. She had nice skin and long well shaped legs. One thing startled me—her bush was bloody enormous, like a hedge. If topiary was your thing, then this was your finest project and I wasn't sure what was in the outback if this was the bush. Don't get me wrong, it wasn't that I had expected it be shaved or anything. I just had never seen such a thing, like a large squashed rabbit, or more like a hare, between her legs.

'They sell knickers at Asda down the road,' I offered, but she only returned one of her looks, sticking her goofy teeth over her bottom lip like a rabbit, squeezing up her eyes. I took this as a look of affection but I wasn't sure. Anyway, I didn't care. I just needed her to stop bothering me and stop using everything and everyone.

So, she was having Simon's child. Great.

'You don't have a belt, do you?'

And she would be walking around Manchester all day with no knickers on and my top on which she was wearing like a skirt, with her all mighty bush.

After a lecture on chromosomes I headed to the café on Swansan Street, a usual hangout for science students. The streets of Manchester were busy with the new first years scurrying everywhere, fresh meat carrying their goody-bags. Rebecca and Sam were already in Warhol's smoking like crazy out back, discussing the merits of reality television. Sam was thinking of auditioning what with the posters everywhere and as she talked incessantly about it I watched men going up to the counter to pay, looking down the back of Sam's jeans to catch a view of her spangling G-string between her buttocks. She was a big girl, her breasts always jiggling about and her long blonde hair and bee-stung lips meant guys couldn't keep their eyes off her. She'd certainly have a chance at the auditions.

'You've got to have a laugh, let your hair down. I mean you can't study all the time; life would become so tedious,' she sighed waving her Marlborough Light around like a magic wand, 'and how's Gary by the way?'

I wasn't expecting this so early in the conversation and didn't feel like going into it.

'He's avoiding me, probably thinks this way I'll run after him.'

Sam and Rebecca looked at each other and then went back to talking about the auditions for *Big Brother*. I knew they thought I was ridiculous to go out with such a loser of a local lad but I was local myself, people often forget that. Why not? Did they think I should only go out with nice Asian boys who were studying to be dentists? That had to be classed a racism, or at least classism. I felt like shouting at them but I just sat there more bored by their banter than by the lecture I'd just been to.

I knocked back my cappuccino then went to the library to prepare my first assignment of the new term. I had a reputation as a real swot and it was true. Let others dream about being on television, in some shit show, I had better things to do.

The library wasn't as busy as it usually is and I found quite a good spot near the biology shelves. I'd been working for two hours when I spotted him watching me. He was pretending to read a book and kept stroking his forehead as if it pained him. I had heard about people who get vicious migraines or start to see round shadows in their vision from too much stress. Clint Eastwood man looked tired not stressed. I thought it would be a bit obvious to just get up and ask him what he wanted. Maybe he was just another mature student, lonely, not from the area, looking for a friendly face. Had I impressed him at the talk at the community centre and he just wanted to talk about it?

The funny lights in the library were beginning to annoy me but I knew if I went home now Simon and Tamar would be making a right

163

noise fucking like pigs in shit and I had to get on with things. The only thing I'd had to eat was an apple and it was way past lunchtime. I looked up and he was staring straight at me from his desk. He tried a smile but it didn't really work, as if he had had stroke and couldn't really control his face. I gave one back and saw the light shine in his eyes. When I looked back, after collecting all my stuff together, he was gone. I felt slightly lost, as I was going to ask him to come for a coffee. What did he know and what was he trying to tell me? Maybe he was just shy. Why did I have to read so much into everything?

The lift was packed, someone had farted, and a bloke with long greasy hair stank while a young girl with a shaved head reeked of cigarettes. Young people of today, hey, they don't wash, or they can't wash. I blame their parents. I wasn't into Freud or that socio-biology stuff but people needed a good start in life, like me. My parents had been strict. All right they had gone too far but it was their choice and, when it came down to it, it was my choice too. When the doors opened Clint was standing there.

'Yasmine, that's your name, right? Sorry to bother you but I need to tell you something, can we go somewhere quiet for a chat?'

As he spoke his eyes burnt right into my soul, as if they were embers from the origin of the universe, his face wouldn't have been out of place on Mount Rushmore. The man in black was cool and had an air about him. I led him to Warhol's, knowing it would be quiet now, all the *Big Brother* wannabe contestants having gone home to dream the same dream of being television stars. Before he sat down he pulled out a chair for me, ever so politely, like a real gentleman, or just a patronising sycophantic old fool, it all depended on how you viewed it. Lisa, the girl behind the counter, gave me a wink and I grinned back. This guy had real deep level charisma, like an Old Testament prophet without the axe to grind, crossed with a hero from some long forgotten Western town like Tombstone.

Fetching the coffees he plonked a file on the table, expecting me to look at it. I flicked through a stack of the A4 sized black and white photographs of Simon and Tamar. There were hundreds of them some so close up you could see their greasy skin. Who was this guy, some kind of pervert? He hadn't even told me his name yet, still trying to be some long lost stranger who rides into town. A lot of the photographs were just boring. I was in some of them and we were just sitting in Simon's car. A lot were of him with a large joint in his mouth. After the fortieth or so they started getting interesting. I took a slurp of coffee, and began to relax into them, trying to read them with more attention, to sense the environment and feeling of the zone depicted. There were twenty or so taken at some festival that looked to be in the countryside, some kind of rally with lots of flag-waving. I got from the photographs leading up to them that they were in a field near a place called Clitheroe that had a castle and was north west of Manchester somewhere, real country bumpkin land.

'Do you get it yet, Yasmine? What Simon did the other day wasn't just play-acting. For him it's for real. They're both trying to become top dogs in the ENP. This is for real.'

Like most people, Yasmine hated appearing thick. She'd never heard of the ENP, but she could take a good guess: The European National Party. It all seemed to fit together now. That's why Tamar was here. And was the baby really Simon's?

'That girl Simon is with, I'll admit it, she's my daughter by my first wife, Amanda. I haven't spoken to either of them since I left, over nine years ago, but I've been keeping track of her, sending them money. Josie went on to marry a neo-Nazi type she met over in Holland, a real head-banging lunatic. He's managed to indoctrinate Tamar and she's done the same to Simon.'

This was getting a bit too weird. First we have rallies, then we have mysterious babies, and now we have neo-Nazis and indoctrination. When were we going to get terrorists, shoe-bombers, nail bombers in Soho pubs, and aliens, I wanted to ask, but I stayed quiet, like a good little girl.

'Sorry, let me tell you who I am, pretty rude of me, I suppose. I've lived on my own for so long I forget normal manners, no excuse though. Reuben Fuertes. I've lived in Manchester for over forty years, but like you people still think I'm a foreigner. My father was Mexican. Your house mates are mixed up with some real lowlifes, you know that?'

After he spat out this final comment Reuben sipped his black coffee and let his revelations sink in. I tried to think of anything Simon had done to give it away but he was a good actor, always camping it up, fun to be around but never really real, whatever that was. Why should I believe this old Mexican freak that had just appeared from nowhere; then again, why shouldn't I? What did he get from making it up? Behind the coolness, he seemed desperate to try and get his daughter out of the group she was involved with and start again. I had to admire him. He was up against something huge.

Going over things I could see that the way Simon just seemed to have plenty of money whenever he needed it was odd for a start. Maybe they were paying him? But how did this involve me? It wasn't that crazy, making a film about an Asian girl being attacked, even if they did broadcast it on the internet for nutters to obsess over. And what about the child they were having together? Don't tell me this was the saviour of the Aryan nation? If it was anything like Tamar then we were all doomed, whether we were Aryan or not.

'It all seems a bit off the wall to be honest. I'm not saying I don't believe you; it's just a bit crazy, that's all. And this Tamar, she's your daughter you say? She doesn't look like you at all. You know they're having a child together.'

For once, Reuben looked away and I waited for his response, which I was not expecting at all.

'Sure, I know, Yasmine, but it's not Simon's. The guy thinks it is his, she's told him that but it's another guy's. A bloke called Sten, she met him at the University of Leiden at some conference on ecology, a tall Dutch bloke who speaks English, Spanish, Serbian and Russian, as well as German and Dutch and French. He's the father, but he doesn't want to know her anymore. Not after, well after what happened.'

He left it hanging there, like someone clinging onto a cliff at the end of a Hitchcock film, the villain pressing down ever so slowly on the tips of his fingers as he desperately holds on, staring at his face in shiny black shoes. Sure, I would ask him what happened. But I could wait. I didn't want to play the little girl in need of help, if that's what he wanted. I could be an enigma just as good as he could be.

27

THE SULTAN

'I thought you'd never show,' said Yasmine, brushing down her skirt and trying not to smile with relief, as Gary kissed her gently on the cheek. She'd been sitting in The Sultan for over half an hour waiting for him, the queue of hungry people getting longer and the management trying to make her feel us unwelcome as possible, asking her every two minutes if she would like to order or have another drink. Snippets of bitchy conversation floated her way, but she was never the one to get paranoid and was able to block the rest of the world out when she could.

'Chris and Buzz had a problem that only I could sort out, now what's this about Simon? I don't want to rub it in, but I always told you the guy was an idiot.'

When Yasmine showed him copies Reuben had made of the photographs Gary grew less cocky. It was impossible to believe that this had been going on under his nose and he knew nothing about it.

'You do need to order now, mister,' barked the harassed waiter, emphasising the mister as if it was an insult.

With that, Gary took her hand and led her out the restaurant, Yasmine throwing down a couple of quid for her drink as they left.

'I need time to think, let's walk.'

Manchester was not as mad as they both had expected, the streets *not* covered in crowds of semi-naked girls, rolling drunks and blokes with bright coloured shirts hanging out of their trousers, but just the odd group of lads and lasses, nothing major. They needed some plan, some way of getting to Simon and finding out what really was going on but they didn't want to give it away. Reuben was onto them, but he was too conspicuous. Perhaps someone Gary knew?

28

ENTERING THE DREAM

There was a Glaswegian lassie, one of the reasons why we taunted her, who worked late at night in the petrol station, selling Rizlas. Mrs Brucciani got a hell of a lot more shit, for being Italian, wearing a moustache and being tight on the chips she dished out. Late in the evening, whole parliaments of crows were pecking at used condoms outside the service station. Lassie, as we called her, had the type of hair that women fought over, those tight red ringlets, natural, falling down like a waterfall to her waist, unfurling so beautifully it made us ashamed to look at them.

The furnace is the rectitude, I muttered to myself, a segment of a novel I had once looked at as I went through the possessions of yet another poor student as we moved across the road in the direction of the river, hunting the skins not of animals but of the paper kind. The ineluctable modality; I never knew what this meant, the word ineluctable with no tangible synonyms, but I could never resist using the phrase, trying to be clever to impress the women, no doubt. There was a friend of mine who had studied language and went to work on antonyms but we had lost touch. I had not met Yasmine yet, who taught me everything. So there we have it, Joyce and Beckett, his nibs, so they call him, they call them so, the soft cheese in the right places, plays and far up and away on the left side of the road the faraway tree and inside the fallen bucket the faces of all the fallen and the race to the centre of the world, the earth should I say, lifted and separated and then divided into private, mostly digitalised mores and the first thought had been felt the moment we leapt to your defence and do not say it was not, and this was it, the dried up eyes, the smashed bones, the skin sinecure with mud or without, the night we attacked the petrol station was a night we will always try to remember, try to remember, try to, Buzz placing his arse on the glass, and all the rest of it.

Like we had fits, and the moment we saw Buzz had diabetes we didn't resent the fact that he had hogged all those drinks for so long and there was his brother Harry who had got into God, studied *The Bible* night after night, day after day, kept on telling us to repent, to find the light, to see the truth, to know God is light, because he says so, on and on, like a tape gone wrong or right, who is to tell, and I find myself being careful what I say because you never know what will get back to the lads.

That night I burst into Yasmine's room, like any other robbery, but this time she was studying the Koran. The room seemed so peaceful, like one of the temples you only see in a dream, almost translucent.

'Sit down over there,' she said gently, not an order or a request just part of the natural order of things.

It was clear to both of us she had been expecting me. I was really stoned, like usual, but could feel her love, if that is the right word. Sweating and feeling like a sheepish fool, I took the steaming peppermint tea and slurped it as if the concoction was my life blood, was the very air we breathe.

'What you reading then?' I uttered like the softest of soft lads.

She held up the cover. I could see it was in Arabic and looked into her black eyes. They were not like pools, more like oceans, far distant oceans that sang and danced to their own tune and the fresh gusts of sea air that moved around their cusp. We'd met before, outside 'Top Man' in the Arndale centre. It must have been about four years ago. I remember thinking then she was the cleverest person I had ever met in my life.

'I'm thinking about doing a PhD in religious studies, feminism and bioethics. It's a long way off, but I'll get there.'

I gulped the tea down now, even though it was still scalding. Why was she telling me all this stuff? She went on about people and theories I had never heard of, about speceism and the idea that we never formulated why humans were superior to other animals, we just assumed. I remembered reading that bit in that book Buzz lent me about mice being in control of things really. Was this what she meant? This all seemed like a test, some kind of human experiment that I could feel I was failing horribly. I was flunking one exam in burglary only to be losing in this other exam. The room was so neat and it smelt so clean, something I just wasn't used to. From next door I could hear *Oasis*, 'Turn Up The Sun'.

'That's Cecil. He's a mature student, about fifty. Thinks he has to try and look cool. It's pathetic really but we try and humour him and not to be too unkind.'

With that she whacked on the wall and it went dead quiet. Cecil, being thrown out for not paying the rent, had replaced Simon. I wanted to kiss her all over. She had such a beautiful face. I wasn't good at controlling my feelings the way most people do. We get so much in the habit of wearing a disguise before others that we eventually appear disguised before ourselves. Then I remembered Buzz would be waiting for the spoils. Could I still manage to steal something when she was not looking?

'I know why you're here. Take this. I don't need it anymore.'

She handed me fifty quid, two twenties and a ten. I wasn't sure if this was a trick, one of those games where if you refuse you keep getting more. But I wasn't thick. I could see she wanted me well out of there and fast. Why hadn't she got on her mobile and rung the police? Something was here between us, I could feel it, sense it in the air, smell it in her hair.

29
THE FUTURE OF FOOTBALL

When I became a teaching assistant I never imagined I would arrange the football matches and then I made Samir the man of the match, even though she was a girl. She had saved a dozen goals, but only let one in. She was in tears when she let her goal in, and like everyone focused on mistakes. I told her she was the man of the match and handed her a tiny plastic cup and the tears ceased. One of the boys who could not play for toffee I made the time keeper. Sometime was for a lick and a promise, the way you have a little wash in my Welsh grandma's language. I was conscious of everything, the sweat and the chest and the hand, yes the hand, I enjoyed all that. Why say so and question it? The world existed, didn't it, you stood apart from it, to a degree you had to.

On the hillside in Sardinia in a dream where the beaches, not the bitches, are the best in the world, we played football in the over-grown graveyard. The priest didn't mind. He told us he had once visited London and had gone to sit in a graveyard to read. To him this was normal, as it is in many cultures around the globe. There was no difference between the living and the dead, that's the way it should be, but the horror story happened. A mourner came and was horrified by him sitting there and told him to get lost and so the beautiful day still remained. As with God, nothing can separate me from the past and the future, only the present the TV was on the blink how could he do that to his family, the Church? And so the argument is, he ended up in a loony bin and found a mission, George Bush and football, the life of Christ, stages of the cross done in such a way that each stage eats at our heart.

There is the Golgotha Goal, with a Goth inside it. The Goth is a woman in a burkha, very freeing, a whole pitch of them, and one of them might be Beckham, we do not know. All we know is that in a room in Morocco, with the windows wide open, a woman is having it

171

with two men in one, and she loves it, yelling for dear mercy, the first or last to cum, we do care, and so the tide turns, all the cum ever shot in the world is the ocean, we came from there, and the island we circum-navigate in our brain, the world, the universe, is one brain, a small one, and we sit within that knitting our sequences, our flesh and bone, over our skeletons, on an album cover, doing it, no need to quote Shakespeare here. Who do we fear, exactly? That is not a question.

A women's football team, group showers, the lights go out, and where is she, nobody knows, not even visible to herself, no blue string, although there is wherever I look, I see blue rope, and hairy beasts, or beasts on a rope, Abraham's son turning into a lamb. That's what she said. Keep the faith, the intensity of incense, the insensitivity of our way of battling sensitivity, and up the front the elaboration given to us. He went to Luton Millwall in a Burkha, they searched him and the police were then done for sexual harassment. In one match of the women she was kicked in the gut, had a miscarriage, abortion, not knowing you are pregnant, the beaver, the question, how tall before you fall, we stopped, the fields smothered with sunflowers to the sky, our essential shapes shadows on the lawns of the mansion house, lying lonely and dormant inside a fridge, inside his Special Brew and Crunchies, in one bedroom a page three model from yesteryear.

For thirty minutes they searched for her on the beach, found her sitting in the back of a car, playing with a dog, whose owners were playing with a kite, while the sun burnt itself. Wotan, that one, they made statues to the famous ones. Let's drink to that. What else is there to do on a Saturday afternoon, drink shout fight, but do you fuck or give one? Should you fuck? Nobody gives a flying one.

Why not let me know where you sit. They discuss the language of the game, and people know it is important but let me tell you one thing, you had trials of course, back in the day, a farthing a week, not a camou-flaged Bentley or some Aston Martin. What are they like? Fit like anyone we know? Of course, let's not think about it, can he play in Trieste, London or Vienna, can she play, once they have had a sex change or once they have had sex. What are the rules exactly?

One had become a copper, and then brought allegations of abuse, or discrimination or trouble with raising an eyebrow; there were plenty of those people, with the great eyebrow raiser in the sky. I must have been about nine, watching Dennis Waterman play in a celebrity football match at my sister's school, Hillside. Wasn't he charged with something, like the rest of them, charged up, like the lunatic on the bus? I am about to eat people who have popped their clogs, and so on and enliven our riches. Keep me from temptation to pull every papa, every page from every holy book, cut it up and splice it together.

What is the passion about? There has to be some reason and some overarching illumination before we treat the foot. They interview folk in cupboards, are we interested? We are filling an opening, you have tried every position, I am willing to bend over backwards. I was told she was the kind of person with nothing there, a Frankenstein of a figure, way up there in the cloud, everything was kept in the cloud, and they could gamble on matches before they began so to speak, I love to hear you speak.

I never wanted to write about football, but I still have the signed photo from Brian Clough–'Be Good Jason!' Is it my most treasured possession? No. We went to a Billy Bragg gig and we got chatting to a guy in a wheelchair who was an English teacher who used to play for Luton Town. At the end of the gig we used him to get to the front of the queue to talk to Billy about working with Muslim community groups. There was a guy totally paralysed, more or less, who was in a wheelchair, one of those electric ones, and what did he do? He wanted his carer to be able to put his condom on for him; apparently they are not allowed. But what if both people are paralysed, from football, violence, drink or birth? Isn't someone going to help?

30

TALKING AT MACHINES

He took his headphones out, and could see better. Took his, or hers, you know what? That old brown football, out there, four of a kind, a windswept moor, the bones of a sheep, or the carcass, and the village played across the country, no boundaries, no tears, no real teams, no audience as all were players back then, no elites and this was the start of theatre that came from religion and never lost its staging. Yes, there is something utterly engaging about all this.

Buddha, fingers in the clouds, goal posts, yes they are, you score, again and again, drugs, women, goals, souls and eternity, through the posts, the pearly gates, that levitate, fallen blossom camomile. The leviathan a monstrous ball that goes round and round the earth, or the earth a football, without a goal and what about the end of the universe? This is the goal people pray for or work for to prevent, the planet where everyone is a Sabutteo player. Awesome times awesome, awesome squared, stuff of awesome.

Dogging in the car-park, streamed live to large screen television in the stadiums, between the action and I hate all those books about football, about fathers and sons, daughters and mums and dads, giving everyone something to do, something to obsess about over the weekend so they don't cause a riot. Derby fans, so 1980s, trashing Cardiff town centre, others arrested for violent crime, forbidden their own clothes and televisions.

'Prison is not a holiday camp,' yells Teresa May the Home Secretary.

'Welcome to Teresa's, never mind the weather, when you come to Teresa's the holiday's forever!'

It is not participating is it, just watching, like the telly or the bars on your cell which you draw, like the first monkey. But you are there. You see the fat gross pig northerner, his shirt off, gut out, bouncing up and down, his nostrilic hairs so long, you can tie them, and he can tie them under his nose.

There have been an enormous number of arenas since the beginning of time, maxima amount, where people became gods, slaves gained their freedom, and the crowds breathed deeply blood.

I am sitting in the family section at Watford, checking my phone, where swearing, or was it breathing, is banned and some complete arse is going on and on about his trip to Rome, or about his mate's trip, I can't make it out, as John Tao appears.

31

WHEN IN ROME

There was something peculiarly laissez-faire about my attitude, James commented, after I mentioned Hermione had single-handedly selected Rome for our summer city break. He knew she was taking a doctorate in Italian, so I don't know why he was shocked.

'It was supposed to be a magical mystery tour, but I found the guide-books in Charlie's rucksack. I thought we were going to Barcelona, a damn foolish guess seeing as she's been there three times already, on mad hen nights, racing around with pink wings on, drunk as a bloody skunk no doubt, male strippers' fluorescent g-strings between her teeth, and all the rest of it.'

I staggered, while James strolled, back into the busy changing rooms, swallowing the heady blend of body odour and Hugo for Men. The match had shattered me, and I wondered why I put myself through this hell once a week. Was it just to boost James' already inflated ego, or did I have a streak in me that loved self-humiliation?

We yanked our gear from our personal lockers, and I felt a moment of bonding. A long mirror at either end offered the ideal opportunity for voyeurism. I surreptitiously watched James go through his toiletry like a Prada model, as he simultaneously cupped his genitals as a way of reassurance.

While he was six foot four, muscular and dark skinned, I was fair, with an ill-defined body, less than five foot six without shoes. Whatever the differences in us physically, we were both excellent at our jobs, and while others had been lost to the wayside, we were here to stay, two of a kind.

Back in the dealing room, I felt far more in control, the excessive exercise loosening my body, my mind now buzzing with numbers and potential deals. James, however, would not leave off his badgering.

'Are you sure you're feeling all right, Rupert old boy, letting a little woman take the decisions for you. I hope you're not losing your touch, hey?'

He barked his jibes ebulliently over his screen, as the whole floor frantically mouthed into phones, simultaneously banging away on keyboards, monkeys composing post-modern versions of *Titus Andronicus*. I refused to proffer him a glance, desperately involved in attempting to decipher the reasons why stocks in JB Holdings had plummeted for the fourth day running, despite my forecasts to the contrary. John Tao, the footballer never out of the paper, had told me to invest here, so I was slightly miffed. The brief rush from the sport had evaporated. I now nursed a nauseous feeling in my lower abdomen, and the jerky nature of the squash had screwed up my dodgy knee again. Was that arrogant vain bastard right; was I really losing my touch?

Escaping dirty old London, on what could be interpreted as an educational trip, part of the process to enlightenment, was the perfect tonic, to leave the stinking office behind, James' annoying puns, and everything associated with that den of rampant iniquity. As we swooped into Roma, cars shimmering on the ground appearing like giant circuit boards, even the suburbs looked possessed with joy, magical.

Rome felt, smelt and appeared like a half-remembered dream, where everything and anything is possible and turns out well; a cornucopia of potential delights. Hermione had selected the flights and destination, the hotel; she had even purchased the Euros. This was our first holiday away from Charlie, who was already two and a half. But it was I who felt like a small boy in the hands of his all-knowing mother.

We both had been working hard and deserved this time away. Over the last year we had been skiing in Austria with friends, where I damaged my left knee, plus there was our timeshare apartment in Florida with Hermione's sister's family, where Hermione suffered severe food poisoning, but none of this was just the two of us. We had lost time to make up, lost lovemaking time, as we had often been too tired, too busy or just too pissed off with each other to even touch, let alone go any further.

The heat in July, the architecture, the temperament, the romance in the atmosphere, the beauty, the language, everything pointed, like the finger of God in that most famous of paintings in the most famous of chapels, to love, so of course, when in Rome . . .

'Prego, you are most welcome, sir, welcome madam,' said the charming man on the doorstep of Hotel Tomasi, as I nearly walked past the small entrance.

We were to stay a stone's throw from the church of Santa Maria Maggiore, originally titled Santa Maria della Neve, of the Snow, the most important church dedicated to Mary in Christendom. According to legend the Virgin Mary appeared on the fourth of August 358 AD to Pope Liberius and John, a patrician of Rome, telling them to build a church. In the morning, miraculously, snow covered the area where they were supposed to build it, despite the time of year.

I was a cradle Catholic, having a Spanish grandmother from Santiago in Northern Spain. Hermione was a convert to the one true faith, hence she was often a fanatic, insisting Charlie go through all the rites and attend a Catholic nursery, but sometimes she held onto her Protestant roots, and placed deeds above faith. She loved telling me about the three hundred Protestant martyrs killed by Catholic Queen Mary at Spitalfields, London. I gloated over telling her about the persecutions of Catholics from the time of Elizabeth over the next one hundred and fifty years and the still latent prejudice in merry old England.

'But it's good to die a martyr for a noble cause, such as one's faith,' she would reply, after Charlie was fast asleep, and we would indulge in bouts of drinking to relieve the tension of work. By the sound of it, her awful PR firm was worse than my lot, but I still envied her ability to shine in any company, her chameleon way of getting people to like her, whoever they were.

We entered the elegant hotel room, absorbed the chilled atmosphere, and stripped simultaneously, knowing full well why we were here. Kissing desperately, I felt so relieved to be alone with Hermione in this darkened icebox.

'Are we allowed to use these things, when in Rome?' Hermione whispered, as she handed me a golden wrapped condom.

I quickly stood, ripped the packet with my teeth, eased the thing on, and snapped the window shutters shut, total darkness swallowing us.

Part of me imagined this was wrong, maybe this act would lead me to hell, that Dante's inferno was lurking in the all-consuming blackness, like a weight, but the mechanical nature of donning the processed plastic alleviated my fear.

We both abandoned ourselves to this moment of forgetting, and went at it hell for leather, if you'll excuse the phrase, the pent up frustrations of the previous months dissipated in this frantic activity.

Rome amazed me, more than I ever could imagine or describe. Shelley, Byron, and Keats had all fallen in love with the city, and you would have to be a Philistine not to see why. After a siesta, we strolled by the Forum, a romantic testament to Rome's past greatness, then over to the famous Coliseum, the largest amphitheatre ever built by the Romans, copied all over the Empire.

Laughing, we watched tourists take photographs of men dressed up like gladiators and Julius Caesar, and at last managed to enter this evocative building, one of the most magnificent on or off the planet. Inside, at the second level, it was easy to envisage the arena, Latin for sand, soaked in the blood of animals and criminals. I imagined them now, knives gouging guilty and innocent eyes, axes cracking skulls, swords buried between shoulder blades, fifty thousand people of Rome roaring at the slaughter, lusting for more. Hermione wanted to take notes for her next essay, but I told her to put her notepad away and just enjoy the moment.

We crossed the city to the Pantheon, the largest single standing dome in the world. Here we indulged in rich chocolate and pistachio ice cream and a bottle of Geographico Chianti, the smoothest wine I have ever tasted. James would be envious, I thought. I even considered texting him! He would probably take it the wrong way, show it round the office, and then where would I be? After this indulgence, we raced back to the hotel for more frantic lovemaking. It was as if these were our last moments on earth, and we both were yearning for final pleasure.

Surfacing in the late evening for a meal in a street-side café, we were serenaded by boys with bongos, receiving many delicacies, 'from the home', as the waiter put it. Behind us a drunken Englishman, who I at first had mistaken for a local because of his dark skin and thick black hair, berated his shattered looking wife, raising his thumb at the waiter constantly for more wine and beer, making me feel ashamed to be his countryman.

Day two of the three-day trip consisted of entering and ascending St Peter's, marvelling at the view of the city, and the gardens that surrounded the Vatican, imagining what it must be like to live in this private world. Inside, hordes of tourists received talks on how the bones of the founding leader of the Holy Roman Church were buried a mere thirty-five feet below the altar, the largest bronze sculpture in the world that could fit into the highest point of the dome. The scale of the church was staggering.

'Are you supposed to drink Holy Water?' asked an American mother with a gaggle of kids wearing hats with solar powered propellers on top, as I filled my plastic bottle from a fountain within the Vatican.

We ate an early lunch, cramming in the mozzarella and caper smothered pizzas and a salad of artichoke, olives and bitingly fresh tomatoes, washed down with more Chianti, and then roamed the streets of Rome, feeling the heat burrow into our bones and thaw the repressed Englishness. This had consumed us over the years; a way of being that had felt necessary just to get on in life, to have a home in dirty old London, to become people worth something.

Hermione was becoming more enlivened by the minute and went on ahead, gabbling to beggars with their plastic bags for shoes, patting dishevelled and flea bitten dogs, becoming the mad woman of Rome, with an authenticity Michelangelo would have admired. This was the greatest education she could have.

We crossed by the Trevi fountain, threw change over our shoulders, and scurried about the small streets, letting fate guide us, and in these unfathomable moments I realised that this was a time of perfect freedom, that anything could be done or said or thought, or even believed.

I came across a large screen in a wall of a baroque building, and admired the incongruity of the ancient meeting the contemporary. Blood-red three-dimensional shapes made up of lines like arteries meta-morphosed into each other, supposedly suggestive of particular feelings, such as deep horror, joy, sadness, the whole gamut of emotions connected to the viewer via sight and touch in technological art. I shouted up ahead and told the disappearing shape of Hermione to wait.

We moved into the cool art gallery and Hermione began a discussion in Italian with the curator, while I hung back, the ignorant tourist, watching her gesticulate wildly as she began to become enthused by the innovative nature of the place. I knew this was perfect for her dissertation on contemporary Italian art.

'This is for you, inner beauty. He's given me outer beauty,' she sniggered, handing me a key with a small blue picture attached, as the eyes of the young curator caressed us.

'We must enter a room and go to the lockers in the centre and find the doors that match our key and feel inside the boxes, but not remove what is there, and this will reveal to us the emotion on the key-ring.'

I felt this was particularly appropriate, given I had deadened my emotions over the years. Could this be my salvation? Quickly, we passed through four corridors, containing minor modern pieces, and found the large room. Nine enormous screens surrounded an onyx box with innumerable doors. Four circular couches were positioned to enable the viewer to watch the screens. We heard footsteps that interrupted our almost religious contemplation.

'I forgot to tell you that the theme today is inner beauty. You see the man's key here will open most of the lockers. Please feel free to stay here as long as you want. I believe this is the best piece of installation art we have had so far in the gallery.'

'Grazie, grazie, grazie,' we both exclaimed simultaneously to the young curator, impressed by his deep enthusiasm for the work.

A pink ball appeared on the first screen and then elongated into a shape that crossed to the next screen, and then moved around all nine, twirling and twisting, with more colours, growing as it went, green and blue and orange being added, all to the accompaniment of moving contemporary classical music. We stayed in this room, chilling out as they say, for what felt like an hour, and then slowly moved out, like an animal, after the kill.

Downstairs a canvas covered in the scribbles of visitors awaited us, plus an invitation.

'You can add something yourself,' suggested another curator, this time a tall American woman, Elizabeth, with waist length streaked hair, an angular face with green knowing eyes, wearing a black velvet dress with straps that crossed over her full breasts. I felt my heart momentarily stop. She was breathtaking.

'I can't draw at all,' laughed Hermione, sketching a small round bumble bee, one of Charlie's favourite things.

Feigning interest in the other exhibition, just to overcome my embarrassment at her beauty, I asked a question and Elizabeth explained to me what was occurring in the pictures.

'Time is battling with space. The artist uses computers to draw the lines, and colours them in using a machine, and tries to show how interiors have a sense of consciousness.'

Really? Sixteen canvasses covered the walls and each was either an empty interior or empty landscape, and each was going for fifteen thousand Euros. She continued along these lines, her eloquence profound. Hermione sat down with an espresso, nursing her sore feet, while I tried to control my excitement.

'If you like the man's paintings, why not come to a party he's holding tonight at Castel di Sant'Angelo, it will be quite exceptional, I can assure you.'

'I would love to, love to,' I stuttered, mopping my brow with an old bandanna I had taken to wearing whilst playing squash, spying Hermione flirting with the waiter, who was now trying to read her palm, gently touching her finger tips.

'You have such delicate fine hands, the hands of nobility,' crooned the Latin lover.

The image of Elizabeth, a post doc fellow at Princeton, stayed with me for the rest of the day, her powerful grace, her vibrant inner beauty and her phenomenal outer exquisiteness.

The Castel was originally structured by Hadrian as a mausoleum, but today the view from here of the sunset over the Vatican made any doubt in the divine mere stupidity. We arrived at the party with the heat of the day still pressing. Many had removed their garments and stood by tables covered in dishes of fruit, pretending to be still fully clothed. Hermione removed her dress, bra and panties as soon as she saw the etiquette. I decided against this, knowing it would be impossible to hide my excitement if I came across the American girl.

'Hi Rupert, Christ, you've still got your clothes on, get them off, come on dude, don't be a square, we're not in boring old England now,' shouted Elizabeth, approaching me with her large breasts bounding now free of their constraints.

'If you insist,' I muttered, still embarrassed by the naked bodies around me and the spicy smell of charged flesh.

Three couples had begun to place ice cubes in interesting places in each other's bodies. As I slipped out of my boxer shorts, and placed my clothes on a stately looking chair, I failed at first to notice that the cubes were not melting.

'What's with the ice cubes, are they fake?' I asked Elizabeth, but she turned to mutter to Hermione, holding her elbow as if to steady my wife, pulling her towards a painting by the same man who had the exhibition, Giuseppe Radolphi. I stood there stark naked and wondered what to do next, desperate to scratch my crotch, realising that this was not entirely appropriate. If only I hadn't given up smoking, the last dregs of my glass of wine splashing down my bare chest. A waiter shot by and I managed to grab another glass, and then heaved a sigh of relief as I knocked the warm fruity liquid back.

Seventy or so people filled the room, with only two now clothed. Short fat men with large bellies that fell over their appendages, young delicate girls with breasts that pointed to the stars, and strong angular-faced Italian women with hair as black as night, all mingled and chatted, discussing art, architecture and love. I peered about the room, aware that I was possibly the only non-Italian speaker there, and felt a desire to run.

Towards the back of the stately room I could just make out a smaller area, dimly lit, shut off from the main room by luxuriously thick ruby curtains slightly ajar, where people appeared engaged in carnal activities. The more I tried to not think about this, the more I found my feet shuffling to this zone, just to take a look, just to be sure I wasn't imagining it.

'I think I'll join you,' said Elizabeth, taking hold of my semi-engorged cock in her left hand, gently pressing her nails into me.

As I entered this segment of the room, everyone stopped moving, moaning, heaving, licking, kissing, touching. This was a moment that felt to me like a brief glimmer of eternity.

'Lie down here,' ordered Elizabeth, pushing me forward as I sat down and moving her perfect form on top of me, her body hair shaven but her long mane brushing over my face as she lowered her neck forward, gently tickling me with the strands across my chest.

'Rupert, you need to relax more, honestly relax man. I've spoken to Hermione, everything's totally cool.'

I jokingly squeezed her rubber-like buttocks with both hands, and felt the slight bump at the bottom of her spine, a magnificent coccyx. My hands slipped further inside her. I felt compelled to glance over at Hermione, who was in the corner of the room with the waiter from the gallery.

She was moaning louder than anyone else, as if she was on stage, trying to project her voice into the street for those who had no ticket for the performance. For a brief moment, to hold my climax, I mulled the paintings we had observed, the empty rooms, the people-free land-scapes, and wondered what would inspire such lack of inspiration in the artist. Before I took a job in the City I myself had aspirations to go to art-college, a dream of joining the Royal Academy, but my father had just laughed in my spotty face.

'Don't be such a damn pansy, Rupert,' he had said when I was eighteen, waving his index finger at me, 'It must be your mother's fault for giving you such a wet name. Christ, you didn't get it from me, that's for sure.'

A loud screech rammed into my eardrum, like a car alarm gone berserk, skewering my momentarily slipped brain. The creature on top of me went into spasms, jerking like a washing machine out of control, then morphed into the inner mechanisms of a machine, an exposed circuit board.

The smell of whirring metal filled my nostrils and lungs. Something had short-circuited and skeletons of machines lay all around me, the bodies now absent, while Hermione's moaning became louder, honking like the sound of migrating Canada geese.

'Don't stop, don't stop,' I heard her cry in both English and Italian.

Glancing over I could see a metal object thrusting itself into her, a blur of metal out of control.

I tried hard to free myself from the machine, but the weight of the object was too much, pressing me down powerfully into the frozen marble floor. Small crackles of circuit boards filled the room with pungent smoke. Green eyes had shrivelled to silicone and there was absolutely nothing I could do. The shutters in the room began to ease back automatically and St Peter's appeared, the sun slipping behind the dome.

For a brief moment orange and blue and black coalesced. There seemed to be a face on the giant half egg mounted with a golden ball and cross, a leering smile that looked like a cross between my work colleague James and the man I had once called uncle, the person who originally got me my job in the City. The sky was a pure sheet of steel.

I could feel my hips now being crushed by the dense machine on top of me, the incessant screeching like a strangled bird, and something gnawing at the end of my penis like the teeth of a demented rat.

'Bring me some more Chianti,' I felt like yelling, but my mouth felt tied, my jaws clamped. I wanted to blank it all out, but the more I tried, the more I felt the intense pain in my groin.

'Science needs rules, Rupert, my boy,' came a fatherly voice from the window, 'but art is free flowing, hence so dangerous.'

These were the final words I heard, as I managed to free myself from the machine, sliding out across the floor, stumbling, and making it to the window.

There was a wide ledge that I needed to avoid, so I jumped, springing as if from a diving board, my arms outreached, expecting to be taken up on the heavy currents of the late evening air.

I was now an angel, but I could not fly. The only place I could go was down. The machines were left inside rumbling mechanically, holding onto my tethered wings, pumping faster, and faster.

As I fell to the stone pavement I remembered the day my father, a biologist, told me about the birds and bees, the way in which we are programmed to find the nectar.

'Whatever the cost, we must gain the honey,' he used to mutter, from behind a large book, never allowing us to read the content of his eyes, the colour of his irises matching that of his thoughts.

'Don't stop, please, please don't stop, please, please, don't stop, please don't stop ever,' yelled Hermione, her accent now like a Speak and Spell machine.

In the corner I could see John Tao, the famous footballer; was he human?

I did not stop, plummeting through the ancient cracked stone, tumbling into the regions we pray do not exist, for all eternity.

32

DON'T CUM A-KNOCKING

Spooney came to Le Clinique and asked for more hair, stolen by a grandmother, you get what you pay for. I became a woman to get more sex, simple as that. It's not that I had always wanted to be a woman. As a man I was always on the hunt for fresh meat, but it was hard. Not my dick, the actual hunt. People thought I was a pervert, as well as being repellent. I tried to wash, I washed all the time, but I couldn't get rid of the smell. Now I'm a woman, you know what I love best? It's hearing that bed-board banging against the wall, being really pounded. I'm a road and they're a pneumatic drill making it flat, so other vehicles can travel on me, and underneath the tarmac? Well, you know the M6 was filled with millions of pulped copies of Mills and Boon. It turns a lot of blokes on to know I was once a man, and I don't hide it or pretend I'm now a total woman. I don't see a difference to be honest. It's pretty obvious really I was once a 'man'. I'm so not deluded. I know I'm a right dog. But blokes will fuck anything, won't they? Usually women are fussier and I think that's what Stephen Fry was getting at, but then he got pummelled by so-called feminists, as if he was saying women were naturally not into sex and men were. That wasn't the point at all. He was basically saying women are more selective, which is a compliment, isn't it, and biologically correct. Men are driven to impregnate everyone, but women must be more careful, that need for the best sperm of course.

I try and have sex with a different man every week. It keeps things all nice and fresh, you need fresh meat, and it keeps me feeling young and sane, the variety I mean. And it makes me personally feel safe, deep down. You might think this was dangerous, how can you trust all these people to be intimate with them, but it's the opposite. As I say it keeps me safe. I don't really have to get personal, do I, go into the details about myself establish a long term commitment, where we have to explore

186

ourselves mentally and spiritually as well as physically? It's physical, so it reminds me I'm human, and anyway it can be spiritual and mental just seeing someone once. I don't get lonely. Funny I have to tell you that. I just thought you might be judging my behaviour, thinking I am looking for love through all these people but never finding it, but I respect myself enough to know I'm doing the right thing for me.

I have regular lovers and friends as well. If you're with the same person it can get really mechanical, machine-like, you're both behaving ritual-istically, which is human I know, but it's also so robotic, like you're not even there. This might be what you're looking for–transcendence–and OK it might get deeper, but it can become stereotypical, and remind you that you may have no autonomy. That's why people are afraid of robots, or cyborgs, as they remind people how stereotypical they are and how autonomy may be fake. What I like about what I do is that each time it is intense, each time I am reminded about who I am and who the other person is, as if I'm reborn each time, if that makes sense. I think I'm being more honest than those who opt for the known. I'm always seeking the unknown, exploring, searching, like a pirate for hidden treasure. If you're always following the map, you only ever see the map.

I put on some perfume, but I don't wash that often. The skussy smell can be a turn on. I know a lot of men like sloppy seconds, or thirds. They can eat out of my pussy if they want. It's well made, I'm proud of it. In this respect I am like a cyborg I suppose, a more advanced being. I didn't want to go through the two year psychiatric assessment in the UK, so I went to Bangkok. This was a service to England as well, to the NHS. The fifty thousand the state would have spent on my op can now go to a cancer patient. Bangkok was great. I banged my cock as hard as I could before the op. I know you'd like some juicy details, but I won't go there, not for now anyway. Sometimes I miss my balls, slapping against someone's arse. But now it's good to more fully feel someone else's balls, slapping against mine. You lose some, you gain so many more. It's like that cartoon. A little boy is showing a girl his penis and he says: look I've got one of these. The little girl says: yes, but look, I have one of these, and with one of these I can get as many of those I want.

I love balls. They are so real and yet so intangible. Dunking the biscuit; you know that? We are all happy, so nobody else can judge. I still go to mass, say prayers to Mary. I think she liked me as a man, but she loves me more as a woman. I can understand her more. The pressure she faced from men, from what seemed like the masculine God who demanded here to have a child. I sense there was some resistance there, like Jesus who didn't want to be crucified, but it's been written to suggest she was totally in agreement, and subservient. I still don't get why Joseph agree to separate from her before they were betrothed if she was pregnant. Why does that make him so noble? I serve on the altar, what we call an Extraordinary Minister. I hand out the flesh and blood. If ever the priest didn't show I could take the mass, but I couldn't bless the bread and wine, just use the stuff in the tabernacle. I like the ritual. The priest wears what looks like a dress, as well as a dog collar which is a bit kinky. I'm not campaigning for women priests, or gay marriage. A lot of my best friends do. The thing is about the church they say it is for everyone but it does have its own rules. If you want to be in the club you have to abide by the rules, don't you? Or you shape it to your own beliefs. As we evolve institutions evolve.

33

WE LOVE TO HATE YOU

If I had the wings of a sparrow, if I had the wings of a dove and wait for it, I would shit on the bastards below, below, pull back, pull back pull back my foreskin for me, for me. The crowd, they were one, alone, singing songs of hatred out of love. For the first half they were on form, meaning they were clearly visible doing something, not that they had form. They might have done. Certainly some people in the crowd did. But now, despite their numbers, it was as if they didn't exist. They were swallowed whole in their own light blue, a wave of blue light unconsciousness, and the heavy draw of the waves feeding back and forward. They're walking straight back into the supermarket's own brand primordial soup, waving a basil leaf. We played a game, back in my childhood days. You know those blue ropes you see hanging like lifeless limbs on trees all around the country. Well it had nothing to do with them, nothing to do with tying people up, for vicious sex, or suicide, for little or big deaths. Nope.

If I say wet the biscuit, you should know what I mean. Us lads at school stood around a cookie, with our cocks out and we masturbated. The last one to cum ate the cookie. And the guy who ate it the one time I took part didn't really mind. He'd already tasted a lot of it. Mine included. So to him it was a delightful treat. But he couldn't show this to the crowd, could he? Remember back in those days any showing of feeling was frowned upon. We'd come out of a war, where things were thought best hidden, kept under the carpet. Not like today, when everyone tells all and sundry about their inner feelings. In a way I can see it as a more honest and genuine time. Your feelings showed, but in your actions, in your body and your features. They didn't come out merely in words, words, words, which can get distorted and might have been mangled, and been dishonest anyway.

So the great apes had smaller testicles than man, and had to impregnate numerous females, and early female humans would have had sex with many men. They would need to have scored lots of goals, and if they had an orgasm it would have been more likely they get impregnated. So the roar of the crowd causes the goal, the whole stadium, the one body, trembling with delight.

There were plenty of people at the match, but not watching the match, not really making a sound, but did it matter? Their presence influenced the game, their warmth, the power they generated to those around them. Their trembling lip, their dribbling, it all counted. Whether the trembling and dribbling was from someone locked in a wheelchair, or free on the pitch, for the eyes of the crowd were on them. They had forgotten to wear each other, unwell. Open your eyes, and sing to me.

34
GOD'S DOGS

They had put a doggy bag, not the food type, half way out of the bin. A sign, and there was a Goth girl, all over the place, with smudge mascara and stinking armpits, and a girl with brown leggings on who looked like she'd just washed her hair. She was smoking. He enjoyed it. She was small. The back of her pants were saggy. Did she have any knickers on? Maybe she didn't know. Didn't know that the back of her leggings were saggy, and whether she had any pants on her not. She didn't seem aware. But she was aware that he was trying to hide his I-need-to-fuck-you look and by doing so was giving it away. The return of the repressed; whenever we try hard to hide things they come back to bite us on the neck. When he'd asked his woman last night where she wanted it he got no reply: was it in a blender, in a box to look after? Not everyman worried about having his cock cut off, it was unnatural. Perhaps partly that was what circumcision is all about. Forget the desert and keeping it clean, or being part of the tribe, it was an attempt to overcome the innate fear. And there was the boy with trousers so low down he couldn't walk. And yes we all knew that this was prison fashion, so people could get in and out faster, not in and out of prison of course because with trousers like that you'd be shuffling over the wall for a year, but fuck each other up the arse faster. But it stopped him from walking properly. Maybe this was a pretty good thing. We all went too fast these days, steaming around. For John his career was over way before it began. He wasn't going to sit talking shit on a couch, or be a manager. He just couldn't face it. The suits, the ties, and the endless shaking of hands, and the legs blurring on the bright green pitch; he had enough of it. He wanted to get back into science, maybe not criminality, maybe look at genetics. What made us a man or a woman, or a good athlete? The pitch was beautiful, a dream, a sea of green. Why did people have to spoil it, as they spoilt

191

everything else? There was the dream of the fast car to do what exactly? One of the spoils of playing well: to murder, maim. How many had died in Vietnam, eight hundred thousand, wasn't it? And two million Americans had died on the road, in car accidents, let along the numbers maimed. The car was worshipped, sex was worshipped, and death was worshipped, and football was worshipped, soccer, call it what you will. What was it about football? We wanted to belong, feel part of a tribe, and anything could happen on the pitch. That's if it wasn't fixed.

The doggy bag was still there, when he left the stadium. He'd heard that in some suburban nightmare the council had the lovely idea of painting dog shit pink, just to bring it to people's awareness. Paint it pink, to make the boys wink. A kind of shit pride: we all battled with dog shit, every day, real or imaginary.

Who were these people who preferred animals to real friends, or was it practice for the real thing, when massaging the anal glands of their pet pouch seemed more innocent, allowable, or getting an erection from a cat sitting on your lap was much less noticeable. Who was anyone to take this relationship away from them? What made this relationship lower or higher than any other? To judge would be to prescribe and dictate what the best form of relationship was and this wasn't right, was it, because the relationship existed in and of itself and those outside of the relationship just could not know.

35

DIG OUT YOUR HOLE

My first review was of Jules Verne's *Journey to the Centre of the Earth*. My teacher gave me a B and corrected the title. I used the title from the cover of the book I had, but it was American, and being an English snob he hated this. The book could be a metaphor for all books that take you into a dark and dangerous world, they let you understand the regions we seldom know are there, or want to go to but are secretly pulled back to. And now, all I can think about is whether a man's anus is significantly different, and I was going to say more dangerous, than a woman's. Why should it be? The pink flesh, that poem by Craig Raine, making it all so beautiful, but he wasn't the first, was he? Allen Ginsberg got their first. I like to think when women shit they don't really go for it, for some reason. I suppose, I believe, at every turn, men are more violent. And it's true isn't it, they are? Think of all the rapes and wars. So even, when defecating, men are having a little fight with the beast that is battling to stay within, and a fight is on. When having sex men would just prefer to shove it in, that's it, right. Some people only shit in a public toilet. It gives them greater satisfaction. Hitler liked to watch women crapping on a glass table while he lay beneath it. According to his driver he had the odd temper, but never ate the carpet. You can use the word crapping, it appears on *The Simpsons*. When I was about seven I found a pack of cards my friend's dad had that had pictures on of people pissing on each other. I must have been the warmth of it that was part of the pleasure. A friend told me how she would put her hand in the toilet after taking a crap to feel her stool. What was she looking for? Maybe I should answer her. They used to test the king's stools and diarise his activities in this area, so unconsciously perhaps she was just trying to examine her own health. What if she had found something, what would she have said? The Dirty Protests in Northern Ireland had involved those on hunger strike in the cells, smearing their excrement on the walls. Life, and who we are, is contained and encapsulated in what we keep and what we give away; how we negotiate defecation in all its forms. In what holes will be buried what we see as the important elements. It is in these decisions that we carve our very existence. Whether we want to make music in the shape of a square, or want to define the painting of a flag as a flag, with the form being the content. The act can be a message that is meaning in and of itself. As a child we give these presents to our parents, we give them our meanings, and they are proud and woe betide anyone who tries to remove this narrative.

36

TO PARIS WITH HATE

It was wonderful, that hour of repose, before the match, when you drift into a world of sounds, senses and smells that take you away from the moment and back to the moment, and back again, like the waves of the ocean. I had decided to listen to the radio, but then was disgusted by the flow entering my holes in my head, a penetration I could have done without. Instead of turning off the radio, I turned it up. There was some sketch show on about a right idiot of an old man who was ringing a man called Miquel. You've got to realise that this itself is funny, given *Fawlty Towers*. Miscommunication and people deliberately locked into their own perspective, that's what is funny, but that's the state of the world, isn't it? The man's partner picked up the phone, a bit unrealistic, I know, given landlines are a thing of the past, but we'll forgive that. The joke was the old man takes the woman answering the phone as a woman, but then states it could be a castrato. He corrects himself, allows the possibility. Anything could be possible. The humour was in him, an old traditional man, even considering this. He knows that sex changes take place and even suggests this might be someone who has had one, perhaps. It's also in the notion that someone, everyone, is deceiving him, having their balls cuts off to get a lower voice, the charlatan! As if this was the only reason to have this done and his outrage at this is what is supposed to be funny. We know this from the canned laughter, and inside the can, as well as kosher ham, might be the sliced off balls. And what is supposed to be really funny is the way he says castrato, in an ignorant way, so we are laughing at the old, the ignorant, the prejudiced, the fanciful and the working class poor arrogant bastard. The cunt. It all works. With the radio off again the world was different. There was still penetration, deep penetration, with the engorged lips sucking the dick in, so the plunger is complete. I tried to block out the cars blurting

195

along the foreign streets, everything foreign, even friends, the sirens, the panting of the whores under the bridges, and in the rooms along my corridor, the fellaheen. These were the sounds that were spray-painted across the canvas of my mind, ejaculated, immortal, and although the shapes were already instilled there, genetically, they failed to dictate. In the Seine creatures were developing that were evolving into forms that might one day send e-mails and then devolve back into the waters, taking their electronic commands with them. You are never free. Freedom is a delusion. To seek freedom is a delusion; the prison of your skin. I had no real or unreal sense of time, or space in this moment, before millions of eyes devoured me, watching my every move, but not really seeing me, just seeing their pre-programmed picture of me, which was reassuring.

37

LOVE HANDLES EVERYTHING

What can you hold onto these days? Pull your knickers up, why don't you, and make us all a cup of tea will you, love, and bacon sarnies, or we can put a few miles on your clock, you've been around the block, so a few more won't matter will it now, darling? A few more Hail Marys is all you want, but you might as well be saying buy one get two three, the Holy Trinity. The universe is a noctary, it dreams who we are, and God holds the universe like an acorn. Are you saying only God knows the truth about you, the real truth. Is that what you're saying, that without conception some truth comes around, so God is born without male human intervention only with the spirit of God. The thing is, Mary, there is always chaos with engorgement. The one who everyone sees as the greatest mother, how do they know exactly? That she found herself pregnant and it was God who had impregnated her, and she did not complain. Is that the sign of a good mother, a good woman, someone who doesn't complain? They assume a lot, but that's what faith is, isn't it, accepting what others may find preposterous. I find it weird how a woman would get pregnant by God but just say it's true. Then Jesus isn't really a man is he, and all that he went through on the cross doesn't really matter. Of course paradoxes do happen. Someone can be a man and a God. We go back to the definition of what it is to be human.

If someone is made in a test tube they can still be a human. It's not how you are made, where you came from, but how you come to be, or are becoming human. So it is the process itself. That's what's important. And people confuse being human from being humane. Who is the Marian figure that appears to people on the ocean, Stella Maris, the Queen of the Sea, of the Stars? The Devil Woman in the Book of the Apocalypse with the stars of the universe crashing around her head? We have quarks between atoms, and there is scope for invention, and if we want to see the virgin we can see the virgin. She calls to us, she needs us, and we need her. You know that film when Terry fucks the mother, the father, the daughter, and then your man, his cock was so damn beautiful, and I don't mean elegant. I didn't like the thought of five willies up her, so they fitted like a glove, but I've seen the video of two cocks up her. I was interested in the position of the men, how they did get their members in the same hole. The kid, the son of a bitch, first hitched her skirt up, then a lift, with his finger probing. He saw a statue, a mystical statue, on the dash of the car, a statue for protection, not Mary, but St Christopher, probably. He was about to show the driver, but the driver shot him. He was a paranoid cop, and had been dealing with angry people, all day. Self-defence, you may say. He thought the guy was pulling out his gun, stroking the truth. Travelling high speed in another the lift, holding each other, the names, the handles, they discussed their tutor who was always asking the girls out for drinks, as if there was something wrong with that. He knew they were thirsty for hot cum down the back of their throat and through their eyeballs. Maybe he was lonely, although you can come to love loneliness like a gift from God. And, he was all over her, so she said, she said so. She wished. They all wished for someone to be all over them in every respect, hands here and there, dicks here there and everywhere, and it's all over she said, and the car accident and the sex change, the teacher.

They are at the party, you can find them there if you look, and they are arguing.

'I don't like you.'

'You don't even know me.'

'I mean if I did like you.'

'You mean if you did know me.'

'No, get a grip on yourself.'

'I mean if you liked me you would know me.'

'What's like got to do with it?'

'You like whatever you want to like, you don't like me.'

'And love?'

'Same difference, there is only one love, and that has nothing to do with you.'

'I'm outside of love?'

'Yes, that's why you can see it.'

'Take me there, will you?'

38
JUST TWEET IT

A mother bought some sperm off the internet from a Dutch site, and then got her fourteen year old adopted daughter to impregnate herself. When she was seventeen she gave birth.

'No breast feeding, we don't want that attachment stuff!' yelled the grandma, who wanted the baby all for herself.

Social services got a whiff of it, grandma goes down for five years. Someone felt like some wine, another like a cigarette, another felt like sharing that a girl of fourteen had been raped by twenty two men. Numbers, statistics, and the Fibonacci sequence, all the code of the universe in a petal, and an uncle of mine in his nineties was a recluse, more or less. When my mother tried to see him he would lock himself away. He played Sudoku all day. I mean, I can't even understand it.

Bingo is enough for me. Fill in the gaps, and mind the gap. And he shops for himself. He likes to do his own thing, a freedom in everyone you know dying off. When his wife, my Aunty Sheila, was alive she used to bang on all the time, an incessant yacking, like a high pitched drill, usually celebrity tittle-tattle, absolute gob-shite. She was a journalist, felt she was in or on the scene, know what I mean. To give her some dues, she did have great blonde hair, staggered up, not a beehive, just stacked up, and she was interesting.

'I've got to interview the band, The Fleece, have you heard of them?'

She meant The Police. As a journalist, accuracy was not a top priority. One thing I remember she said that did make sense was that Proust's *Remembrance of All Things Past* was the greatest thing ever written and if you did anything in your life you had to read it, which makes me think of roads in France, with trees. She said this as we were coming into a chav type carvery in Borehamwood in the 1980s. I know Professor Chav thinks using that term is as bad as using the N word, but I like it. I'm proud of being half chavy myself, that's why I play for the team I play for.

So back to the tweet, they do create a kind of cloud of knowing, a form of Godliness. People can pretend what they want, but isn't that what people do anyway, put on masks, then the mask is how they become authentic? Is it wrong for a white man to pretend he's a black man, or a black man to pretend he's a white man, or can't we just do as we please, do we really have to always worry about who or what we offend? There was a story today about a preacher in America who had been campaigning so hard about atrocities in a country nobody knew existed who had a nervous breakdown and was found naked, breaking into cars and masturbating. The question is, was he really masturbating or just trying to make his penis look larger so he could feel more comfortable with being naked, that's the question. Same with the charity work.

The same thing happened to the actor Keith Allen, who was on a show working as an electrician, and one day he decided he'd had enough, took all his clothes off at the side of the stage but was concerned about the size of his knob so starting playing with himself and the girls doing the act saw him and the audience saw their shocked faces. This was an odd threesome. Perhaps there was more to it than meets the eye. Let's get behind it. The show was a Max Bygraves' nightmare of a show, probably celebrating jolly old England, because if you don't you're shot, and how everyone came together.

But let's take things back a bit.

Take Peter Pan for example, where we have the money shot scene of topless mermaids fighting with Wendy for his love. You can't get better than this.

'Did you miss me?' asks one, and the dog is dressed as an old woman, with the crocodile, the *vagina dentate*, attempting to eat Captain Hook, the hook symbolic of castration, his wig identifying him as a cross-dresser, the sea the unconscious. It is also so blatantly obvious. He is desperate to capture Peter Pan, like the mermaids, Pan, the name the Greek God, is his desire, and he is desperate to contain his desire and yet the desire, weirdly, is childhood innocence. What this proves is Freud's polymorphous perversity, and it wasn't Cardiff town centre smashed up by Derby fans, but Blackpool. The connection being Freud made a trip to Blackpool, as he had a brother in Manchester.

'Welcome to the Freud archive,' barks a man in black framed glasses so big they need a passport all of their own.

'Each item stored here is a part of your unconscious and tells us about your desires for your mother. Clearly, you latch onto unattainable people because you were never fully loved as a child and just repeat this as an adult and this is damaging.'

Mist brewed up today and the skies then were filled with an endless timeless spaceless blue that sat on the horizon, her eyes when making love full of the depths of the universe and beyond that lap-dissolved. That decision that always creeps up on the ant hill and stamps down, allowing for them to disperse as Darwin received the letter that showed someone had developed his theory simultaneously. He wanted to be first, everyone wants to be first, but he was a gentleman. Today, we would just have burnt the letter or deleted the e-mail and pretended we never read it. Darwin was a friend of mine, I mean a literary friend. His life seemed to mimic my own, with children dying so young.

39

THE EYE OF THE CAMERA

And when they saw the man, if that's what he was, beating the other man, if that is what he was, with a stick, if that is what he was, they were sorry for it. They were sorry that their eyes had witnessed it and thus made it truthful. They could tear their eyes out or shed one two or three tears, over such eventualities. A taxi driver had told them never to look left or right. Never to contemplate bare legs, or buttocks, or anything other than that which had been accepted, for it was forbidden to explore. And who knows, you might enter the Mersey Tunnel and never get out again. From time immemorial people had witness it all, and the creatures that circled God, with eyes all over them, was it the same in China, where cameras were being placed everywhere so all could be controlled from a central control room, and the person watching, what about him, was he there, or did this space become a place that itself was controlled by that which it was observing? Freedom could only be gained by such subservience. Let the state intervene, or a company, or a combination of the two, and whatever individual existence you experience could be removed. And then you could thank them, for you would never need to feel lonely, and if you forgot something or wanted to relive something you could rewind, just to check things out. And you did this anyway, didn't you? The funny thing was you used to do more of it, go over what you'd said or done. The Jesuits have a term for it. The Examen, or more fully The Examen of Consciousness. At the end of the day you are supposed to go through the events of the day and see what pulled you away from God, or, thinking positively now, what pulled you back to God. The grace of God was higher than any law or any self-willing activity, so in this sense it was kosher. The cameras functioned in this way, purging people from any unsavoury activity, and then the images could be pored over, as the Jesuits pore over the images of their day. And in this way, find what led them astray. This all made sense. What was needed was irrefutable proof, and the image had a higher status than truth. Give me a penis that talks and a vagina that photographs, give me everything, and inside we will send a camera, so it views the internal organs of your body. Down your penis, it looks good, the glistening pink flesh, a tunnel to a better world. Better than any wet spunk filled vagina? In the orgy scene, bodies were strewn at specific angles, which made it cinematically more appealing.

40

BLOW UP DOLL

I was in the room, you know the one; we've all been there, the one without any doors or windows, performing gratuitously and flirtatiously with a blow up doll by the name of Priscilla. Well, that's what she told me, but she could have been an invention, a concoction or a breath of fresh air. I was so shocked when I watched the film *E.T.* again with my young daughter and the boy in the film, Elliot, calls his older brother penis breath. Maybe I'm just a prude. What I don't like is going to a restaurant in China Town and being asked to pay before the meal. What if I don't like the meal? It might be like throwing up into a sock. Sorry, there was no blow up doll, so don't get all sweaty, no need to turn your heart beat up. It was with some head of department, but it might as well have been a blow up doll because it was all role play, as if everything isn't. A bit presumptuous that. I'm not saying I wanted to blow them up with dynamite, or anything, but it had really crossed my mind viciously. Not just like a ball of straw going down the middle of an abandoned town, but more like a jumbo jet landing in your eye. That's the way it had crossed my mind, dissected it, the scalpel, the trowel of a surrealist painter in Sicily contemplating where Plato had thought, crossing his thoughts off one by one. My mind was a giant noughts and crosses game, spinning and revolving madly, one of the ones you get in playgrounds, large wooden bricks in a frame spinning insanely. Blow up a football stadium, one two three, that's an order, say a command, command it, from above. Instead of forcing that dirty angel face between your legs get them to help you with this mission, we all need help, don't we, and if we don't then that's our problem, too much of a loner, dangerous I would say. Real results come through group think, and group action. Think about those idiots who got caught trying to set fire to their shoes on planes, rubbish like that, they didn't have a clue. Think about blowing up a football stadium, having it, large. Not in your mind but in reality, a solid supporter. A prime target, or prime suspect, I would say. So many clubs had recently gone out of business, into liquidation as if everyone had just stepped into a blender, and just before the huge stinking shit hit the insanely revolving fans the directors had been creaming off their cut, feathering their nests to buy their own blow up dolls, and yachts, and villas in the sun, and planets, and universes, and space stations, and tickets on intergalactic trips or just a shared in some seedy club in London, Birmingham, Manchester or Glasgow, and lines of coke the length of the equator or the distance to the moon and back.

Why hadn't anyone thought of it before? The idea lying dormant, sleeping in a hotel room with the shutters shut and the mini-bar empty and the girl slipping out the room before dawn, waiting to flip over, the salamander of destruction. Forget the Bradford fire, or Hillsborough, the stabbings and the crimes and the drugs and cunts and fuckers, this was fifty five thousand people, running for their lives, screaming for their souls if you believe in such things, not for their clubs or flags or religions, trampling over young children, scrambling out of the stadium, before the next explosion and the next, blind, deaf, legs and arms blown off. Perhaps they had but we would never know about it, would we, not ever, because that level of fear is too bad for business, although the police make a great deal of money out of these events, so the more the potential fear the more overtime. At the same time, privatisation makes this kind of security really good business; get in there, my son. Get your spunk right up that dirty hole of a business. But how dangerous is it all? All these people focused on the match, obsessed, absorbed and fanatic. If you've ever been to a match you'd know how crazy that sounds. Nobody watches the match. They fiddle with their phone, watch the giant screens scattered around the stadium, and think about the scores at another match. They think about getting another pint after the match, or whether they need to go to the loo now or later, or who to shag and when to shag it. They study the programme, the form, in depth and they learn everything about the players they didn't want to forget, but no matter how hard they try then always forget mostly everything. Something like false memory syndrome; who are these people with fast legs and quick heads and sharp elbows: homo foot erectus. This sounds almost erotic, as if they should be posing like statues in the gardens of Italian villas. The fans are cramming obsessively for their exams, an oral. Which one can be the most eloquent in the pub afterwards, after the pints and the crisps, the roar and the piss and the smoke? Everything's a competition, whether it's a Tuesday or Friday evening kickoff, or a lazy Saturday afternoon—all a competition. There's nothing like Saturday afternoon though, the moment in the week where you are most free from work, from family, from anything that might hold you back. So no wonder the men, and the women, and the children, roar with delight, returning to our deep dinosaur roots. The ball could be the equivalent of an egg they need to score with, the whole game a re-enactment of a fertility ritual, getting one in for the team, striking one home, making sure the tribe gets up, the league that is, the survival of the fittest. Supporters compel the ball, the sperm, on. Someone might run on the pitch with a knife and cut the ball looking for the yoke, and smear it all over their body, naked. And then rub themselves all over a canvas, and this can be hung in Tate Modern, and then fetch millions, and the cash can be used to buy a golden rabbit and people will then be sold tickets to try and find the rabbit, and guidance will be given, weekly radio talk shows, and internet television shows, and we shall see how much money is raised by the rabbit, the great rabbit that talks to no one but sees everything.

There's been a study done about learning in crowds. You just cannot do it. So this blow up doll is sitting there and I have to pretend she works for me, corporate training they call it. The whole thing is a disgrace, a real disgrace. One woman was kicking off about it.

'These people are a bunch of jokers,' she yelled.

'I'm not doing this anymore, you can't do this to us.'

She stamped out of the place, without batting an eyelid.

We call decamped in Starbucks and realised if we didn't go back we might not keep our jobs as it was part of our contracts to do the training.

41

DEAD SEX

On the hill, overlooking the bay, sat a Methodist Church. I was on an adventure with my nephew, who was eight at the time. We were looking for snacks at the local supermarket and had drifted away from the pack. I only had a five percent share in the club so didn't really give a fuck. Jumbo was the largest shareholder with forty percent. I think he did it to try and pull the women. He'd heard about that guy who owned a club in Ibiza who every night, as regular as clockwork, would shag his wife live on stage, in front of the crowd, as they were going nuts to Fat Boy Slim. My dad was right, that was a stupid name. The couple in question used to wear masks, but I suppose it turned them on. At least all the fanny farts and the squelching were drowned out by the beats. The thing is though, watching others have sex, be it pornography or live, is just not interesting, even if you're out of your head on drugs or drink, or about to have sex yourself. Some people who never got a taste might find it a turn on, the closest they could get to the real thing. The thing was though this was the owner, so whatever he did you had to approve, just to get close to the centre of power. So back to my little adventure, I was trying to explain to my nephew the differences between the denominations, and why there were so many different brands of Christianity. I'd seen on *Russia Today* that in certain parts of Russia there is only one brand of Cola, or anything else, and as soon as they start to introduce a choice people get unhappy. Choice does not bring happiness. We might like to think it does, particularly when it comes down to sex and partners, but that's a particularly Western idea. Anyway, I explained that John Wesley tried to get Christians to go back to their origins and tried to form a particularly methodical way of worshipping and meeting, hence the name. 'Method of Death Church,' came his reply, which I thought was entertaining and worth remembering to tell his mother, my sister. The beach, with its dark sand, looked ominous. I was thinking of the tsunami that had swallowed part of Japan, and how, as if from nowhere, everything you held to be normal, and by normal I mean sacred, disappear in a breath. The Methodist Church on the hill was abandoned, but maybe the prayers lingered, along with the breath of God, whispering somewhere in the gallery on the second floor. There were high arched windows, and the building had about two acres of grounds, still reasonably well kept. The idea came to me fast. Why not buy this place, turn it into a retreat, away from all the beach apartments and bars, somewhere relaxing to really meditate, paint, read and write. This had to be the future.

42

THE BIG GIVE AWAY

All sides like Watford and Crystal Palace and those higher or lower good game good game, or heaven or hell in a Dante style way gave away tickets and had a disabled area, as if it was a special enclosure for another species of people or for animals. A day out at the races, but instead of seeing slick beasts running around a track, you watched shaven haven folk running around a pitch, seemingly randomly, unless they'd received a bung like cricketers, that is. Lord Sugar and Clough, the former claiming the latter met people in transport cafés and accepted bungs for transfers. It made me feel sick, really, if I'm honest, which is seldom. For honesty is what they ask for under torture and it is never the truth and why the need for it?

I could pick up a copy of James Joyce's *Ulysses* of course in an honest book shop, down a lane in Dublin, a shop that stinks of mould and rot and bad guts, and randomly go through it for key lines, words and phrases of significance, that might stand out, trigger words and hooks, but would you then think that this was a particular enclosure of language, for example, a compound? Importantly, language is always enclosed in artificiality, a type of bubble wrap that is the brain, and that's the beauty of it me old fruit, the playground of words spinning round and round and nobody knows where it will stop.

You, of course, might be like that mean kid who hogs the swing or the slide of the roundabout and says it is yours and nobody else can go anywhere near it. It's like the man who thinks he pronounces words correctly, or the north is superior to the south, or vice versa. He's got a big chip on his shoulder and he's going to use it to fry others, if not chop them into little pieces, dice them into carrots. Back to the compound, the accessibility was one aspect, for sure, but often it had nothing to do with this because they put wheel chairs right at the back, and sometimes rightfully so, so people could get a better view of the game, and it wasn't just about the people in wheelchairs, it was about those with them, taking care of them. Everyone was in on it, so to be in on it you had to be out of it, and it had a lot to do with health and safety. People were really hung up on that.

Taking care of them; we all know that has another meaning if you're a gangster. My sneaky feeling was that they wanted to put everyone who was so-called different into one compound so other people didn't have to mix with them, didn't have to look at them, smell them, feel their presence or be disturbed by them. Nothing should interrupt the beautiful game. That was an interesting approach wasn't it. Given football was supposed to be a game that got everyone together, that transcended race and class, if not sexuality, gender and disability.

The great game was slow to catch up.

43
CLEAN IT OUT

Before he got in to porn, as a regular star in films, he wasn't sure how they kept all the anuses clean. And bleaching, well that was way out of line. He wasn't certain he wanted to do any rimming with anything too dirty. He'd been kicked out the club for not producing the goods and he'd already been getting offers. People had always commented on his cock. They'd seen it swinging around in his shorts and wanted to see more of it. It wasn't that fat, just long. Even from a distance it looked silky, even pretty, one might say. He was happy to oblige, felt he was doing them all a favour. Girls didn't often go on about wanting to see more pornography. Usually they were saying how demeaning it was for women, but with him it was different. They wanted to see his cock, something they had only ever dreamt of. It was like that game, one potato, two potato, and with him they could play three potato more.

Women had had tattoos of his cock entering their arses and vaginas, and it made him proud to think that really he, or at least his cock, had become an icon, like David Beckham. Pornography was a physical sport, like football, after all. You had to keep it up, you have to perform for the cameras, and if you shot too soon and missed you were sent off and a substitute came on.

He got to do a shoot in LA, but he did have limits. He wouldn't do it with other guys, or go on any reality television shows. There was no point going totally public about what he was up to. His grandmother wouldn't approve. And part of the allure of it surely was that it was still kept slightly under wraps. OK, it was everywhere and people could instantly access the stuff on their phones, but they still had to search for it, it wasn't plastered on cereal packets, not yet anyway.

Tenants beer when he was a teenager had girls on the cans, but this was somehow so seventies. Everything was so in your face these days, all mystery had been removed. The secret was to keep people guessing until the final minute. Would he come in their arse or shoot his load in their face? Keep them guessing. The money shot they called it. He felt slightly sorry for the women. They had to be covered in the stuff–all the cum. Of course, some loved it, rubbing the sticky stuff all over their tits and never washing, or so it seemed to him. Some believed it was good for their skin, rejuvenating. So when it came to cramming his stiff rod up a tight anus he wasn't too keen as it didn't seem natural, even if what was natural was debatable. But, if the money was good, like all of us, he would do anything. He had a sister who was dying if she didn't get his money, and he had never taken out any insurance when he was playing, which was kind of illegal, so he never wanted to go on about it too much.

44

ON THE RAMPAGE

She has a Hugo Boss pinstripe on, and she's part of the Inter City Firm. Five pound tickets to watch Arsenal Ladies versus Everton Ladies at Borehamwood FC haven't materialised yet, and nobody is complaining about it. She's out for violence, for blood, and she's looking, hunting, for the Chelsea Head Hunters. She's renamed them the Chelsea Giving Head Hunters. She takes men down back alleys, undoes their pants bites their cocks off. We've all done it, in our dreams. They deserve it of course. She's in there, like a rat up a drain pipe, in there. There will be blood. The score doesn't really matter. If they win, they are over the moon and need to do some damage, go on the rampage. If they lose they need to take it out. Whatever happens, trouble commences, especially if it's a draw. There's nothing worse than watching a match where nothing happens. You feel your life's slipped away and you've nothing to show for it. Sad but true, but we can't always go with the Tao, with the flow, and say the destination is the journey, as we really want results, we want something outside of us to show us that things are meaningful. Maybe that's where we have it all wrong. It needs to come from inside, not from shelling out a meaningful amount of money and expecting something meaningful. So I'm down this alleyway, and he's got his trousers down. It smells like he hasn't washed for a month. He's not a Chelsea fan. He's Wolves for God's sake. He's got their stupid top on, and he's as pissed as they come. A few reports about someone biting cocks have appeared, but he's too pissed to stop me. Then a group of seven blokes materialises at the head of the alley way. I can see the shape of a Stanley knife. They're tooled up and look for business. Seven blokes, and a pissed mate of theirs being attacked, and me, a woman on a mission in a Hugo Boss suit: if you could out on a bet now would the odds be obvious? This feels a bit like garbage in and garbage out, down the back alley, their mate an old sack that I'm punting. I can hear the expletives, but I'm not listening. There's nowhere to run, I've got to take them on, take them down, one after the other. Eliminate them, maybe two at a time. I've got a handmade shank, and some acid that burns the skin like nothing on earth. If I can make a proper semi-circle with the bottle across them I can blind six of them in one foul swoop. Then I can put the boot in. My heel cracking their faces, splintering the bone, ringing Dr Gunter the anatomist, pumping their bodies full of red plastic, so we can see their arteries and put them on display, turning every corridor into a gallery and museum so every child and every senior citizen will visit them, so they become passage ways to enlightenment.

45
RIMMING OR FISTING

There were lots of ladies running about with their twitter accounts on their sleeves, waiting to be fingered or poked or raped, something that filled the gap. Mind the gap. Listen, guys, or ladies for that matter, if someone says *no* they mean *no*. It isn't a come on. Some blokes think it is a type of tease. I found all these books on football and porn sites, rammed them all together with a lot of penetration and engorgement, and lo and behold got a result. It's a real shame that women appear in what is known as scenes, by that read a porn film, and then their vaginas and anuses get wider and wider, then they have to spend any money they have made on getting plastic surgery. Match this with a boob job and you see how they get in debt worse than a student, but this is what keeps the capitalist system going, isn't it?

John Lennon had a whole flat in the Dakota building for his fur coats to be kept at the correct temperature, and Elizabeth Taylor designed one for Richard Burton that cost the same as a house at the time. If we love until it hurts there is no more hurt only love. So, this my friends is the answer to everything, pain and hurt. Why do you think people spend time in the big house having the words love and hate tattooed on their fists? This really should be love and hurt, but they are too proud, too puffed up with their own pride to use the word hurt. Hurt is close to suffering and sacrifice. Some hurt themselves on purpose, you know. It helps them feel alive. Some hurt others on purpose. It helps them feel alive. And some people try and numb themselves from the pain. They do anything to escape it, even so-called healthy things like work. When you're travelling around the country watching your team there is a healthy type of masochism. You're shelling out on tickets, transport, beers, and everything else. You're depleting yourself, so you can be filled with what? Like a bird being shafted. You're being shafted

215

alright, but you feel it's all reasonable, all part of the process and you will hand this feeling on to your son and his son and his son, until the past and the future unite. Hindsight, where you went wrong, foresight where you are going wrong, and insight, how far off you've been. You know nothing about all three of these. All you know is the game. You've read about it all before as well, the firm and the tribe, we can't just call it a gang of hooligans with knives, cock replacements of course. Nothing like it. The coppers are missing out these days. No one hard enough to kick in. They've all gone to seed, they've got mortgages on estates like Organ Hall in Borehamwood, and town-houses made of red brick with gardens for the pit-bull and a mock fountain. They've BMWs in the garage, along with porn films. They get drunk, do all manners of misdemeanours, but the days of kicking the shit out of someone just because he's a northern cunt are over.

Or are they? Isn't that what the government's doing, but by other means? Removing the benefits from those who can't get work, and the disabled, kicking them when they are down, worse than using fists? We all became working class Torries, remember that; owning shit was supposed to make us happy. But it made us more possessive, more focused on the box, more aware of wars going on around the globe that we couldn't stop. We knew our taxes were being spent like this, and what were we supposed to do, other than buy a pint or ten down the Crown, leer at the eastern European barmaid then dream about banging her over the bar while the manager's Alsatian licked its lips, sending dildos in the post to some posh cunt at work, just to watch him as he opens the box and laughs awkwardly and then tries by any means possible to work out who sent it to him. Back at Organ Hall you are making a move on the girls who've moved in next door.

'Alright, darling, I've seen you in films, haven't I?'

I'm having a fag in the garden, which is a mess. Keep meaning to go to B and Q with all those other cunts and buy loads shit which looks good for a week then fucks up again.

'You shouldn't be watching those kind of films,' titters the fat one, tits like barrels moving up and down creating some kind of tsunami, and I wouldn't mind her over a barrel.

'Let me know if you want me to join in at all, if you're looking for a length. I've got some stamina and experience, and I'm not shy of cameras.'

216

Barrel tits smiles at me, and I can't work out if it's a come on, or sarcastic. She's got my number. Knows my sort, meets blokes like me round the back of the boozer every night of the week. Funny thing is, no bloke seems to mind that her pussy is now so big she may as well not even be there, like fucking a load of candy floss. I suppose it's the dyed blonde hair, the stench of perfume, the sexiness of it all.

'Why don't you come over later and fix our plumbing,' laughs a little girl who could be barrel's daughter.

I take the final draw on my fag, wishing it was a spliff, and just nod as if I couldn't give a fuck. Inside the results are on. All these twats in suits lined up on Sky as if they are about to cum if a bloke gets a corner. It's a joke. Some results interest me. I remember going to this shit places and giving a kicking or getting a kicking. The wife's out tonight, at bingo or something. I don't bother asking these days. We never speak about anything other than the kids. Jensen's seven, and slightly backward they say, Melissa's twelve and good at everything but gets bullied for it by the thicker kids. That's what it's like round here. Borehamwood. People speak like they're from the east end because their ancestors were. By the time the kids are asleep it's well after nine. I've got a pizza in the oven, as it's healthier than the ones you get delivered; less salt. You would have thought the ones that deliver would want you to live longer to buy more pizzas, but maybe they've got a deal going with the funeral parlours and the church. Remember that guy somewhere near Preston who pretended his dad was still alive and claimed his benefits for him. The sick fucker used to make his daughter walk past her granddad's dead body every day for about six months. When the son finally went to jail his brother said the sentence wasn't long enough. It's raining badly, but I still pop into the garden for a crafty fag, or is it a cheeky one? Cheeky sounds something more like a bird would say. Next door the three birds that have moved in are dancing naked in the rain. You wouldn't believe it. Sounds like some fantasy shit I'm making up. It's not. And it's proper dancing. They're in training. They do some cabaret act. It's all the rage now. Turning sex into art and back again; people pay more for this shit than going to some live sex act. When you're watching a real sex show you might as well just be doing the real thing. This is more like art. They know I'm watching, and having an audience just makes it better for them. It's like those pandas in zoos. People say they don't fuck because they have an audience. Fuck off. They're animals.

They're not aware of having an audience. It's humans that are so god damn paranoid that we've invented God to keep an eye on our every thought, and cameras rammed everywhere, just in case someone misses something.

46

TENERIFE OR BUST

I pulled the cheeks back, as requested. I was vulnerable yet hard, vulva pulsating, a spaceship if paradise is half as nice, and all that. Who was I kidding? My palm was stinging, red raw, as was her sweet white ass. Did she not feel anything anymore, was I the only person in the world with any feelings anymore, was that it? So she had read Virginia Woolf, had lived on a farm in France, knew the name of every punk band. But she didn't know what to do with it, you dig? She was the girl in the lift, with the lovely lush faux fur jacket on, the interesting glasses, and the mauve and black hair, the cool boots, and the skin that wasn't just porcelain, it was Elizabeth Taylor as she always should have stayed. That's the way it is, and the funny thing was I was pretty certain none of it was real. Her, my emotions, anything, it was all a diversion, a total waste of time, but a good one at that.

'Keep the faith, brother.'

Letters from the graffiti juggled in my bloodshot eyes. I couldn't wait until daylight, until the moment I could hit the Blood Mary's, and pretend to be sobering up, when I was really entering the zone of no return. I'd never been so fucking pissed in my existence. Perhaps nobody had in the whole fucked up existence of the world. I'm not going to apologies for swearing, I mean you said I could be as open as I wanted to be. I had started over a week ago on the old booze; just a cheeky double gin after lunch with Jim, a neighbour who'd lived out here for over twenty years, maybe you know him, then a bottle of local red with Jose, the head green-keeper and a close mate, and I had never looked back.

'What have I lost? What the fuck have I lost?' I kept on repeating this mantra like a mad man, until nobody would listen. I knew I looked like a prat who had totally lost the plot, gone loco and bamboo and berko all at the same time. When you are in such a state you don't really think of what others think of you, like when someone dies, which actually might not be a bad thing. I think people worry about others too much, don't you? My mind was like a rat in a trap and I couldn't see a way out, an obsession going round and round and round. This was all I could think about, a worm gnawing at my soul so deeply that nothing else mattered.

Would anything else ever matter?

47

THE LOSS

I couldn't really tell anymore. When you lose something so huge you start to doubt whether you really had it in the first place. My legs were broken when playing for Villa, but it was nothing like this. I could go over our life together and re-arrange it like a jigsaw to fit any pattern I wanted. Nothing mattered–you tell yourself all sorts of lies. I had given everything up for her, and now this. Everything and nothing perhaps; all I knew was that the heat was now intense and there was no cloud on Teide. It was all burnt up, like me. Sanity you could never lose out here, on the equator, as nobody really had it.

From my adobe-white villa next to Fairways Apartments at Amarilla Golf and Country Club, I could view the central mountain Teide, a dormant dragon quietly smoking. I too was smoking now, yet again, but not so quietly. I had given up just over seven years ago. I'd also given up my family twelve years ago, at what seemed like her insistence, but it was probably due to my own guilt.

Back then it seemed like something I had to do, to prove to her that she was really the only one I had ever really wanted, that she was my dream, not just my dream woman, but my dream, and my reality and I now had to live my dream and everything else was really bullshit, that I did love her without question, that it wasn't all a fantasy, that it wasn't all a game at all that we were both playing, that I wasn't using her. Now it didn't matter. Nothing mattered. And who had used who? My kids would be fifteen and seventeen now. I'd come out here to find work and give them everything I'd never had, but then I hadn't seen them in ten years. Their mother refused to let me go near them.

And all for what, exactly? Her well-thumbed fat novels, lying around the kitchen, were offensive. They resembled her in their obesity. In their multiple pages lay the history of her life on the island, the smudges of sun cream and chocolate, the lazy hours spent lounging in the garden, or by the communal pool, listening to Moby and other meaningless music that had become a soundtrack to a billion other consumers' lives. I didn't want to think about whether she'd been fucking the pool man, the gardener, and every Tom, Dick and Harry. Some might say it was a fantasy of mine; you might say that? We had a loyalty that went way beyond that anyway. I wasn't the sort of guy who acted on jealousy anymore, even though I was insanely jealous, so jealous I used to go into a rage if she spoke with anyone. Sure, I had my fantasy fears, like any other man, but I blocked them out with work and drink and other fantasies; nobody likes to face the truth, do they? I suppose her reference to porn when we first met had given the game away but I was too dumb and love struck at the time. She'd given me a lobotomy just by looking at me, and I never really recovered.

Trash, the whole lot just trash, containing stories about stupid people for stupid people—I wouldn't even take them down the book exchange at the local bar, The 19th Hole, just throw them in the bin without recycling them. Why should I inflict them on others, even in a different form? I needed to take control, pronto. Even if people wanted this stuff they should be protected from it. It was time for a total clear out, big style, all her dresses, pathetic knick-knacks, every tiny piece of crap she had accumulated over the years. All her Pilates DVDs, and all the knock-off gear, the detritus of over a decade in the sun, everything had to go. I didn't even care if some of this was from her grandparents, knowing that she treasured it because they had been so close, knowing they had basically raised her, or that this stuff was the only link she had to her past. Why should I care? That was her problem now. The photographs of her family—burn the fucking lot, and be damned, just like I too was now damned, absolutely, no going back now.

A song lyric, something from our duets together in the clubs around the island—first you've got to make it then you've got to break it till it falls apart, my broken heart. At three-thirty in the morning, after twelve double vodkas, a vat of wine and barrel of beer, I would be emotional, and she would love it.

'You look just like a little boy,' she'd say, staring deep into my eyes, stealing them and my soul, that I'd protected until now from everyone else my whole life, and she managed to take it all with her cat-eyes as we made love, deep sweet love, her heavenly juices flowing, and she'd tell me sweetly to cum totally, totally, deeply inside her, within her. I was putty in her hands. I was the twat more like. At that moment of what I had thought was true love I truly hated myself, more than anyone had ever hated them self for being so fucking vulnerable, for truly loving her, completely without any reservation.

I wasn't sure with her whether everything was an act or whether she realised how much power she had over me but I had no way of holding back. And I didn't care in the end. For years I had been someone or something else, an observer, watching other peoples' lives, but somehow, in her own way, she had managed to reach me. And I fucking hated her for this. There was something deep inside of me begging me to destroy, deeper than the desire to do monkey chants had been on the terraces at Elstree and Borehamwood FC twenty-five years ago with the Barmy Army when I was a kid basically with a bunch of nutters leading me on, way before I was an entertainer, a crooner, swapping a hooligan lifestyle for a cabaret lifestyle blessed by the endless sun.

We had sung together, made love together, got drunk together, abused people together, abused each other together, we'd been Siamese twins together, lived and breathed each other, and now I was having nothing, absolutely nothing, to do with her. For me she was a stain in the apartment that had to be removed, every little piece of her, forensically. I became a scientist removing the spore of a creature or biological culture that may destroy the planet if it is not destroyed first. I began to scrub the toilet. The white porcelain confronted me in all its brightness like an accusation, a perverted work of art. There were invisible fragments of her shit, I was sure of it, positive. She had sat there, changing her tampons, like Queen Boadicea, smoking Dunhill International extravagantly, like a film goddess, ranting on the bloody phone, doing god knows what. She wasn't one of those people that hid in the toilet, like it was a room that could transport her anywhere, but she did make a meal of it, like with everything.

She had a way of turning everything into a drama, and, if I was really honest, that had been part of her I loved so damn much it hurt, and why I had been such a fucking fool. She was a film-star of sorts, she turned heads with her gorgeous figure and face, every head and I mean *every* head, man, woman, and beast, and when she walked into a bar men wanted her, women wanted her, they couldn't think of anything else. I knew what this was like, because I had once been one of these men and for me, as well as many other men, it had been love at first sight, a huge tornado of love that I'd never experienced before or since.

My jealousy drove both of us crazy, but for all this time, as far as I knew, she'd been loyal, despite my fears and fantasies. I had to hold on to that. I had to eliminate her there was no choice, every trace of her–it was the only way. Her three pictures of dogs playing pool were supposed to be ironic. I used to ignore them when he took a shit but now they seemed to mock me. I hated them. I took a knife to all three of them then added them to the fire next to the barbeque in the garden. The fire felt good, even with the smoke in my eyes. Pain was significant. The tears and cough seemed genuine.

Neighbours left him to it and knew it could be worse. They wouldn't complain. That was one of the things I liked about this place on the edge of the world. You never really understood it until you lived here a few years and became truly part of the place. There was a different kind of respect than people had back in England. Everyone here kept themselves to themselves, like in England, but it wasn't due to fear or paranoia or just a lack of concern. When someone was way out of hand, a tourist too pissed for his own good, a bloke beating up a woman, then that was different. A few residents would sort them out. But resident would never turn against resident. It was an unwritten law and it was sacrosanct. Nobody had gone up Teide to receive the commandments about it–'Thou Shalt Not Be A Cunt' but it felt like they had.

In fact it was more powerful this way. They all knew the rules, even if they weren't even written on paper. As soon as they got written down there was something dodgy about them, people wanted lawyers and religious people to argue about what they really meant, turning this way and that with the truth. But you can't argue with the truth. This wasn't a cult, just a group of people that supported each other or left each other alone when necessary. And that was that.

Mother had used powerful chemicals back in the day to clean her curling-tongs, so from an early age I knew a thing or two about deep cleaning. I was turning Villa Acanto into a spotless temple to nada, to absolute zero, an existentialist's dream palace, to eliminate the past as far as possible. Pour away her favourite booze and all the other tipples they had enjoyed together or chuck away her favourite food? No, that would be a waste, but once it was gone it wouldn't be replenished either. I sat on the sofa and knocked back a quick Sambuca. I loved the way this spirit hit the brain and made things look different, for a moment anyway. There was something beautiful about the process of removing every trace of the past, not cleansing and cathartic, but more spiritual.

My parents were both quite religious, with my mum being a reader at the local Baptist church and my dad being an elder. I could take it or leave it as a kid, but I liked Sunday school as a few nice girls attended. I remembered the story from *The Bible* about Jesus' parents going to the temple after he was born, and offering a dove to Simeon because they were so poor they couldn't afford a larger creature for sacrifice. The story was strange. I understand the connections. Later Jesus was to be the sacrifice so nobody had to make all these animal sacrifices anymore. And the fact that his parents were poor was symbolic. I wasn't sure about what I thought about Mary being so young and Joseph so old. Today that might be frowned upon, but a lot of successful men traded their wives in frequently for a younger model. It seemed to be part of a culture of status symbols.

A more interesting question I thought about as a kid was who cleaned the temple and was there a word for it? There may have been in the Aramaic, but they hadn't bothered to translate this into the English bible. This was how I felt, like that poor sod who had to clean the temple day in day out, after some horrendous blood sacrifice, sheep skins or pigeon entrails everywhere. Perhaps they saw it as a privilege. I stared at the bed, what used to be our love nest, and it made me feel nauseous. She had this way of scratching herself when drunk which was annoying, even when I still loved her. But no matter how I tried, I couldn't help but feel sadness and regret for the end of all the magical experiences that had taken place here. I was never as experienced as her, but it didn't matter. She loved being tied up, loved tying me up, and loved riding me, wildly shaking herself all over me.

Jesus, it pissed me off this was now over. Over the years I'd got used to it, her whole act in bed, her shtick. It was like she had learnt what I liked instinctively and did the business, as if going through a ritual. I liked to think it was all for me but I was deluded. The ritual was like the act in the temple, spiritual and animalistic. But the fact that it was known didn't ever make it less exciting. It disturbed me to the marrow that it was over. And what was I supposed to do with the bed, burn the mattress? That would create havoc, the smoke bellowing out across the neighbourhood like a huge symbol of devastation. I could dump it, let some other cunt deal with it, but it had cost a fortune. It was one of those mattresses that shaped itself to your body. Maybe her body shape was still indented in it. I couldn't bear to think about it; it made me feel like topping myself.

The more I tried to not think about it the more I did. All those years of being not just close but one and the same, like twins. We had a certain telepathy, we were that close. I felt the raw agony in the pit of my stomach, like a chasm had been opened up. Drinking would not solve anything. At the same time I was getting an unusual clarity right at this moment, as if someone had cut open my head and a jet of air-conditioned air was being spurted in, like on a plane, and this was firing directly into my brain. All the sluggishness I had felt for years vanished.

Our life of singing in bars meant we usually went to bed about five or six in the morning, after fucking and drinking wore us out, rising at one or two in the afternoon and going back on the sauce. With her gone, I was following a routine that matched most of the rest of civilisation; in bed by eleven and up at seven. I went for long walks by the sea, chatting to neighbours more than I had ever done, got a dog. I rang up old friends and family in Tenerife and in England and all round the world, like Australia, people I hadn't spoken to in years. I didn't care what they thought of me and anyway they were really pleased to hear from me.

'You're lucky to be shot of her, that old slag, she was leading you to an early grave, mate, I know you really loved her, and she was gorgeous and everything, but it's time to move on,' was the normal response.

My spirits lifted up and, like the long blue skies that normally sat across the South Tenerife coast, they seemed like they would stay raised up forever.

48

UNNATURAL PURITY

Her unnaturally white skin was so pure, so light and delicate, it was as if the sun was an over-protective father and once saw her as too precious for his rays so he could never touch her. The skin was translucent and at the same time you never wanted to stop kissing it. Her lips were so rich I wanted to have her there and then, as she stood. You can't help who you fall in love with. I realise that now. For years I believed in free will but that's just nonsense.

I'd been on the island about a month and this was my first gig, The Lounge Bar, not a bad joint, opposite Casablanca's at the far end of Amarilla, which sat between the airport and Los Christianos. The place only a few of the regulars came in, but as I was just starting out here I didn't mind at all, it gave me the chance to build my confidence up and my reputation. They'd done some good promotion, so I was pleased about that, even if it hadn't really paid off in the number of punters. My fee was fixed, a paltry sixty-five euros.

I'd started with a few well-known Andy Williams numbers, a guy called Jed with a goatee and a seedy history sorting out the backing track on a huge Casio organ, and it seemed to be going well. Like any musician, I would slip in some of my own original work between the well-known tracks, and sell my CDs, so I had to go through this tragic routine first. I was conscious of what I was doing, liked the irony of it all. To me it was art, but it was always commerce first.

'Red golden nights, when we were one . . .' and then she appeared in the room and stood by the bar, just staring.

From that moment on everything changed. Not just for me. For everyone in the room, you could sense it. The atmosphere shifted, something magical was happening, for once in this what was really a crappy dive of a bar a major event was occurring. I tried to resist my feelings but I was being pulled in, there was no way I could resist. I don't believe in astrology, or anything like this, but I could tell this was an epiphany, a real moment I had been waiting for. Something deep down inside me broke and tore. It was like the years of holding things back inside just couldn't be sustained anymore. I didn't know what was happening to me only that this woman, this totally amazing woman, who had appeared from nowhere, had caused it.

Miraculously, I continued singing after a little stumble, a kind of pregnant pause I could build into the theatricality of the act, so that nobody really noticed. At that moment it didn't matter what was coming out of my mouth. Most of the men, and many of the women, were too enamoured by her to even think about me. I did my best to hold the note at the end of the song and put some real emotion into it, as if I was performing just for her.

'What can I get you, darling? A double vodka and tonic, is it?'

Jesus, get a grip, telepathy already–come on, man, stop looking at her lovely breasts. How I longed to caress and kiss her gorgeous breast. Everything about her was speaking to me. She was fulfilling the living incarnation of what I wanted in another. How did she know? Stupid of me, she could have just asked anyone, the barman Tony, or one of the regulars. But whatever, she was slick, a real charmer who knew not only how to work a room but to rule a room.

She had an enormous cat-like smile that made me want to be with her and do whatever she demanded, and beautiful black hair that rested on her shoulders. Why was a model like this in a dump like this? A tight black and purple velvet dress hugged her perfect figure and her tasteful silver jewellery made her look so good, it sounds like a cliché but it is true: she was a fucking goddess.

I'm not that good with words, singing is my game. That's the best way I can put it, a fucking goddess. I'm usually a geezer, one for the birds and the lads, and with a lot of gab in me, a lot of mouth, plenty of the verbal. But for the first time in years I was literally tongue tied, I must have come across as a right Muppet. We took our drinks onto the veranda and she offered me a Dunhill.

'We could make a fortune doing this, you and me. It's like pornography.'

Did she say pornography?

'What?' I managed to choke.

'Pornography. Don't try and fake shock, Jason, I can tell you're the kind of bloke who's watched a lot of it. You've probably been addicted on occasions, right? It deadens you I know, kills the soul. But what I'm getting at is that people love to see a couple pretending they are in love on stage, performing, singing all their old favourites. It gives them hope. Better than religion. And you're good, you're really good.'

Despite being what I thought was a hard man, I was blushing in the dark, drawing hard on my smoke, watching the moon and stars in the cloudless sky, finding Orion's Belt, the Big Dipper, the Plough and the Bear, and trying not to stare at her as I knew just a glance would give me a huge erection. She was that sexy. Jesus, I can't begin to tell you how sexy. Take your fantasy of the perfect woman, and then think about meeting her in the flesh and finding out that not only does she look incredible, she has this way about her, something indescribable.

Unbelievable, right? But believe it, this night it was happening to me, and not only that but she wanted to go into business with me, becoming my partner so that's how committed she was, right away.

'And I'm not so bad at singing either,' she added.

I don't know if I want to say here that we made love that night all night long, until we were both soaked with sweat, and she screamed again and again, that she told me I was the greatest lover she had ever known. I mean it's not really any of your business, is it? If you want to know what it's like screwing the sexiest woman alive then make an effort, go out and do it yourself, don't just read about it here, you fucking pervert.

We didn't do it, if you must know. Feel any better? Less envious, or did you want all the juicy details, the way she kept on pushing my hands down onto her sweet arse, and made me hold it tight, the way she kissed my ears, and did anything and everything. But it was better than sex. We took four bottles of wine down to the seafront and sat drinking and talking until the sun rose, planning our life together.

The water had never looked so powerful, and nothing was more beautiful than it was that night. I wasn't really into women at that time. I don't mean I was gay. I mean I was just a bit wary of them and wanted a break, so I wasn't looking for love and it wasn't a good time. This was one of the reasons I'd come out here in the first place as things had gone wrong with a previous relationship. But that night I was even more flustered. She was just too sexy. You know how some women are too beautiful it's intimidating you don't feel up to it. I didn't feel good enough, not worthy to be with her, inferior if you must know. People try and find equality but deep down each one knows there's always bit of a competition as to who is in charge, who is being looked after, who really needs the other more.

When I looked back at her she was gone. Had it all been a hoax? I knew I wasn't that mad. OK, I had a drink problem, who didn't? It would be a problem if you didn't have a problem because then all your demons would appear, the inner critic would start to really put the boot in. The next thing I heard was a splash. I spied her pile of clothes on a rock, her knickers sitting there, and yes, she did wear knickers, perched, shall I say, resting there. As the waves lapped, the moon shone on her underwear. Many men would have gone insane at this. Maybe picked them up and sniffed them, certainly jumped in the water and tried to have sex with her in the waves.

I can't begin to tell you what those knickers did to me.

They are weird things, knickers, or panties, I hope you'll agree. Some of course are way too big; they look as if they could have helped Columbus discover America. Others are a piece of string, more like a tail, that could easily disappear up your crack. Like with everything, you need to have a happy medium and it is difficult, at the same time not be too boring. It sounds like I'm a total pervert. I'm not at all, I'm a real nice guy, trust me, and in fact it's the opposite. Most of us go around noticing very little, just oblivious to it all. I'm not blaming people or claiming I'm superior. It's just I noticed all the panties when I collected my laundry once a week, so I'm a bit of an expert, see; the same faded underwear seem to carry a distinct history, a secret history. Imagine being that underwear, sitting there. Maybe that's too much for anyone to imagine. Like an idiot I just watched as she swam, battering the waves, as if she'd been in training. She wasn't inviting me in, and I wasn't going in. I could sense this was something sacred between her and the sea and I would spoil it if I interfered. At one point I saw a man sitting on a rock, and thought it was a night fisherman, but it was only a shadow, a trick of the night.

We kissed ever so gently as we finally went to bed, separately I must add, neither of us were that easy, not then anyway, with the morning's German golfers trundling by in their ridiculous outfits, the sprinklers already having done their business, moistening the fairways, wetting the greens, spitting out the precious fluid. I collapsed on my dusty bed that morning and shut my eyes and only thought of her, how amazing she was, how lucky I was, what things we would do together. I could not have wished for anything better. I never doubted then what was happening. She was all I saw. And for the next twelve years she was all I saw; nobody and nothing else mattered. I know I sound like a fool, an idiot. Other people put their energy into their jobs, families or wider projects, like saving the planet or at least some kind of charity work. They do it because they want to, because it makes them feel good. And then others are just selfish. What motivates what we do deep down? I haven't answered that one yet, but I'm trying.

49
ALL THAT IS SOLID

We'd been together for over twelve years when she disappeared. I thought it had to involve someone else. It always does, doesn't it? This wasn't like that girl disappearing in Portugal or that one in England who was found to be hidden by her actual family. I was jealous and I was weak, and I had always feared abandonment, a textbook case you might say; but it is my theory that what you can imagine always comes true. Throughout my distant learning courses in psychology and psychotherapy I had studied areas such as synchronicity and the way people manufacture fatalism. My worst fear had come true of course. It always does. If we put our energy into even thinking something will happen then it will; good or bad, it's always how you see it, even after an event–change your thoughts and you change your world. Yes OK, don't look like that, I know it sounds like new age mumbo jumbo but there is a lot of truth in this. We were both too old to start a family together but it didn't stop me having fantasies about it. As you know, I never really got to see anything of my kids growing up and it wasn't unusual to be an older father. And then she was gone.

I had my small practice now, seeing regular clients for treatment and my own supervisor, before I met you that is, as I think you know. It's weird the way it all works. They didn't like the way I had changed from being a Borehamwood hooligan, fully-fledged member of the Barmy Army, worshipping John Tao and all the other overpaid tribal warriors, into a cabaret singer doing a double act with the most beautiful girl on the island, into a therapist and counsellor. The three faces of man. Nobody here likes change, nobody anywhere really likes change, and they don't like it when others get further up the food chain. I realised a long time ago that it isn't basic jealousy; not everyone feels jealousy but everyone feels something when someone else is showing them up. It makes them feel like they should be doing better, that they shouldn't be where they are when really they are stuck, all of them. Whether they came out here to run a business or not, they were always escaping something, usually themselves, and of course wherever we go we take the weather with us.

That night we first met, I said I watched her swim naked in the moonlight. You like romantic stories; who doesn't! If you know anything about the sea, and coast around Amarilla you'll know that's a lie, or a very tall tale. Even during the day I've watched helicopters circling exactly in this spot, searching in vain for the corpse of sailors. So at night to dive in, unless you're a mermaid, would be certain death. I'd like to say we made love all night long on the soft green under the myriad stars, the Big Dipper, caressed by the silvery fingers of the moonlight, and awoke up to the soporific sound of sprinklers, and the faraway barks and echoes of abandoned dogs. I'd like to say she whispered in my ear so lovingly, 'You're the best.' There is a lot I would like to say but it isn't really what is said, is it? The point is what we do not say. That's what I have learnt so far. I know I am still a novice, if you'll excuse such a religious term.

I'd like to say that. But I'm cynical now, totally cynical. Even if she had done what I said, would I have believed it, would anyone have believed it? Part of me would of course, but part of me would have doubted it, doubted it to my very soul if I believed in one. Like everyone, I've re-jigged my memories to suit what happened since. There's a necessity for this, re-jigging memories, I mean. It's not about deception, self-deception perhaps, but not deception of others. That's the reason why we think the way we do. The memories pop up and we crop them and re-style them; that's what we all do, nobody is any different.

I had a friend who I grew up with from about eleven to nineteen, when we lost touch. We did everything together. He was more practical than me, I was always more artistic. He got into trouble, stealing petty stuff like microwaves, and was expelled from school. He was a close mate, so I was really upset about it, but couldn't show it of course, that's the biggest sin when you're a young man, showing any feeling is bad. He told me that he was born in South Africa, and when he was little his mum and dad split up, and his mum returned to England and left him with his dad there. His dad just left him in a boarding school from the age of six to eight, and didn't visit him once. Can you imagine that? At the age of six you never see your mum or your dad or anyone in your family. Then when he eventually was got by his mother and returned to England he got abused at school, people calling him Paki, stuff like that.

None of this is unusual. Who wasn't bullied at some point or who didn't bully others? He can't remember a thing from before he was ten. Maybe it's best. Keep a lid on things, no point prodding around in things best forgotten, right? But the truth is, doctor, they don't get forgotten, do they, not ever! They dictate how we later feel, think and behave and all our later relationships. The damage is done and then we damage others. I know you know all this. You don't know this specifically about me. You know this from all your other supervisee. Sad, isn't it? We all think we are special, all think we are intrinsically different, when in reality we all have the same issues. Maybe that's not so sad. Maybe it just shows us we are part of the same human race, and really we should cooperate more and find time for each other more.

What you really looking for here? Maybe you want to hear more about what it was like in bed with her, all the ins and outs so to speak, how sticky and sweaty it all was, as if this will explain the attraction and the madness. I've changed, you know that, I'm no longer the hooligan I was or the singer, and now I'm trying to be different, you don't you think it's appropriate for me to not buy into all this self-exposure. The thing is if you want to hear about threesomes, about me fucking some girl up the arse and then her giving me a blowjob, want to see a photo of her Dirty Sanchez, after we'd drunk a bottle of tequila, you'll be disappointed. Everything we did was pretty tame really. Some people fantasise about what other people get up to, maybe that's what attracts them to our profession; but I am not one of them.

Honestly, I don't think it is right to go into detail about a woman's pussy, the red cherry or the black cherry, or their arse, their perfect ripe arse, although of course it was perfect and sweet, so damn sweet, it was the best damn arse you can ever imagine. I'm not sure if I want to share that with you. Picture it, if you will, like a guided meditation. I'm not going to delight you with every detail. You'll have to use your imagination. I'm not going to rub over every image, over every tiny detail. Not yet anyway, too tempting for you. You'd be titillated, even aroused perhaps right in the moment, but you know how it is when you read a novel and the couple keep going to bed, even in a novel that's a private act.

If it was a painting or photography or a film you wouldn't call it erotica, you'd call it pornography.

Let's not be too common about it, sex wasn't a distraction, or even a form of entertainment, it wasn't as if we were locked up in an attic while the Nazis were invading. All that had been and gone. We fucked until we were red raw, but it wasn't enough. There was always room for more, and I loved the fact she was so demanding, and she talked dirty. I realised then that I was so inexperienced. Neither of us cared about the pain and we both just wanted it to go on and on and we could have done if our everyday lives hadn't got in the way.

'I can feel you,' she always said.

We did it mainly in the villa, with the shutters down as if the sun never rises. There was the true beauty of being tied up and it was true she did most of the tying, but I got my own back, using her scarfs, making her blindfold and tying her to the bed. She said she got all these ideas from her gay friends. I'd tolerate everything, everything other than her talking about her former lovers. I just couldn't stand that, and who knows if she was telling the truth anyway.

'What did she say?'

'I knew you'd push me on that, penis size that kind of thing. How she once met a builder just hanging around a street corner, took him home and how she held his cock and not even her two hands could hold all of it, and she's got huge hands, massive.'

'How did that make you feel?'

'Angry, and it made me wonder whether she'd been a prostitute in a previous life, I mean why was she hanging around on street corners?'

'And what else did she tell you about other men.'

'She talked constantly about two or three, one she nearly married. A guy called Ed. She interrupted his wedding and broke into his house and tore up all his clothes. There were so many blokes she'd slept with, she couldn't even remember how many, had given up counting which made me sick, but only a few she'd really loved.'

'Did this help, knowing that?'

'A bit, I try not to get so jealous these days, I've learnt to relax more, meditation helps, I've grown up a bit, I don't let myself get swallowed up by my feelings.'

'Why do you think she killed him?'

That one stumped me. I paused. I was usually garrulous, could go on and on about the ins and outs of relationships. I knew she was capable of anything but I didn't really want to admit it.

'I'm not convinced she did. Maybe to get at me; in any case she just wanted to get away from him, to have her life back, he had become more obsessed with her than even I was, than any man before, which was an achievement of sorts.'

'So her action was reasonable?'

'It had logic to it, but please, don't put words in my mouth. If you'd ever seen her in her black fur coat, naked underneath, her gorgeous beautiful body, her perfect breasts, her perfect body, then you'd know why obsession is logic as well. There is only one way humans can achieve anything. Everything worth doing involves obsession, don't you think?'

And so we continued this discourse deep into the night, like a type of tango.

'One thing is for sure, she put a spell on me, you know like a black magic woman, in that Carlos Santana song.'

'I've heard your act and you don't do any Santana.'

'You're really sharp, you know that.'

When she told me she wanted us to run a brothel, of a sort, I didn't even bat an eyelid. What does it mean running a brothel, there were websites now for everything, it was so in your face, but back then, even a few years ago it was nothing like it is now. Kids today think porn stars are the norm and they are the abnormal ones. Saying all that, there were so many lap-dancing bars and clubs that it wasn't a problem. My first wife's dad had made a killing in Australia by investing in a legal brothel. After we got married he gave us seven thousand pounds and some of that was probably gained from that brothel, so we had been living off the sex of others. Funny to think that, an illicit orgasm, a sweaty, but an otherwise respectable suit-wearing nine to five man, had financed our very lower middle class lifestyle. It seemed that it didn't matter how much you earned, the government would take it anyway.

Gambling, sex, all the many ways people distract themselves, some of it is pretty and some of it isn't. By that stage she could have told me the Queen of England was a lizard from another planet, as David Ike the former footballer and television presenter preached, and I would have believed her. Not just pure putty in her hand, salivating like some puppy over her gorgeous body but far more than this. I read a novel about an artist who is locked in an asylum after killing his first wife and using her head in a sculpture, literally tearing her eyes out and moulding her head like putty. He then has an affair with a psychiatrist's wife, escapes and we think he is going to do the same to her, cut her head off for the sake of art. Well, I was like her sculpture, without her having to physically cut my head off. Do you get where I'm coming from?

'You're sort of nodding, thanks for that.'

50
MELTS TO AIR

It is funny thinking about where all the time went and seeing how you become a parody of yourself–easily done. Even in this game, when you think you're reflecting, going into depth, it doesn't happen that easily, and you might be conning yourself. What's wrong with acting instead of thinking, and is therapy a type of voyeurism? These questions always haunt me. Ours is a confessional culture but has it actually got us anywhere? On the terraces I was into voyeurism, staring at the game, but you also felt part of it, especially if you gave someone a good kicking. As a singer you're the centre of attention, so of course you feel part of it. As a therapist you stand outside the equation slightly, even though you encourage the transference, making the patient feel things for you that are important, that might be elements of how they feel about significant others, and you deal with the counter-transference, when the patient starts to become something for you. It's complicated, but then again very obvious.

Like the wisps of cloud that often appear early morning around Mount Teide and then vanish, burnt up as the sun is pulled across the sky, she disappeared without a trace, not even the lingering smoke of her cigarette remaining. When she had arrived it never crossed my mind that it was odd that she should just appear like this, I never questioned whether it was planned or not. Despite my rampantly excessive jealousy, I am not one for conspiracy theories, they are of a Cold War period and I never saw any reds under the bed. What I saw were folk desperate for the easy life, for just relaxing in the sun, and not having to worry about anything. Is this a crime? My job was to help with this, I know. Nostalgia, is it a crime? They say that islands like New Zealand and Guernsey are stuck in the 1950s, and Tenerife seemed stuck in the 1980s in a way. Remember the 80s? Bad haircuts, exploitation, no morals; whether we liked it or not, it was that period that defines us now, and it was that period that led to the collapse of the world economy. Some of the music wasn't so bad. But I digress.

Can you hear me? Like a stuffed dummy, sitting in a chair, or a murdered mother upstairs, anything can be useful if you want it to be, if you care enough. The simple fact was there were too many distractions. Once the businesses kicked off, the club Technology, and the other areas.

'Can I just interrupt you there, you said you got distracted? Are you saying you were never distracted before, wasn't your relationship a distraction?'

'A distraction from what exactly; no I can't say it was, I might even go as far to say the opposite was true. It took us both closer to reality rather than away from it.'

'Like therapy, you mean.'

'If you want to bring everything back to therapy then yes but it was less artificial than therapy, given therapy has its own literature, and framework, and payment method, and is by nature a consumer sport. Whereas love, if it is real love, is freely given and freely received.'

I had to play it carefully because if I put a foot wrong I might be out of a job. This was the final part of the process and I was being judged. I could disagree this was part of the game. But I couldn't dismiss it completely. We are in a truly ridiculous position if we can't be honest so we can enter an honest profession, and we all have doubts about what we do so why not express them as much as you can.

51

BRACKEN

I would like to say there was something significant about that day, or at least the day was the same as any other. I had enjoyed managing low league sides, after the high times at Colchester and Elstree. My retirement was, at first, just as peaceful as I could wish for. I'd never trusted God, so I had turned to Buddhism. In Buddhism patience is more importance than kindness, and I can see why now. It is easier to give, to try and act, and do something, than to wait. You feel in control that way.

Let me see, why was that day significant? The horizon was sharp, the outlines of container ships lining up on their way to Harwich, then on to Africa and Russia having vanished in the dawn. These behemoths were replaced by corporeal beasts on the shoreline of the human and animal variety, if there is a difference. Once, out for a walk with Jasmine, a friend's collie, not as bright as she should be, I had had the same uneasy feeling in my abdomen as I got from watching Pete's dog Bracken a lurcher race all over the grass that fine, almost too perfect, summer day.

'Help,' croaked a weedy voice, with no real exclamation. It was as if she had no intention of being found at all. She would just lay there, waiting for moon and the tide, and pass down the river Styx, majestically. The word for assistance was being mouthed, but it symbolised nothing, demanded nothing. Any response seemed almost obscene.

This particular southern end of Frinton-on-Sea, by the golf club no less, had a range of ostentatious beach huts selling for over twenty grand, while less than a mile and a half away they went for six hundred quid. There was nothing especially pretty about this area or of note. Some old wooden barriers in the sea covered in seaweed and sea creatures; a sandy and stony beach with an alarming amount of foamy sea water; and a concrete path, that went all the way around the coast to Clacton.

You could laugh at the golfers, struggling on the Lynx course to hit their shots through the sea wind, or be amazed at the hardiness of families who sat right by the sea's edge as if it was actually warm. But familiarity and habit had made me come to love this area, having been brought here by my parents as a child. I now live here, just opposite this small coastal area, in a Spartan two bedroom flat on the second floor facing the sea, the golf course and the Union Jack permanently displayed to my right. And I am content, more content than I have ever been.

'Help,' it came again, not exactly annoying, more like a background meow of a lost cat who hopes it may find food or attention, but does not really care either way anymore. Nature can seem more robotic than technology and more of an existentialist than anything humans dream up. I could ignore this semi-feline cry quite easily, and carry on my merry way regardless, stretching my legs behind Jasmine sniffing out her familiar trail. That was one option I honestly did contemplate. But normally when you see an accident and consider getting involved your excuse is that a number of other more qualified people are already there helping. Here, alone, I had no such excuse.

Moving down the concrete slope, for wheelchair access I presume, I came across the woman face down on the hard grey surface, her left hand twisted doll-like behind her back, her right knee bloodied. A gull, sitting on a beach hut, observed the scene mechanically, its head slowly falling from side to side, as if its eyes were cameras transmitting our behaviour to another world. I had trained with St John Ambulance but that had been over forty years ago. I didn't dare touch her now, remembering nothing from the training other than the fun in molesting a rubber torso. Mobiles weren't my thing. I wasn't one for gadgets, one of the reasons I had moved away from London being to get away from the future.

The grey concrete she had kissed matched the grey endless sky that hovered oppressively over the Essex coast. At least I realised that with injuries of this kind you had to be careful, as you could do more damage than good moving someone. Another excuse for doing nothing, some might add. Looking down at her, with her eyes clenched shut, a holiday in Austria with my family flashed into my head, memories of when I had knocked my head on the ex-Olympic swimming pool floor aged seventeen. A farce was then played out, me being shoved up and down, with my father insisting I should sit up and an Austrian man insisting

241

I shout lay flat. Despite my head, this was great exercise, like military training old school.

Today, if you intervene with someone else's child, they arrest you for things like that, and your face is in the papers or name tweeted about, if that's the right phrase for it. If someone were to come along right this minute I could envisage this scenario being played out again in Frinton. I'd be accused of knocking the old woman down on purpose, mugging, or even raping her. As if. I can honestly tell you no such thoughts like that had crossed my mind at all, not even in my wildest imagination. It was frightening how blank that part of me had become, a tabula rasa some might say, like the white sheet on an altar in a church with nothing on it.

52

TERMINAL

I was out for a walk with my friend's dog, an old chap who was finding it hard to get about, and this slight inconvenience of a fallen woman was breaking my usual routine. That's about as far as my thoughts went. I'd already had a cup of tea, but no breakfast if I remember correctly. I hadn't even established what I was going to do that day, apart from a vague plan to transcribe my parents' war diaries, which had recently been sent to me by my younger sister who still ran a clothes shop in Brighton and was into collecting. My father had been stationed in Italy from 1941 to 1943, doing some kind of office work, not fighting, and both had kept very detailed diaries. They had only been together a year or so when the war started, my mother already pregnant with me and working on her family's Essex farm, just outside Wivenhoe. They were very much in love, always were. They didn't make a point of demonstrating it too overtly to embarrass others, but one thing I always found fascinating about them was they never argued.

Every woman I had ever known intimately I had argued with like crazy, especially with my wife, Tabitha, who had died seven years ago of lung cancer, having smoked two packs a day, every day. Tabitha and I got bored with each other early on, and lived an open relationship with the tacit agreement that as long as we didn't screw someone in the marital bed or get diseased then it was fine who we fornicated with. There was one more important rule. We weren't allowed to go on about it with anyone. Tabitha of course broke the rule, frequently bragging about her conquests. But in my parents' day marriage was for life and was all about monogamy, no questions asked, a bit like a dog isn't just for Christmas today. I remember hearing Germaine Greer say that in America more money is given to animal charities than it is in total to charities that protect women from violence.

'Had a leaving do for my oldest pal Frank; the entire team were there, which was wonderful. Lots of drink, even more than usual and a few skits; Frank got very drunk and then tried to get into bed with me. This spoilt things a bit. I was disgusted by this, to be honest, and pushed him out. He slept on the floor, snoring noisily. Not sure if I will see him again.'

The injured lady, for that's what she was, was slightly different to your usual Frintonian, if such a creature exists. If you don't know Frinton let me explain. Despite it being by the coast and not that far away from Clacton, there are no gambling machines, you know fruit machines, one arm bandits some people call them, or other similar types of entertainment, and up until recently there was no pub at all, not even a chip shop. The idea was to keep it purer than pure, so the riffraff would stay away, and only former majors and the daughters of vicars would feel at home here. Burger and ice-cream vans are not allowed to this day and the whole town is protected by the station and the now iconic white gates that guard the entrance.

This, for some, is a haven that keeps undesirables out and maintains the class of the place. For others, it is an enclave for pompous hypocritical bigots and racists. I am somewhere in the middle, sitting on the fence like a typical liberal, unable to decide. I like the way the English can take the mickey out of everyone, including themselves but I don't like the way that some English people take their hobbies so seriously. Everything then becomes a competition, such as who has biggest marrow, the best score at golf, which takes the fun out of things.

Her clothes were more than your standard grey slacks, floral blouse, and brown raincoat. Her hair had a hint of red, and was blown dry, not just by the wind, bouncy and still thick at the ends, as if she had recently had an expensive cut. The maimed woman donned a luscious black theatrical coat, with high leather boots, despite being in what looked like her late seventies. Even with her eyes tightly shut, and a wincing look of pain, her face looked surprisingly familiar, echoing back to me a wealth of information I hadn't quite put my finger on yet. The pale skin and Elizabeth Taylor style demeanour stirred something deep inside.

Then it dawned on me—Frinton Summer Theatre, no more and no less! Melissa St Claire, the once famous starlet from soap operas and trashy seventies horror films; her picture was all over the town, had been

244

for months. There was something really glamorous about all this, amongst the plethora of charity shops and blue-rinse cafés, and determination to live a limbo existence where anything interesting is forbidden, only allowed in depraved London. Interestingly, Harwich around the corner was closer to Holland, not known for its repressive way, than it was to London. In the early twentieth century Frinton had been a playground for the rich and famous, the Prince of Wales holding wild parties here. An architect had tried to build a utopia, with pure white Bauhaus style homes dotting the side roads off the seafront over towards the Walton end, but eventually giving up after just six were built. Melissa was a direct line to the heyday of Frinton, like meeting Zelda Fitzgerald. What a find!

I had a number of options that I now listed to myself mechanically, like a man going through clubs in the different leagues to stop ejaculating prematurely: go get help; help her myself; walk on by, and some others that slip my mind now. I tell you all this because today, as I now visit Pete the Beat who is comfortable I can assure you, I remember this incident and it blurs in many ways with Pete's story I am about to tell you.

Like me, Pete loved dogs. Before retiring, I worked on tabloids in the city, first *The Express* and then *The Blob*. Trust me, when I worked on these papers they still had some esteem, and they weren't just full of celebrity tittle-tattle. I missed the companionship of work, and when I was out for a walk used to strike up conversations easily. You make a community amongst other fellow dog walkers and I preferred this to the formalised rules of official sports like golf or cricket.

'How's Bracken today then, she seems sprightly enough.'

It was mid-summer and the tide was out. Pete was racing Bracken across the greensward that sat majestically above the Frinton coast. Families were just finishing their picnics and a group of youngsters were sitting in a circle singing. I thought I heard a smattering of French and something about Jesus.

'Look at her go, there's no beast who could out-race her,' purred Pete, in his strong Lancashire accent.

Pete had moved to Frinton once his wife had passed away, but having come original from Lytham St Anne's on the Lancashire coast this was a home from home. And he was right about Bracken. She just shot along, without a trace. The sun was past its zenith, and the porcelain blue sky was mirrored in the water. This was the perfect day and the central reason I had moved here.

I had already spotted that one of the families with a picnic had a young girl around four, who was interested in investigating everything, her mother frequently calling her to not run off.

'Amelia!' shouted the mother. Well I think it was that. I couldn't really tell, the name not being that familiar to me, and my hearing not being what it was. At this moment, the mother seemed overly stressed for the situation, over-reacting to the child who was just practicing her walking and testing boundaries. The father kicked back on the grass drinking from a can of Stella, singing songs with the older boy. Of course, I identified more with them and their behaviour. I've always thought life is way too short to get stressed about things. My father was the life and soul of any party. He embarrassed my mother who hated his exuberance. I had wanted children so I could play the fool, but it just didn't happen. This lack of children gave me a certain freedom and objectivity, whatever loneliness it also brought with it.

Bracken was picking up pace now, her tongue appearing from time to time, shooting and darting across the grass, as if at a race track, looking so sleek and svelte, totally majestic. Despite the speed and the heat of the day, she wasn't tiring. Pete had been out hunting rabbits with Bracken all over Essex and Suffolk. It was in the dog's blood. This wasn't cruel, just the way of nature. Who was I to judge, one way or the other, I was friendly with Pete and could see how much Bracken meant to him now his wife wasn't with him.

The family continued their post-picnic games, and the mother seemed more relaxed. I think she was now drinking some white wine, but I couldn't be sure of that. They had their backs to the girl, who was walking off investigating like usual. Now they trusted her a bit, and wanted to spend more time messing about with their son. By the time I looked back Bracken had the girl by the throat, and was whisking her away. The family hadn't noticed. Pete just watched on, as did I, not wanting to make a sound that might alarm the family. The dog pounded away further from the family across to the far side of the grass, shaking the child in its jaws from side to side, like a rabbit. There was no way I could see the whites of the girl's eyes, could I? My eyesight was also going, so this would be impossible, and yet I thought I could, as if I imagined them. Still the family hadn't noticed.

'You look sweet, talk about a treat,' I could make out the sounds of the father and son doing a musical routine, with the mother occasionally joining in.

They were having fun, who would want to interrupt them. But Pete, he was now running to where Bracken was 'playing' with the lifeless child. Finding a stick in a bush, he began beating the child relentlessly, his violence unbound, and it was this I just could not tolerate.

'For Christ's sake Pete, stop,' I yelled.

And then the parents turned around.

You know how they say when there is a road accident that just after the crash there is an uncanny silence. This may or may not have happened. The father was now running, I was running. The mother and boy stayed frozen. For some bizarre reason I started thinking about Frank. Maybe Frank was always running away from those that didn't accept him and I bet, underneath it all, there were many Franks in Frinton. What if my father had felt violent that night Frank had just wanted some comfort, what if he had beaten him with a cane? Or, what if my father had accepted Frank's affections and had never come back from the war, never known his son or had a future daughter? Personally, I wasn't against homosexuality, never had been. Even at my strict private school I had argued in class that some people were born homosexual, so to say they should choose not to be was ludicrous, and in any case you fell in love with the person. This again wasn't really something you could choose, and it didn't matter if they were a boy or a girl. Love chose you, not the other way around.

Despite my age, I reached Pete before the father, and wrestled the stick off him which wasn't as easy as it sounds. Pete's a big bloke, his father was an old fashioned policeman, and Pete himself had been an amateur boxer. Bracken was jumping up at us, as if this was some new game we'd invented. I didn't want to look at the child again, but it was impossible not to. Her skull and grey brains were smeared on the green grass, her orange dress with butterflies a bright red. I didn't get it immediately, but within minutes it dawned on me that Pete had been trying to save Bracken from being put down. Like Jesus, he was sacrificing himself. He didn't mind if it meant him doing a life sentence for murder. He was old anyway, past it, he would say. And the child was already dead in the dog's mouth so he wasn't doing any real violence. There was a clear logic to his behaviour, something noble that I actually admired. Was I sick, or him?

'So would you say Mr Longmead is an entirely rational man?'

I wasn't sure how to answer that one. The inclusion of 'entirely' threw me, because nobody is entirely rational; we wouldn't be human if we were, we'd be more like a machine. The prosecution barrister was trying to establish whether this event was out of character, and as a character witness as well as an eye witness it was up to me to make some kind of judgement.

'Pete's from Lancashire, where they call a spade a spade.'

This got a murmur of laughter from the court room. Being in the limelight like this was not something I wanted and I didn't want to play to the audience. I hadn't intended it to be funny at all, more factual I suppose. I spotted the father staring blankly, as if he had just switched off his humanity once his daughter had died. Maybe I had done this also, but years ago. I don't like expressing my feelings much, probably comes from my schooling where if you did you were hit and told to stop blubbing. Pete and I got on because we had a range of subjects we felt comfortable discussing, but not others that touched on feelings. I couldn't exactly say that in the court, could I, but my phrase that caused some titters I had hoped summed this up.

I really don't think I helped Pete much, but by that stage he didn't care. His mind was made up that he had done the right thing. There's no arguing with someone like this, they have to believe it, even if it is verging on the psychotic.

'I saw her little face, and then her teeth were coming out of her mouth, blood out of her ears, it was terrible.'

An old woman sitting on a nearby bench reading *The Blob* had seen everything anyway, and she made it perfectly clear to the court that Pete had bashed the child to death without the dog's intervention. She described the way he had found the stick and used it methodically, clumping the child's head. Despite what she was describing, this obviously wasn't premeditated and there was no cause or motivation, which in some ways made it even more sinister. I could see the headlines now in my mind's eye–The Mindless Evil of an Old Man. There could be a feature on how mindless violence wasn't just conducted by the youth, as in *A Clockwork Orange*, but part of human nature in general, just like war. The older generation were clearly worse, because they couldn't deal with their feelings, they couldn't sit in television studios and pour out their feelings of self-loathing while the audience in the studio and at home condemned them.

More interestingly, it came out at court that the child, Amelia, was an advanced and avid reader. She had kept on wandering away from her family to read the signs dotted about the grass, such as 'Danger, Keep Off' positioned next to the top of the cliff, as if curiosity and knowledge were now already putting her in danger, like the tree of knowledge and of good and evil. Pete's defence tried to argue that the child was at fault here, that this was really an accident, and Pete was trying to beat the child off his dog. Plus the parents were drunk, weren't they? Getting pissed while your child is first mauled by a dog and then beaten to death is not the perfect way to spend a day near the seaside, but it is memorable. Nearby is Frank perched on a bench, dreaming of my father or another man, or nursing a small flask of whiskey, his days in the civil service and war still a strong memory.

And I never told you what happened about the other accident, did I, in case you were wondering. I did help Melissa up after all. What do you take me for? As if I would leave her there. Her injuries weren't too bad and they brought us together, like a common enemy. She had grazed her knee, which looked worse than it was, and a fractured wrist, nothing that serious, and she still looked damn gorgeous. I took her to A and E in Clacton, and they patched her up as best they could. The attitude of some of the staff dismayed me, but I wasn't the sort to complain. From what was going on there I knew they had their work cut out and better things to do. Melissa didn't want any fuss either and just wanted to be out of there as quick as possible. I could smell the gin on her breath, above her heavy perfume, so this probably killed off some of the pain.

Back at her one bedroom seafront flat which had an interesting turret and was crammed with old movie posters and photos, she stripped off naked after I ran her a steaming bath. Before that moment I had never really lived. We both got in, smoking Gitanes and drinking a cheap bottle of Chilean I had had rattling around in the Volvo for months. I'd never been up close to a woman with a tattoo before, and I was fascinated by it. On her left buttock she had a horseshoe with the word 'Lucky'. I'm not going to tell you what happened next, of course. I'm a gentleman, and an OAP, and I don't think it is right to go on about genitalia, all the ins and outs of it. I might not be a paid up member of the golf club, but I don't have pampas grass outside my abode either if you get my meaning. I wrote for the tabloids once, of course, but I'm retired now and I don't even engage gossip. If you were to ask me who the latest celebrity caught with their pants down was I couldn't tell you. It just doesn't interest me. So you can use your imagination when it comes to what was going on between Melissa and me. That will be good for you, instead of me spelling it out.

I will just say, if that's OK by you, that it was the best sex I have ever had, and I'm seventy nine next Tuesday. I don't exaggerate. Bracken's still going strong by the way. Melissa and I take her for a walk every morning, bright and early, and she chases the seagulls and whatever else she can find, leaping and bounding like you wouldn't believe. I try to keep her on a muzzle and lead whenever children are about, of course. Pete, friend, I know you will die in prison, but at least you know Bracken is still free, enjoying his early morning run. And not only this; because of Melissa's film and television connections Bracken now gets the odd part and does a bit of acting himself. Pete, you're now playing the part of a prisoner. Perhaps we're prisoners in Frinton. There's a theory that it is when we are acting, putting on a mask, that we are truly ourselves. I still have baths with Melissa, wonderful baths. I let her go on about all the roles she's had, all the people she's known, even all the men she's had. And I'm not jealous of her fun. I'm too old for that. I'm taking vicarious pleasure in her re-telling of her pleasure. But, to be honest Pete, sometimes when Melissa and I are making love, truly lost in the moment and I feel at one with Melissa, I just wish Bracken wouldn't watch.

Melissa's niece Caitlin switched the digital recorder off. At that precise moment the manageress of the Glencoe Hotel, Frinton-on-Sea, brought in afternoon tea.

'Will that do? Sorry to ramble on a bit, just talking brings back memories and I thought Pete might like to hear it.'

I was aware I had been slightly sexually explicit, but Caitlin was no longer a child. Sun was streaming in through the large windows that looked over the lawn. Soon they would be turning this palace into retirement flats, so I was making the most of it. I could tell she thought I was a doddering old fool, but there were parts of this that would make a good story for the magazine she worked on in a lowly position. I was doing this for Melissa's sake and I knew her niece loved her, so this was fine.

'As long as you put Aunty Melissa's name in there somewhere, reference a few of her films and plays, I don't really mind what you do with my story. I was kind of a bystander in a whole series of events. But she wants to see the edited version before it goes to print please.'

I was trying to tread a thin line between assertiveness and politeness, something I found difficult with the younger generation who often seemed to have all of the former with none of the latter.

'The print version of the magazine probably won't want it, but we have a chance with the on-line,' Caitlin grinned, flashing a lovely smile within which I could see Melissa and only then did I realise how young she was, probably sixty years my junior. Like everyone, she was acting a part, but she was doing it exceptionally well.

'I thought it quite revealing that you never really mentioned much about yourself, other than Tabitha, your wife. You know the best bit was the smidgeon about Frank. It's sad your father rejected him. Were there any other letters or glimpses of Frank in any of the materials your sister sent you?'

I wanted to explain to her that sometimes people try to write people out of their lives as well as in, and what really went on with Frank we'll never know. My father was actually pretty tolerant, certainly not a prude, and in his own way loved people. All the same, I found it odd she was heading in that direction.

'There could be a whole different approach to this story, couldn't there? I mean late in life you met my Aunty Melissa and I am sure her glamour had something to do with your attraction to her. Frank had something about him, too, something glamorous, and your father just had to stamp out the fire before it go too hot.'

I had thought of this, of course. And how did this relate to a dead child? Well clearly the child was clever, and the parents were into amateur dramatics, as was my father. Just because you're into the theatre it doesn't mean you're a queen, mind you. Still, Caitlin was making me think.

'John, would you like me to find out more about Frank? Maybe he's still alive. I'm good at research and I wouldn't charge you or anything. I'm just intrigued that's all. A few lines in a dead man's war diary, it's not enough.'

I hadn't expected this at all. After she kissed and hugged me goodbye, as if I was her grandfather about to snuff it, I took a long walk down the beachfront. Families with young children about to enter their lives played on the sand. There I was moving amongst them, about to move out of my life, now with someone stepping back into my life piecing it together, creating a new pattern and picture.

Melissa was waiting with Bracken. Not only was I content, I was happy.

About the Author

Jason Lee is the author/editor of 15 books, with work translated into 12 languages. Previous novels include *Unholy Days* (also published by ROMAN Books), and *Dr Cipriano's Cell*. Other books include *The Psychology of Screenwriting, Lost Passports, Seeing Galileo, Pervasive Perversions, Cultures of Addiction, Madness and the Savage,* and *The Metaphysics of Mass Art.* He is Professor of Culture and Creative Writing at De Montfort University, Leicester.